A Novel

Letters from Shadow Oaks

K. L. Small

Cover design by Lidia Puccetti

This is a work of fiction. All characters and events portrayed in this novel are either products of the author's imagination or are used fictitiously.

Letters from Shadow Oaks

Cover design by Lidia Puccetti
Editing and formatting by Kingsman Editing Services

ISBN: 979-8-9900863-4-0 (paperback)
ISBN: 979-8-9900863-3-3 (e-book)
LCCN: 2025908163

First Edition September 2025

www.kathleenlsmall.com

Dedicated to Kelly, my daughter,
who has an artist's spirit

CHAPTER 1

Thursday, September 1, 2023

NINA HATED TO SAY GOODBYE TO THE APARTMENT THAT had been her home for over thirty years, but retirement and condominium conversion forced it. The bare walls and empty rooms hurt more than she expected.

She trailed behind the property manager, who scanned his final inspection checklist. *He's young enough to have been my student not too long ago.* As they moved from room to room, he marked his form, and Nina fought back tears.

In the bedroom with the lake view, while the property manager opened the closet door and added a check mark to his paperwork, Nina gazed out the window and sighed. *The sunlight twinkles on the water like diamonds.* She loved to watch the sandhill cranes stroll along the shoreline and the alligators float in the shallow water. She had sketched and painted them many times, along with the sabal palm trees and Florida sunsets. *Until my arthritis got too bad.*

"Ms. Kos . . ." The property manager fumbled with his form. "Ms. Kossell . . ."

"It's Koscielniak." Nina walked away from the window, her footsteps echoing in the barren room. "Please call me Nina."

He flipped over his paper. "I'm sorry you're leaving. Our records show you've lived here a long time. We would have enjoyed having you in our new condo community."

She nodded and headed into the kitchen, where the last box of her personal items sat on the countertop. The room smelled of cleaning products, rather than the many international meals she had cooked. All her exotic spices now resided down the hall with the young newlywed couple, and her pottery from around the world had been donated to a thrift shop. Another sad decision.

The property manager cleared his throat. "Since we'll be doing a complete renovation for the condo conversion, we'll return your entire security deposit."

"Thank you." Nina picked up her box and headed to the door. "I have to go. The car service is waiting for me at the curb." *I will miss this place.*

"Let me help you with that." He hurried to open the door. "Did you leave a forwarding address with the office?"

"Yes." She sniffled. "Shadow Oaks Senior Living Home."

ON MONDAY MORNING, THE SUNLIGHT SLID THROUGH THE blinds into room B12 of the Shadow Oaks Senior Living Home in Tropical Springs, Florida. It brightened the simple interior, streaming across the floral comforter on the single bed and the leather recliner. The sunshine gleamed on the silver picture frame atop the nightstand beside her bed and brightened the pencil sketch of Nina in her younger days.

Despite the pain, Nina flexed her arthritic fingers. *Forty-eight years of teaching art, and now I'm paying the price.* She shook her head. *Three Teacher of the Year awards. Where did the time go?*

Ingrained from years of practice, her hands braided the long strands of hair without looking. She twisted the silver locks into a single thick braid that she wore to the left side of her head. *What color would my mother's hair have been if she lived as long as I have?* She still grieved the loss that had left her alone in the world in her twenties. No parents. No children. No family.

With stiff fingers, she draped the silk scarf around her neck and tied a French knot in it. The fabric's brilliant claret color brought back memories of drinking Bordeaux red wine at a café in Paris. And of André. He still made her blush. *Best not think of him. Besides, he's probably long buried. I was such a crazy college kid back then, and he was wise in the ways of the world. My older man.*

Nina straightened her shoulders and left her room. The beige walls and brown carpet of the hallway irritated her. She had selected this facility because of the bright flowers in the garden, the friendliness of the staff, and the moderate price. Her room was spacious, and the other residents were pleasant, but after three days at Shadow Oaks, she detested—no, hated the wall and floor colors. The framed pictures along the hallway screamed at her with their garish imitations of the great art masters. *Perhaps I was too hasty in deciding I couldn't continue to live on my own. I should have found another apartment.*

At the end of the hallway, she took a deep breath and entered the gathering room. "Good morning, everyone." She almost misspoke and said, "Good morning, class." *After all those years of teaching, it's inevitable.*

Nina scanned the seating areas. Sunlight streamed through the large window and spread across the carpeted floor. Centenarian Liz, in her wheelchair, stared out the window. The sunlight gave a halo glow to her white hair. She wore a pink sweater and a patchwork quilt draped over her legs.

A pair of sofas in chartreuse-and-marigold-striped fabric faced each other in the middle of the room. Two couples—the Turners and the Denzels—chatted together on the sofas. Four card tables filled the far end of the space. Rosemary, Emmett, and Mike sat at one table.

"Over here, Nina," Rosemary called. "We saved you a seat."

Nina strolled past the sofas. *I'm falling into a routine after only a few days here.*

Emmett rested his hands on the card table and rose feebly. He pulled the empty chair away from the table and gestured for Nina to sit. "Please join us, dear lady. You're looking as pretty as a peach this morning."

"You need your eyes checked," Nina said with a smile and joined them. Emmett attempted to push her chair toward the table, but it barely moved. "Bless your heart."

"Such a gentleman," Rosemary said and raised her teacup in Emmett's direction.

Mike guffawed. "Fancy pants Southern ambulance chaser."

Nina chuckled at their banter. *The same every day. Sweet, caring Rosemary. Emmett, the Southern gentleman, retired lawyer. Mike, the disabled Vietnam veteran. How did I fall in with this odd trio?*

Leaning over, Rosemary patted Nina's arm. "You are looking lovely today. What a beautiful scarf."

"Thank you. It's from Paris."

"What about me, Rosemary?" Mike stroked his beard and puffed his chest.

"You're my hero, as always. And Emmett, you're a treasure."

"What's that?" Emmett cupped his hand to his ear.

"I said you need to change your hearing aid batteries." Rosemary blew him a kiss.

Nina smiled at their exchange. *I'm still too new to join in; maybe next week. Right now, I'd rather sit with Liz by the window and watch the birds in the garden.*

Activity Director Emily Carson breezed into the room with a red bag. Her brunette hair rippled with each step.

Late twenties, I'd guess.

"Mail call." Like a drill sergeant, Mike's voice carried across the room.

Rosemary bent closer to Nina again. "I'm sure Emily will have something for you today. It takes a while for forwarded mail to catch up with you when you move."

Nina nodded. *No one is writing to me. No family members. No friends.*

Emily opened her bag and removed a handful of letters. "Mr. Emmett Myers, Esquire."

"My, ain't we fancy," Mike said.

Emmett took the three letters the activity director handed to him. "Thank you, Miss Emily. You're looking as pretty as a peach this morning."

Rosemary leaned toward Nina. "He says that to all the ladies."

After reaching into the bag, Emily removed a gardening magazine. "Mrs. Elizabeth Campbell." Emily walked over to the window and placed the magazine in the elderly woman's lap. "Here you go, Miss Liz."

"Her granddaughter keeps sending Liz magazines even though the poor dear can no longer read," Rosemary whispered.

Her words made Nina look over at the slight woman in the wheelchair. "I've never heard her say a word."

"She hasn't spoken since I've been here." Rosemary counted on her fingers. "Six years now."

"Mr. Michael Walsh." Emily carried an envelope over to the table. "Mike, it looks like a VA document. If you need help with forms or paperwork, please let me know.

"And Rosemary, this one must be for you. It's addressed to Granny Nelson."

Rosemary raised both hands in the air, and her face lit up with joy. "That must be from one of my grandchildren or great-grandbabies."

Emily continued distributing mail, while those at the table opened their letters. For a few minutes, the only sounds in the room were ripping envelopes and rustling paper, followed by excited chatter. Nina sat silently. *Nothing for me.*

One last correspondence came out of the bag, and Emily carried it to the table where Nina sat. "One for you." She held out a beige business envelope.

Surprised, Nina took the document. She read the front of the envelope. *Dear Occupant.* She met Emily's eyes. "Thank you." Nina opened the envelope and pulled out a blue flyer announcing a dry-cleaning sale.

"Look at what my grandson drew." Rosemary held up a picture of three superheroes. "He's very talented."

"How old is he?" Nina asked. She studied the drawing in Rosemary's hands.

"He's twelve. He's the son of two educators. Isn't he quite the artist?"

"May I see?" Nina took the offered sheet of paper. "Excellent use of color, but the proportions of the arms and legs are wrong. He tried to keep the characters in scale with each other, and I applaud that."

"Why Miss Nina," Emmett said. "Sure as the sun shines in the summer, you sound like an art critic."

Nina returned the drawing to Rosemary. "You must be proud of him." *I better keep my opinions to myself.*

"Listen up, everyone," Emily said. "The shuttle bus will leave for the bingo hall in twenty minutes. For those who are going, please meet in the lobby in fifteen minutes, so we have time to board the shuttle. Our driver, Andy, will assist anyone who needs help. Any questions?"

When no one asked questions, Emily left the gathering room.

"Nina, are you going to join us for bingo?" Rosemary buttoned her sweater and got up from the table.

"Not today."

"I'm feeling lucky today," Mike said. He snapped his fingers. "Fate owes this one-legged vet a win or two."

"I've agreed to escort the widow Lynn," Emmett said.

"You're wasting your time with her," Rosemary said. "She's looking for a sugar granddaddy."

Emmett looked puzzled. "What did you say?"

"I said you need to change your hearing aid batteries."

"Oh, yes."

"Nina, one of these days you should join us." Rosemary held her arm out to Mike as he struggled to stand.

"Not this time." She folded the dry-cleaning flyer and

rose from the table. "I have some things to do."

"They can wait," Mike said.

"Miss Nina, don't let anyone discourage you from doing that which you are meant to do," Emmett said.

"Typical lawyer mumbo-jumbo." Mike snorted and limped away.

"No pressure, Nina." Rosemary smiled. "But join us on an outing one day."

Without committing, Nina nodded and returned to her room alone.

CHAPTER 2

Tuesday, September 5, 2023

THE SILVER SOUTH SEAS PEARL NECKLACE ON THE MARBLE bathroom countertop guaranteed Megan success. *It's always worked in the past.* Her eyes shifted from the strand of pearls to her watch. *Four thirty-five a.m., over two hours before sunrise. Everyone in the house, including the cat, is still asleep. Except for me.*

She applied her matte lipstick, adding a hint of rose to her lips. A quick layer of blush finished her routine. She leaned closer to the mirror to inspect her makeup. After a quick spray of her favorite rose-scented perfume, Megan glanced in the mirror again and smiled. *Forty and fantastic!*

She eased into her tailored suit jacket and lifted the string of pearls from the countertop. With the necklace in place, she double-checked the clasp and examined her appearance for a final time. The pearls shimmered against her skin. *Today is a day for pearls. They get me through all the difficult times.*

After turning off the bathroom light, she opened the door and tiptoed into the bedroom.

"Mornin'," her husband said with a sleep-heavy voice.

"Sorry to wake you, sweetie. Thanks for taking care

of the girls this morning." *I sure treasure Steve's help. He's everything my first husband wasn't.*

Steve sat up in the king-sized bed and stretched. "No problem. Does Penny need anything for school?"

Inhaling the hint of his cologne from yesterday, Megan kissed him and pressed his shoulder to lie back down. "No. And she doesn't have to get up for another hour. Jody needs to take an extra juice box to daycare."

"Okay." The sheets muffled his voice. "Good luck at work."

Megan moved through the darkened room and down the stairs. She gathered her purse from the entryway table and headed into the garage. With no traffic to slow her commute to the office, she mulled over the day's tasks.

She usually looked forward to presentation day for new marketing plans. *All the demanding work is done.* The planning and brainstorming would pay off, and the sophistication of the finished materials should please the client. Yet on this account, her intuition nagged at her. *Something isn't right. The financial forecast seems wrong. Today's early start will give me time to review the figures again.*

The decorative streetlights cast a cool glow on the dark road winding through the suburban development. The headlights of Megan's car reflected off thin swirls of fog. She drove past the neighborhood's large houses, their windows still black. *I sure have come a long way from those downtown apartments over the shops. I have a terrific job with lots of security and benefits. Steve is a godsend, a kind man with a sense of humor. We have a lovely home for our family.*

After turning out of her development onto the main road, she headed toward the interstate. *Shouldn't be any traffic at this hour.* As she picked up speed, the volume on the radio automatically increased.

"It's going to be another lovely fall day along the Florida coast today," the radio announcer said. "Light morning fog will give way to sunshine with a high in the low eighties." She selected another station in search of some music for the commute to the office. When she couldn't find a song choice that suited her mood, she switched to the *Financial Security for Life* audiobook and settled in for the rest of the drive.

Forty minutes later, she pulled into a parking spot in the company's downtown parking garage.

The elevator doors opened to the fourteenth floor, and the motion-activated lights snapped on, illuminating the framed awards and samples of marketing ads displayed on the walls. Megan smiled with satisfaction knowing that she had worked on each of the award-winning campaigns. *Not bad for an accountant who started in billing and worked her way up to project manager of marketing programs. And maybe, if Bradley moves up to the executive level soon, VP of marketing.*

She strolled past the rows of cubicles and into her office. Outside her floor-to-ceiling window, streetlights illuminated the empty city streets below. She checked her watch and frowned. *It's too early to be here, but going over the numbers again can't hurt.*

A stack of folders with the marketing plan and collateral materials for this morning's client presentation sat in the left corner of her desk. Family photos occupied the right corner. She started her laptop and connected to the double monitors. While she waited for the system to clear the company's security system, she picked up the photo of Steve. *Our fifth anniversary is coming up. We should plan a little getaway. Maybe a short cruise. Penny is old enough now to watch Jody for a few days.*

Megan put down her husband's photograph and gazed at the images of her two daughters. Jody's blonde baby picture filled a handmade ceramic frame given to her by a coworker. The baby's chubby cheeks were full and round, like Steve's face. *I need an updated photo, but I love that baby look. Can't believe she's four now.* Her attention turned to Penny's freshman high school picture. The teen barely smiled. A hank of jet-black hair hung over her eyes. Eyes that were dark pools, full of challenge. *She looks so much like Peter. That could be why I have such a difficult time talking to her.* Thoughts of her ex-husband always made her angry.

The laptop beeped and waited for her security code. Megan focused on the computer screen and entered her password. *The system sure is fast when the office is empty.* She pulled up the spreadsheet for the new account and reviewed the calculations for the next thirty minutes.

When her neck muscles stiffened, she took a break and went to her office window. The morning sun crept through the city streets. She watched the sky brighten, while the commuter traffic flowed in the streets below. With a sigh, she returned to her desk and studied the spreadsheet one more time.

At the sound of the elevator doors opening, Megan looked away from the numbers. Abbie, the lead designer for the firm, stepped through with a cup of coffee in one hand and a Coach bag in the other. Her signature citrus perfume scented the air.

"You're here early," Megan said.

"Look who's talking." Abbie settled in the chair across from Megan and took the lid off her cup. The aroma of freshly brewed coffee filled the office. "Still reviewing those numbers?"

Megan nodded. "The plan's projections are ambitious for such a unique restaurant concept. I'm afraid we may have exaggerated the customer flow the client can expect."

Abbie laughed. "You worry too much about money."

"Money makes the world spin, pumpkin." Megan blinked. *Why did I say that?* She quickly added, "My mother used to say that all the time."

"Pumpkin!" Abbie rolled her eyes. "The coffee shop is pushing pumpkin spice lattes right now. The place stinks of it."

"Abbie, seriously. I'm concerned about the projections." Megan stroked the pearls around her neck.

"We used what Bradley gave us, and he's the boss. The logo is fantastic, if I can brag a bit. The graphics for the signage and the menu layout are spot on. You've laid out a broad advertising approach. It's one of the best plans we've done."

Abbie's right. All the pieces work. Creative. Upbeat. Innovative. We couldn't have done better. "I suppose so."

"I know so," Abbie said.

Megan glanced back at the spreadsheet. "The company needs a big win." She had been counting on the VP promotion, but the firm's growth had stalled recently and so had her hopes for advancement. Then last year, the company hired Bradley for the position she thought was hers.

Abbie finished her coffee. "When do you meet with the client?"

After glancing at her watch, Megan did a quick calculation. "In two hours."

"You'll be fine." Abbie rose and headed to the door. "You've done a hundred of these presentations."

"Thanks. I'll fill you in on how it goes." *This might be my next step to a promotion.*

* * *

As the first light of dawn peeked through the blinds, the gray tabby cat jumped on Penny's bed and bumped his head against her cheek. She rolled away and tugged the sheet over her head. The cat burrowed under the covers.

"Go away, Goku." She brushed the cat's whiskers away from her ear, but the cat purred louder and kneaded her shoulder.

Her phone dinged with the first message of the morning. Penny groped for it beside her pillow and sent her friend Lacey a sunshine emoji. She read Lacey's response twice.

R u ready?

Ready for what? She typed a question mark.

Soph fun day appeared on Penny's screen. Before she could send another text message, heavy footsteps approached her door.

"Time to get up," her stepfather, Steve, called from the hallway.

Penny blinked and tossed the covers off. *Why is he telling me to get up? Where's Mom?* She donned an oversized black T-shirt and black leggings. Quickly, she reached into her sock drawer and grabbed a mismatched pair while the cat rubbed against her leg.

She sat on the floor and slipped on her socks, one purple with pink dots and the other yellow with green kitties. She wiggled her toes, and the cat swiped at them. A curved claw snagged on the purple sock.

"Stop!" Penny giggled. "That hurts." She grabbed her black ankle boots. "I have to get going. It's Sophomore Fun Day at school, and I have things to do before class."

With both hands, she tousled her short hair and shook her head. She licked her fingers and flattened the cowlick at her hairline. As she lowered her left hand, she glanced at the skull and crossbones drawn on the underside of her wrist.

"Look at this, Goku." She held her hand close to the cat's face. "I did it last night. This'll warn everyone I'm poison."

Penny ran down the stairs but paused outside the kitchen. She listened to her stepfather talking to Jody, her four-year-old half sister.

"Cereal or muffin?" Steve's voice was gentle.

Since there was no response, Penny imagined Jody pointing to her choice.

Cereal pieces poured into a bowl with a plink, followed by the splash of milk.

"All ready. Eat up, Princess."

He always calls Jody Princess. If my dad was here, he would . . . Her mind froze. I don't know what name my dad would use. Would he call me Princess?

She took a deep breath and marched into the kitchen. Her stepfather sat at the oval table with Jody, exactly the way she had pictured them. The strong smell of Steve's coffee made her wrinkle her nose.

"Where's Mom?" she asked.

"Good morning, Penny. Your mom had an early meeting."

Penny sat next to Jody. "How's the cereal?"

Jody offered her a spoonful.

With a laugh, Penny ate the cereal. "Yum. I'll have some, too." She reached for the box in the middle of the table.

"What's that?" Steve pointed to the skull and crossbones on her wrist. "Is that a tattoo?"

"It's a poison symbol." She filled her bowl with cereal and milk.

"I know that. How did it get there?"

"I drew it." She took a spoonful of cereal and raised it to her mouth.

"Your mother wouldn't like that."

"I don't care." With a clink of metal against ceramic, she dropped the spoon back into the bowl and stared straight at Steve.

His face tightened. "That's the wrong attitude, Penny."

"You can't tell me how to think."

"Your mother works hard. She deserves your respect, not your nonsense."

"She's my mother. I've known her longer than you have." Penny pushed her bowl away, spilling milk on the table.

"Watch your tone, young lady."

"Daddy, all done." Jody held her empty bowl for her father to see.

"Penny, I have to get Jody ready for daycare, and you need to get to school."

"I know that." Penny stood up, and the chair legs scraped across the floor.

Why do I always fight with him? Penny stormed out of the kitchen, grabbed her backpack, and headed to the bus stop. Her feet hit the pavement with force. *My life would be much better if my dad was here. I don't want a stepfather. Why did Mom marry Steve? What does she see in him?*

On the school bus, her thoughts continued to roil in unsettling directions until Lacey boarded the bus.

"Soph Fun Day all the way," Lacey said, sliding onto the bench seat beside Penny. "It's going to be fire."

Penny half listened as Lacey rambled on about their plans. Her mind played back the breakfast conversation with her stepfather.

"Dylan and Ashley have everything we need. You'll be helping them."

"What?" Penny focused on Lacey.

"When the bell rings for first period, we'll meet at the mascot statue, rather than going to class. We'll turn that plain white polar bear into a soph superstar."

"How are we doing that?"

"I don't know. Dylan and Ashley are planning something. I'll text you when I find out."

The bus pulled into the unloading area. The front doors opened, and the riders filled the aisle.

"Remember, Penny, after the first-period bell rings." Lacey joined the crowd exiting the bus.

Penny sat a little longer on the bus. *First period is art. I love that class and don't want to miss it.* Slowly, Penny trudged down the aisle and stepped off the bus. Her phone signaled an incoming text message from Lacey.

SEE YOU BY THE MASCOT.

When the bell rang for the first period, Penny skipped

art class and met her friends outside at the seven-foot-tall statue. The white polar bear was between the main school building and the football field, an area not visited during a normal school day.

Dylan and Ashley were already there when Penny arrived. "There you are, Penny," Ashley said. "We were afraid you might have chickened out."

"No sign of Lacey?" Penny asked.

Ashley shrugged and Dylan said, "We don't need her."

"What are we doing?" Penny eyed the three paint cans at the foot of the statue.

"We're going to give this bear some personality," Dylan said. He bent and opened a can of paint to reveal a bright blue. The paint smell rose in the morning air.

Ashley laughed. "You could say a makeover."

"What do you need me for?" Penny's insides did a nervous flip-flop. *I'm not sure we should do this.*

"You're taller than both of us." Dylan held his hand over his head.

"And you're artistic," Ashley said. "You can do the head. Make the eyes stand out."

Penny studied the bear more closely. It was a hulking white figure with small black eyes, a large dark nose, and a thin line for a mouth. Any color on the claws was long gone. There were no other distinguishing features. *Why would they pick a polar bear as a mascot for a Florida school?*

"I got the paint from my dad's garage, but we only have one paintbrush. So, we'll have to take turns." Dylan picked up the brush from the ground. "You can start with the head, and when you're done, we'll take the brush for our parts."

On tiptoes, Penny reached to the bear's nose. "I'm not

tall enough to reach the eyes."

"You can stand on your backpack," Ashley said. "That should give you the extra height."

Dylan dipped the brush into the can of blue paint and handed it to Penny.

"I'm not sure about this." Penny's hand shook as she took the brush.

"You can do it." Ashley flashed a thumbs-up. "I've seen your drawings. You're so artsy."

Penny examined the statue's faded black eyes. *Small and plain. I can make them more visible.* As a hobby, she drew lots of black-and-white renditions of manga characters, all with enormous eyes. *Eyes are important.*

She dropped her backpack on the ground, stepped on it, and extended the paintbrush. Bits of blue paint ran down her arm and dripped on her backpack. Carefully, she spread a layer of paint over the bear's right eye.

"That looks like eye shadow," Ashley said. "Keep going."

With the brush still dripping globs of blue, Penny painted a swash over the left eye.

"That's it," Dylan said.

Where else would a bear have blue? "How about we add a scarf?" She lowered the brush and added a wide blue band around the neck. Her brush ran out of paint and she stepped off her backpack. Bending down, she dipped the brush in the can of paint and scraped off the excess. The fumes reminded her of art class.

"A scarf has long ends." She trailed a blue streak down the bear's chest. "How does that look?"

When there was no reply, she looked around for Dylan

and Ashley. *They're gone.*

Heavy footsteps ran toward her. "Stop right now," the football coach yelled.

Penny dropped the brush, which splattered paint all over the ground. She backed up and knocked over an open can. A puddle of yellow paint spread across the ground.

"What do you think you're doing?" The coach stared at the statue.

"It's Sophomore Fun Day," Penny said in a faltering voice.

"There's nothing fun about vandalism."

"Vandalism?" Penny's knees shook. *That's not what we're doing.*

The coach pulled out his phone and took photos of the statue, the paint cans, and Penny's paint-covered clothes and backpack. Then he placed a call.

Penny examined the bear covered with blue paint. *It's a mess. I wanted it to look amazing, but the paint dripped and splattered.* "But I wanted . . ."

"One day you'll see the world doesn't revolve around you and what you want. Come with me. We're going to the principal's office."

Penny's shoulders sagged. *I'm in trouble now.*

Chapter 3

MEGAN ADDED AN UPDATED FINANCIAL REPORT TO THE folders on her desk. *Glad I took the time to revisit those numbers.* When Megan's boss arrived an hour later, she was ready for the presentation.

"Good morning, Bradley." Megan rose and shook his hand. *He's too young to be a VP. Every time I see him, I can't figure out how he got to be a VP so fast. That should have been my job, but instead, they brought in this youngster.*

"You ready for today?" Bradley walked past her and gazed out the window at the city street below them. He sucked on a peppermint candy, clicking it against his teeth.

Bradley is nothing but direct. "Of course."

"I can't tell you how important this account is." His jaw barely relaxed as he spoke.

Her intuition jumped into overdrive, and her fingers rested on her pearls. "Is everything okay?"

Bradley returned to Megan's desk and flipped through the top document. "Very professional. I admire your team. They're a hardworking group." The mint on his breath spread as he spoke.

Megan read people well, and Bradley was saying one thing, but his stiffness was sending a different message. "Yes, they are." *I hired all of them and got them the training they needed.*

With a soft chime, the screen of Megan's phone glowed. She glanced at it on her desk but didn't recognize the number. "Bradley, is something wrong?"

He shook his head. "Take your call. We can talk after the presentation."

She watched him leave, unsettled by his cryptic comments on the presentation. *He usually has a lot to say.*

Megan glanced at her watch. *An hour until the client gets here.* She grabbed the phone and answered, "Hello, Megan Hinson speaking."

"This is Roger Nelson, principal at Bridgewater High School." His tone was all business.

Megan's heart beat faster. "Is Penny okay?"

"Well, Ms. Hinson, Penny is outside my office. She's fine, but there's been some vandalism at the school. I need you to come to my office to discuss the next steps."

"What kind of vandalism? What has she done?" Megan sat at her desk and exhaled slowly. *What now? Penny's been difficult, but she never got in trouble before.*

Principal Nelson cleared his throat. "It would be best if you came in person."

"I'm getting ready for an important meeting." Megan tapped her foot. *This is the worst timing. Can I get someone else? Steve is so helpful, but I can't send him to school in my place. Not for something like this.*

"My next step will be to get law enforcement involved."

Megan closed her eyes. "I can be there in forty-five minutes—at the most, an hour." She ended the call and set the phone down. *Oh, Penny, what have you done?*

She leaned back in her chair and rubbed her eyes. *Should I call the client and reschedule? Who else can take over the presentation? I'll start with Bradley.*

Bradley's office door was open, but his chair was facing the floor-to-ceiling windows. The corner office provided a view of the city's high-rise buildings and a glimpse of the bay beyond the structures. *A VP's view. One day this will be my view.*

His polished mahogany desk was massive and bare of papers. His jar of peppermint candies was gone. *That's odd. Bradley usually isn't this neat. Maybe he packed things to move up to the executive level.*

"Excuse me, Bradley." Megan put the stack of presentation folders on his desk. "An emergency has come up at Penny's school. I'm afraid I have to go and can't do the presentation. The client will be here in less than an hour."

With his fingertips steepled together, Bradley stared out the window. "Did you ever wonder how one gets into window washing as a career?"

Megan glanced at the clean glass. *Did he hear me?* "I said I have to leave."

Bradley's chair swiveled around, and his eyes met hers. "I heard you. I'll make the presentation. Before you go, please tell Abbie I want her to attend as well."

"Yes, sir." Megan examined the pointed toe of her snakeskin high heels. "I'm sorry."

"I understand. When you get back, I want to talk to you about your future."

Megan's knees shook, and she touched the pearls resting against her throat. *Is this about the promotion I've been hoping for?* "Certainly. I'll be back as soon as I can."

She hurried to Abbie's workspace. Everyone else in the firm had an office or cubicle, but the lead designer had taken over a conference room with props, posters, and even a manikin. Megan spotted Abbie beside a collection of teapots taking close-up photographs. The room even smelled like a tea shop.

"Abbie, there's been a sudden change of plans."

"How exciting!" Abbie lowered her camera. "Will I like it?"

"You need to go to the presentation with Bradley." *If I can count on anyone, it's Abbie. Bradley doesn't know the details, but Abbie does.*

"That's not what I wanted to hear."

Megan almost laughed at the face Abbie made. "I'm not kidding. Something happened at Penny's school."

Abbie took another photograph of the teapots. "Is the client cute? Maybe I can get a free dinner at this unique dining experience place."

"Easy there, girl. Fraternizing with the clients is forbidden."

"And hands off the boss, too," Abbie said with a wink.

They both laughed. As Megan left, she flashed a thumbs-up at the designer.

"Say hi to that charming daughter of yours," Abbie called.

"Which one, Jody or Penny?"

"Both."

Right now, Penny isn't on my charming list.

* * *

Penny sat in the administration office waiting area. She could hear the principal speaking to her mother, but the response he was getting from her was unclear. *She's gonna meltdown over this.*

Principal Nelson emerged from his office. "Your mother is on her way. She should be here in about forty-five minutes. Until then, you can sit here and contemplate your punishment." He headed back to his office but stopped and turned around. "You want to tell me who else did this?"

Penny lowered her gaze to her boots and shook her head.

"Protecting someone who commits a crime doesn't make you a hero. It's even worse because the guilty parties aren't being brought to justice. We know you weren't acting alone. You sure you don't want to share their names?"

Still looking down, Penny said, "No one else was there." *Why am I covering for Dylan and Ashley? I doubt they would do the same for me.*

"I'm sorry you want to take all the blame and all the punishment." He returned to his office.

She pulled out her phone and sent a text message to Lacey.

Where were u?

She waited, but there was no answer. *She's in class, where I should be.*

Her stomach rumbled, and she pressed her hand against her belly to ease the hunger pang. *I missed breakfast because of that argument with Steve. He's going to be mad, too.* She turned her wrist over and admired the skull and crossbones she had drawn. *All because of a stupid poison symbol.*

Could I get suspended from school? Would they send me to juvenile detention? It's just paint. It can be removed.

What's the big deal? She swung her feet. *What happened to Lacey? Why wasn't she there?* She squirmed on the smooth plastic seat. *What am I going to tell Mom?*

The school resource officer led a shaggy-haired boy with gauges in his ears into the administration offices. "Sit here," the officer said to his charge and pointed at the seat beside Penny.

The boy slouched in the chair and curled his upper lip. "Go ahead. Call my ma. She ain't gonna care."

Penny inched away from him. *He smells like one of Steve's beers, and his T-shirt is ripped from the collar to the hem. He looks older, like he's a senior.*

The school resource officer stepped into the principal's office. Their muffled voices droned in a monotone.

"What they get you for?" The boy slumped lower in the seat.

"Me?" Penny's voice squeaked.

"No. The Red Skull." The boy snorted. "Of course, you." He leaned forward and put his head between his knees.

Penny moved her backpack away from him. "Are you going to be sick?"

He made a noise that sounded like a growl, then sat up. "What's your name?"

Without hesitation, she showed him her skull and crossbones. "Poison Pen."

"That's not a real tattoo." He grunted. "I'm Dagger."

They fist-bumped, and Dagger sank back in his chair.

"So, Poison Pen, what did ya do?"

"I got caught painting the school mascot statue."

Dagger scoffed at her. "Is that all?"

Penny swallowed. *That's enough.* She hesitated. "Why

are you here?" *I'm not sure I want to know.*

"Fixin' a jerk's attitude."

I think that means fighting. I wonder who won and what happened to the other guy.

"Then the SRO found my juice."

"Your juice?"

He cocked an eyebrow at her. "Are you stupid?"

The school resource officer and principal emerged from the office.

"We spoke with your mother," the principal said to Dagger. "She won't be coming here. You'll be going to the police station."

"We'll meet the police car out front." The school resource officer waved his hand for Dagger to stand up. "Come with me, Oliver."

Oliver. No wonder he goes by Dagger.

Dagger rose slowly and wobbled. He turned toward Penny with a scowl on his face. "Keep it real, Poison Pen."

She watched him walk away unsteadily, following the school resource officer toward the exit.

The principal glanced at Penny. "Your mother should be here soon. If she hadn't agreed to come, you would've been going with him."

She lowered her eyes. *This is more serious than I thought.*

* * *

THE RIDE FROM THE FOURTEENTH FLOOR TO THE LOWER-LEVEL parking garage gave Megan time to think about Bradley's words. *Was he annoyed I had to leave? But it could be about my promotion.* Her mind shot from one alternative to the next. The higher pay grade that went with a promotion would make a big difference with Penny's college expenses just a few years away. *Wonder why Bradley was thinking about window washing as a career. Why was his desktop empty? Something is going on.*

On the drive to the high school, Megan called Steve. When he didn't answer, she left him a voicemail. *Steve and Penny have such a rocky relationship. I doubt she would have told him what she was going to do at school this morning. But Penny's so quiet, I can't imagine her vandalizing anything.*

She pulled into the high school parking lot and searched for a parking space. *Being here takes me back to my time as a student. How many years ago? Over twenty.* She parked and walked to the front entrance. Her heels clicked against the concrete walkway. She swung the entrance door open and went to the front desk.

"I'm Penny Davis's mother. I'm here to see Principal Nelson."

The receptionist gave her a dark look. "Sign in here." She pointed to a registration ledger and made a phone call.

After Megan signed the list, an older woman came from behind the counter. "Right this way."

Megan followed her down a hallway with motivational posters on the wall. At the end of the hallway, she spotted Penny sitting with another student. Penny's head was down and her legs were swinging. The sign above the office read "Principal."

Taking a deep breath, Megan stood in front of her daughter. *This couldn't have come at a worse time.* "Penny, what did you do?"

CHAPTER 4

PENNY FIDGETED IN THE CHAIR OUTSIDE THE PRINCIPAL'S office. She rubbed her eyes and sniffled. *How did I get myself into this mess? Mom is going to kill me.* When her mom arrived, Penny cringed at her expression. Mom's tight lips and narrowed eyes sent a chill up her spine.

"Penny, what did you do? What's this about vandalism?" Mom's tone was harsh.

"I'm sorry." The tears she had been trying to hold back streaked down her cheek.

The principal came out of his office. "Mrs. Davis?"

"It's Mrs. Hinson now."

"Please come in. You, too, Penny." He led the way into his office.

Penny had never been in the principal's office before, and she blinked at the number of books on the shelf behind the cluttered desk. A limp potted plant filled one corner of the desk; a box of tissues occupied the other corner, and a half-eaten breakfast burrito on a plate sat atop a pile of folders. The smell of it made Penny's stomach rumble in hunger.

"This is extremely serious, Mrs. Hinson. Penny was caught vandalizing the statue of the school mascot. She won't tell me who else took part in this, but we don't think she acted alone. As you can see, she's covered with paint."

Penny squirmed with both the principal and her mother staring at her. She put her left hand over her paint-covered right hand and tried to hide the blue splatters on her leggings.

"We could take this to law enforcement."

Penny's head jerked up, and her mouth opened.

"Principal Nelson," her mother said. "Penny's not been in trouble before. Is there something else we could do? I'm sure she's learned her lesson. Right, Penny?"

"I'm sorry." Penny's voice cracked.

The principal shifted several papers on his desk. "There is an alternative. If Penny completes forty hours of community service and promises she won't do any more vandalism, we won't take this through the legal process."

"That sounds reasonable." Her mother turned to her. "Don't you agree, Penny?"

Penny nodded eagerly. "Yeah."

"I'll hold you to that," the principal said. "Penny, you can pick a community service project, but I need to approve it. If you want a suggestion, I have the address of a local senior center where you can write letters to residents. For every response you get back, I'll credit you with one hour of community service. Would you like the address?"

"Yes, please." Penny took the slip of paper the principal handed her. She glanced at the address printed in neat letters. *I can write letters. That's easy.*

"You need to understand that if you don't complete the community service hours, the school will take legal action. We have everything documented."

"Thank you, Principal Nelson. I'll make sure she follows through on these letters." Penny's mother rose and shook hands with the principal.

Penny followed her mother out of the office. "Mom, I'm really sorry."

Her mother looked away. "I have to get back to work. We'll discuss this when I get home."

With a sigh, she picked up her paint-stained backpack. *And the ice war begins.*

By the time Penny got a pass to return to class, it was lunchtime. The drab gray walls of the cafeteria matched her mood. She wandered through the rows of tables with her food tray and searched for Lacey. When Penny couldn't find her friend, she sat by herself and ate without tasting her lunch.

Before the end of the lunch period, Dylan and Ashley hurried over and sat across from her. Dylan glanced over his shoulder, while Ashley twisted a lock of her hair between her fingers. In frustration, Penny clenched her teeth. She was in trouble because of them.

Ashley leaned close. "Did you get away?"

"No. Coach caught me."

"Didn't you hear me say to run?" Dylan asked.

Puzzled, Penny gaped at him. "You said something?"

Both Ashley and Dylan nodded. "Dylan saw the coach coming and told us to run," Ashley said.

"I must have been in the zone." Penny knew from experience when she was doing art, she rarely heard her mother calling her for dinner. *The zone explains it.* "I thought you just left me."

"We wouldn't do that," Ashley said. "What happened after they caught you?"

"I had to go to the principal's office, and they called my mom."

Ashley groaned. "That's bad."

"Did you tell them we were there?" Dylan asked, staring directly at her.

"No."

He pushed away from the table and jumped to his feet. "Good. Gotta go."

Ashley continued to pump for information. "Was your mom mad? Are you getting detention or suspension?"

"As punishment, I have to write letters to old people."

"That's weird." Ashley contorted her face into a poor imitation of a demented person.

"They have to write back or the school may get the cops involved."

Ashley appeared nervous. "We don't want that. You better write the letters and hope the boomers still know how to write back."

"There may be more." Penny picked up her tray and stood to go. "When I get home, I still have to face my mom and Steve."

Ashley rolled her eyes. "Best of luck with that."

"I know." *The worst is still ahead.*

* * *

MEGAN STEPPED OFF THE ELEVATOR AT WORK IN A DAZE, STILL sorting out her reaction to Penny's vandalism. It was lunchtime, and the office was deserted. Megan glanced at Abbie's workspace, but the lights were off. She dropped her purse off in her office and wandered down the hallway to Bradley's office. *He's probably at lunch with the client.* When she reached his doorway, she stopped, surprised he was seated at his desk.

Bradley gestured for her to enter. "Please close the door."

Megan did and sat in the chair closest to the desk. "How did the presentation go?"

"They liked the plan. Abbie took him to lunch to get more insight into a few changes he wants to have made."

Megan stroked her necklace. "I thought you would have joined them."

Bradley chuckled and took a deep breath. "Normally, I would have, but . . ."

Intrigued, Megan leaned forward and searched his face. "But?"

"You know the firm has been in a decline lately. Upper management accepted an offer to buy us out."

Megan's stomach ached. "An acquisition?"

"They made the announcement right after you left. You and I are redundant. We're being terminated."

In shock, her shoulders sank. "Our jobs are gone?"

"There will be a severance package. I have a couple of documents for you with more details." Bradley slid a large manila envelope across his desk.

With trembling fingers, she picked up the envelope. The papers inside held the last bit of security she might cling to while her future collapsed around her.

"I'm sorry, Megan. You've been a valuable resource for the company. I don't know where I'll land, but if you need a reference, you can count on me."

She twisted the pearl necklace around her fingers. "When does this take effect?"

Bradley stood up and came around his desk. "Immediately. They asked us to leave this afternoon and take all our personal possessions. They wanted to escort us out with security, but I guaranteed we're professionals and that was unnecessary."

Megan nodded, rose, and shook hands with Bradley. "It has been an honor to work with you."

As Megan placed her framed photos and mementos in a box, she fought back tears. *I was expecting a promotion, not this.* She left her security badge on the desk and scanned the office for any personal items she might have missed. She had been thrilled when she finally moved from a cubicle to an office with a door. *That door was a mark of accomplishment. And now I'm going to walk out that door for the last time. How did I not see this coming? I'm normally aware of what's going on with senior management.*

She scribbled a quick note for Abbie and left it in her workspace. Then she collected her box of personal items and took the elevator to the parking garage. Once inside her car, she sat behind the steering wheel for a few minutes as the impact of being terminated overwhelmed her. With her hand shaking, she started the engine.

As she drove the interstate heading home, Megan gripped the steering wheel until her knuckles ached. "It's not fair. I worked my tail off for them for eighteen years. It isn't supposed to end like this. Where's the appreciation for all the hard work? What about all those awards they won because of me? Doesn't that count for anything?"

A panel truck cut in front of her, and she slammed on the brakes. With her heart racing, Megan shoved her hand on the horn and let it blare for a minute. The truck sped up, and Megan eased off the horn. "Stupid jerk! No common sense.

No sense at all."

After pulling into her garage, she shut off the engine and left the box of office items in the car trunk. The house was empty. *Steve's working until five today. Jody's at daycare. Penny will arrive on the school bus around four. For the next hour, I have the house to myself. I could use a glass of wine or bourbon, but I have to pick up Jody.*

Megan slumped on the couch. *What am I going to do? We can't afford this house on only Steve's salary. Where can I get a job fast?* Question after question swirled through her head. Tears trickled down her cheeks. She took off her pearl necklace and held it in her palm. *It's happening all over again.* Her mind took her back to when she was a child.

September 1990

WHEN HER MOTHER STOPPED WALKING, SEVEN-YEAR-OLD Megan stared at the three gold balls hanging from a bar over the tinted glass of the shop. Megan had not been inside this store before. With a sense of excitement, she followed her mother into the shop. As the door swung open, a set of bells jingled.

"Mommy, look at all this stuff," she said. Her eyes darted from televisions, tools, guns, clocks, books, and display cases full of items.

"Don't touch anything," her mother said and took Megan's hand.

"What's that smell?" Megan wrinkled her nose at the musty odor.

"Some of these things are old and dusty. Now, keep

quiet while we're in here."

The pawnshop owner called from behind a counter. "Hello, Mrs. Brown. Glad to see you again. Are you here to reclaim an item or bring in something else?"

Megan tugged at her mother's hand. "He knows your name, but what does he mean?"

Her mother shushed her. "I said be quiet. Why don't you look around? But please don't pick up anything."

Left to wander around the narrow aisles, Megan roved toward the back of the shop. She paused in front of the guitars hanging on the wall. The brown one with the red strap looked like the one Daddy used to play. Beside them was a tall wooden frame covered with splotches of paint. "Mommy," Megan called. "What's this?"

The shop owner laughed. "That's an artist's easel. We get lots of things from musicians and artists. Must be tough to make money being creative."

Megan frowned. "That sounds sad for them." This wasn't like the other stores she had been in with her mother. These were bits and pieces of people's lives.

"What can I do for you, Mrs. Brown?" The shop owner pulled a ledger from behind the counter.

"I want to sell this necklace. Those are real pearls. They were my mother's."

Megan drew closer to the counter. She recognized the necklace her mother held toward the shop owner. "You can't sell those, Mommy. Grandma told me I could have them when I grow up."

Her mother gave a nervous laugh and placed the necklace on the counter. "How much for these?"

The man pulled out a magnifying glass and bent over

the pearls. "Pleasant luster. Decent quality, but they need to be restrung. Common color." He paused and straightened up. "Not much market for antique pearls. Twenty bucks."

"That's all? They're real." A tear trickled down her mother's cheek.

"But, Mommy—"

"Not now, Megan." She put her index finger on Megan's lips. "Money makes the world spin, pumpkin."

"Because you're such a regular customer, I'll give you twenty-five." The shop owner opened the cash register drawer and pulled out two bills.

Her mother took the money and brushed the tears from her eyes.

"Come along, Megan."

"But you can't sell them."

"Someday you'll understand that there's no money to be made being creative. We have to pay the bills. When you grow up, you better get a better-paying job than your father and me." She pulled Megan out of the store.

As Megan looked back, the shop owner placed the pearl necklace in the display case.

Tuesday, September 5, 2023

THE SOUND OF HER PHONE RINGING PULLED MEGAN FROM HER childhood memory. She read the caller's name. *Abbie.* With a sigh, Megan accepted the call.

"I heard a few minutes ago and can't believe it. How are you doing?"

Megan rubbed her forehead. "I'm still in shock."

"If there's anything I can do, call me. I can't believe they let you go. I mean, you're the hardest worker I know. And Bradley, too. Wow, just wow."

Bradley, too! I was caught up in my situation and didn't think about him at all. "I'm sure he'll be fine. He's young and sharp."

"You're young and smart, too."

"Abbie, I'm forty. Where am I going to go that will pay what I've been making?"

The phone was silent.

"How did the presentation go?" Megan asked.

Abbie launched into a detailed description of the client's reaction to the marketing plan, barely pausing for breath. "He loved it, Megan. And you deserve all the credit. Hey, what was the emergency?"

"I need to get Jody from daycare. I'll fill you in when I've processed everything that happened."

Megan put the phone down and closed her eyes. She ran her fingers along the pearl necklace in her hand. *Am I going to lose this, too?*

With a meow, Goku jumped on the couch and curled up in Megan's lap.

She stroked the gray fur. "You know, Goku, you wouldn't normally be allowed to lie on my suit, but today is not a normal day."

The cat purred and extended his neck for more attention.

"I thought the worst was all behind me. Here we are in a gorgeous house with two cars. A kind, caring husband. Jody is a sweetheart." Megan paused. "What am I going to do about Penny?"

She continued rubbing the cat's head. "There's a sever-ance package, and I can apply for unemployment."

Her phone rang again. Megan recognized the name of another coworker but decided not to answer. "Goku, you look comfortable, but I need to get something started for dinner and then go pick up Jody. And I have to figure out what I'm going to do next."

Chapter 5

PENNY HOPED SHE COULD SLIP INTO THE HOUSE AND HEAD straight to her room, but when she opened the front door, she heard sounds coming from the kitchen. Pots clanged and drawers slammed. She took a deep breath. *Mom's home early. Let's get this over with.* She put her backpack down and walked into the kitchen.

Her mom was still in her business suit and peering into the refrigerator. "Stupid, so stupid," she muttered.

Penny edged closer. "Mom?" When her mother turned toward her, Penny gasped. Her face was puffy, her eyes red and glassy.

"I'm sorry, Mom."

"You should be."

Penny hesitated. *I can't tell if she's angry or sad.* Penny lowered her head. "It won't happen again."

"You better believe it won't, because you're grounded."

Penny's head shot up. "You mean I have to write letters and I'm grounded, too?"

"What were you thinking? Or maybe you weren't thinking. Why would you do that? And who are you protecting?" Mom's voice grew louder, and her face turned red.

Penny reeled back, then stepped away from her mother. *We've had words before, but she's never been like this.* "I made a mistake."

"A mistake! You vandalized school property. That's more than a mistake."

"It was Soph Fun Day . . . We meant it to be fun—"

"If destroying things that aren't yours is your idea of fun, then I've raised a selfish brat."

"That's not true." Penny stiffened her back.

"You're lucky the principal didn't call the authorities. You could be considered a juvenile delinquent."

"It was only some paint."

"Was this your idea?"

"Mom, it doesn't matter who started it. I'm the one who got caught."

"You're protecting someone or a couple of someones who wouldn't do the same for you. The world treats you like dirt. There's no loyalty. None."

Puzzled, Penny raised her eyebrows. *What's she talking about?*

Slowly, as if she was running out of steam, Mom exhaled. "You need to be honest and tell the principal who else was involved."

"I can't do that," Penny said. *I can't snitch on Dylan and Ashley.*

Mom glanced at her watch. "I've got to pick up Jody. Steve will be home around five thirty. In the meantime, go to your room and do your homework. You can work on those letters after dinner."

In her room, Penny stretched out on her bed. The cat settled beside her and purred in her ear. *How did I get into this mess? Why didn't I tell Dylan and Ashley I wanted to go to art class instead? They aren't even my friends. Lacey got me into this, and she didn't even show up at the statue.*

Forty hours of community service is rough. What if the old people don't write back? I could write letters all year and never get a response. Then what? Principal Nelson said he would go to the police. Would they arrest me? Take me to jail? Court? How much trouble could I get in because of stupid Soph Fun Day?

She sat up and rubbed the cat's head. "I did something really wrong today. I got community service hours and Mom grounded me, too. No going to parties or the movies or shopping with Lacey. This is the worst day of my life."

Later, Penny set the kitchen table for dinner, careful not to make too much noise. Oil sizzled in the frying pan on the stove. *Fried chicken,* Penny guessed. The smell soon changed to burned chicken. *Mom's standing right at the stove, but she's not even looking at the pan.*

"Mom?" Penny kept her voice low.

"I pulled out a few envelopes for you," Mom said. "They're on the desk in the office."

The sizzling continued, and smoke curled from the frying pan. Drops of oil shot out of the pan and landed on the cooktop with a hiss.

"Mom." Penny stepped closer to the stove. *If she's not careful, the smoke alarm is going to start soon.*

Within seconds, the harsh alarm sounded. Its mechanical voice said, "Alert. Alert."

Mom shook her head and grabbed the frying pan from the stove. She yelled in pain and dropped the hot pan. With a clatter, it fell back on the cooktop, and oil splattered across the surface. Her mother cursed and waved her hand in the air.

"Are you okay?" Penny's heart raced.

Mom ran to the kitchen sink and turned on the cold tap. She held her right hand under the stream of water.

The smoke detector continued to blare, and Jody ran into the kitchen, shrieking.

With her eyes burning from the smoke, Penny raced to open windows and doors to get the air circulating. She grabbed a kitchen towel and fanned the air around the stove. At the sink, her mother was sobbing with Jody clinging to her leg.

The door from the garage opened, and Steve rushed into the kitchen. "What's going on? Where's the fire?"

"Just smoke from cooking," Penny said. "Mom hurt her hand."

Steve hurried to the sink and examined her mother's hand. "Let's put some ice on this," he said.

"They fired me." Her mother's voice cracked, and tears ran down her cheeks.

Wrapping his arms around her, Steve pulled her into an embrace. "It's going to be alright."

"No, it's not," she wailed.

Penny stopped fanning the air. *That must be why she was home early and such a bitch.*

As the air cleared, the alarm silenced. Penny checked the chicken in the frying pan and grimaced. "Um, I don't think we can eat this."

"Penny, order a pizza," Steve said. He held Jody in one arm and encircled her mother with the other.

Glad to be out of the kitchen, Penny placed the order in the app and sent Lacey a text message about the craziness in the family. *Mom getting fired sounds worse than paint on a statue.*

LATER THAT NIGHT, PENNY PULLED A SHEET OF PAPER OUT OF her spiral notebook with a quick tug. She stared at the lined paper and waited for a word to pop into her head. *How do you start a letter to someone you don't know?* She grabbed her red pen and wrote, "Dear Old Fart," then crossed it out and wrote, "Hello, Stranger." She scribbled through that, too. Frustrated, she looked at the manga poster on her wall. *Ashley called them boomers.* "Hey Boomer."

She crumpled up the page and threw it in the trash. With a frown, she ripped another page out of her notebook and started again. This time, she got halfway through the letter before tearing it into little pieces. She wrote another letter and then another. Each one became a ball of paper shot into the trash.

The sounds in the house told Penny it was nearing time for bed. It was dark outside her bedroom window. She listened to more music and did her homework. With a yawn, she stretched. *I don't want to face Mom at breakfast without a finished letter.* She leaned over and pulled a ball of paper out of the trash. With her hands, she flattened the paper and set a few heavy books on the wrinkled sheet, then went into the bathroom to brush her teeth. When she came back, she took the books off the paper and added a final sentence to the letter.

Her red pen hovered over the bottom of the letter. *How should I sign this?* Penny put the point of the pen on the paper and wrote the letter *P.* She stopped. *I could sign it with my full name, Penelope W. Davis, but I hate my first name. I don't know who this letter is going to. Why should they know who I am? Why is this so hard?*

She tapped the pen on the paper, and it left a few dots. With little thought, she connected the dots and drew a skull. She glanced at the faded image on her wrist and added a pair of crossed bones behind the skull. At the sight of the finished drawing, she sat up taller. *I know!* She went back to signing the letter.

With a smirk, she signed: "Poison Pen." *There. That will show them who they're dealing with.* She sat back and examined the letter. The paper was wrinkled and the red ink wavered a bit with the wrinkles.

I need to get a response. I should rewrite this. No. This is who I am. Poison Pen. Whether or not the old fart likes it.

She folded the letter in half and then half again. She crammed it into the envelope her mother gave her and sealed it shut.

Done.

* * *

THAT NIGHT, MEGAN LAY ON HER SIDE IN BED WITH HER EYES wide open. Steve snored lightly beside her. The burn on her hand throbbed despite the pain relief cream and the pain medication. She rolled over and tried to put the events of the day behind her, but the meetings with Bradley and Principal Nelson replayed in her mind.

What could have caused Penny to vandalize the school statue? It has to be the kids she's hanging around with at school. She's more of a follower than a leader. There had to be other kids involved. Why is she protecting them?

The principal's punishment seems doable. Heck, writing letters to residents of an assisted living facility should be easy. Getting responses might be a challenge. If it was me, what would I do? I'd make my letters fun to read and ask simple questions that an older person might answer. I'd start right away. But Penny isn't me.

She rolled over and put her uninjured hand behind her head. *Being fired came out of the blue. I was expecting a promotion, not a termination. I wish my next steps were as easy as writing letters to seniors. What am I going to do? I've heard it takes a month of job hunting for every ten thousand dollars' worth of salary being replaced. That means finding a decent job is going to take the better part of a year. The severance money won't last that long. I'll have to apply for unemployment, too. I never thought I would have to do that.*

She shifted her position again. This time, Steve mumbled something. "It's okay, sweetie," she whispered. *But it may not be okay. Whatever happens, I'm not taking my pearls to the pawnshop. No way.*

CHAPTER 6

THE NEXT MORNING, ON THE SCHOOL BUS, PENNY GLARED at Lacey, who stared back at her. *Why didn't she show up at the statue yesterday? She was the one who was so excited about Soph Fun Day.*

"Dylan and Ashley—" Penny said.

"Don't talk to me about them. They have crazy ideas. I told you they were trouble."

Penny raised an eyebrow. "When did you do that?"

"I sent you a text message."

"When?"

"After we got off the bus. I told you what they were planning wasn't what the day was about." Lacey was wound up and spoke louder. "Soph Fun Day was supposed be fun things, like turning the desks around in the classroom as if the back of the room was the front or wearing weird clothes. Not destroying or damaging things. Dylan and Ashley were taking it too far, and I warned you not to do it."

"I didn't get your text."

Lacey pulled out her phone and scrolled through messages. "I sent it after I found out what they were planning to do. Before classes started." She continued scrolling. "Here it is." Lacey lifted her head. "OMG, Penny. It didn't go through." She shoved her phone in Penny's face.

Penny read the words on the screen. "I wish I had seen this yesterday. I wondered why you didn't show up."

"I thought we would get in trouble. That wasn't what Soph Fun Day was for."

"I did get in trouble . . . and grounded." *If Lacey's text had gone through, if I'd seen it, I wouldn't be in trouble now.*

PENNY HESITATED OUTSIDE THE ART CLASSROOM. HER mother's words still rang in her head. *You better apologize to the teacher whose class you cut to vandalize school property.* Penny took a deep breath and stepped into Mrs. Silsbury's classroom. As Penny walked to her seat, she avoided making eye contact with the teacher.

Unlike the other classrooms in the school, the art room was full of color. Paintings hung on the walls. Paint splatters covered all the desks. Even the ceiling tiles were painted. Soft music played in the background. *Normally, the art room is my favorite place to be.*

When the bell rang to start class, Mrs. Silsbury turned on a light next to a table with a box and a ball. "We're going to continue yesterday's lesson on shadows. You have thirty minutes to sketch either the box or the ball or both. Pay particular attention to how the shadows fall on the object and the surface. Remember, there's a shadow on the object and a cast shadow."

Papers rustled and chair legs scraped across the floor. The sound of pencils scratching on paper grew louder.

Penny opened her sketchbook and fished in her backpack for her pencil.

Mrs. Silsbury stopped beside Penny's seat. "Since you missed yesterday's lesson, let me tell you what you should focus on."

Penny cleared her throat. "I'm sorry I cut your class yesterday."

"I am, too. Principal Nelson told me what happened. I am disappointed."

In surprise, Penny studied the teacher's face.

"To use paint to deface something that isn't yours is a crime. You need to find more productive uses for your talent."

"I am sorry," Penny whispered. "But that bear . . ."

"That bear is the school mascot. If you don't like the way it looks, there are ways you could have handled that. We could have held a contest to come up with a new design for the bear. Or start a petition to change the school mascot."

Penny nodded. "It won't happen again."

"I hope not. Now, let's get you caught up with the rest of the class." Mrs. Silsbury took Penny's pencil. "Yesterday's lesson was on shadows."

Penny paid close attention to the lesson, but Mrs. Silsbury's words kept intruding on her thoughts. *I disappointed her. What would be a more productive use of my talent?*

PENNY SLIPPED INTO A SEAT AT THE BACK OF THE MATH classroom and opened her notebook. Since her pen had run out of ink in the last class, she searched her backpack for another pen or a pencil. *Come on, there's got to be something in here.*

"Today," the teacher said, "we're going to learn about calculating the volume of a rectangular solid." He drew the geometric shape on the board. "Copy this into your notes." He wrote, "V=lwh."

Penny frantically dug through the papers in her backpack and found a pencil. The tip was blunt from art class but serviceable. She drew the shape in her notebook and copied the formula.

As the teacher explained the elements of the formula, Penny doodled on her page. *This reminds me of the box Mrs. Silsbury set up for the shadow lesson. Which direction will the light be coming from?* Penny shaded the sides of the box and added a cast shadow. She sketched more details, increasing the depth of the drawing. With her head down, Penny focused on her page and created a second box.

"Would you like to share this with the class?"

Penny looked up in surprise to discover the math teacher standing at her desk. Her mouth opened, and she stumbled over her words. "No, not really."

"Do you want to show the principal?"

She shook her head rapidly. "No!" *Don't send me to the principal. He won't be happy to see me again.*

"Well, then pay attention to the lesson and save the artwork for art class." The teacher returned to the front of the room.

The class snickered. Penny turned the page in her notebook and carefully drew the rectangular shape and the formula. *I better listen to him. I don't need any more trouble.*

* * *

DURING LUNCH AT SHADOW OAKS SENIOR LIVING HOME, Rosemary put her fork down. "We need to have a plan."

Nina continued chewing. *Now what's she up to?*

"The only way we're going to get Emily and Andy

together is to create situations to make that happen."

Nina picked up her glass of water and took a sip. Over the rim of the glass, she glanced from Rosemary to Emmett and Mike. *The men don't seem as interested in this effort.*

Nina set her glass down. "Rosemary, what makes you think Emily and Andy belong together?"

"They're like Romeo and Juliet, or Scarlett O'Hara and Rhett Butler."

"Those all ended poorly," Nina said.

"Well, they are both kind people, single, and they're here." Rosemary ran her finger around the rim of her teacup.

I bet that description applies to most of the people at Shadow Oaks. Nina nodded and scanned the room with its tables full of seniors. *There's nothing wrong with being single. I've been single my entire life.*

"We can loosen the light bulbs in the gathering room lamps. When Andy comes to fix the lamps, we can get Emily to join us there, too. Then we'll get them talking to each other." Rosemary rubbed her hands together.

"Nina, are you done with your lunch?" Mike asked.

Nina blinked. "Yes. This is more than I'm used to eating at noon."

"Pass me your plate." Mike extended his hand.

What? She picked up her plate with the half-eaten mashed potatoes and meatloaf and passed it to Mike.

He emptied the mashed potatoes on his plate and returned the meatloaf to Nina.

"Here she comes," Mike said.

Nurse Bridger had a tray with little plastic cups. She moved from table to table, handing out the cups to specific individuals. She stood by Nina's elbow and picked up a labeled cup. "Mike Walsh."

"Here!"

With a stern glare, she gave him a cup with an assortment of pills in different sizes and colors. "Make sure you finish all of those." She walked to the next table.

With his spoon, Mike scooped a hollow into the mashed potatoes and dropped all the pills into the low spot. Then he covered the pile of pills with the remaining potatoes.

"He does that almost every day," Rosemary said. "One day she caught him because the blue pill and the red one together turned the potatoes purple. Now he buries them deeper in the potatoes."

Nurse Bridger circled back to collect the cups and check on compliance. She picked up Mike's empty cup, and he made a show of drinking a large gulp of water.

"All gone," he said and wiped a trickle of water from his beard.

"Well done." The nurse walked away.

When she was out of earshot, Nina said in a low voice, "Shouldn't you be taking those pills?"

"Sometimes I put them in my pocket, and Emmett and I play poker with them."

"Nina, you'll get used to it here after a while," Rosemary said. "We do what we need to do to make the time pass."

Nina scratched her forehead. *That sounds miserable. Is that it? Life is over and we're here passing time until the end?*

After lunch, Nina strolled through the gardens. A light breeze shifted the leaves, and the sun sparkled through the branches of the oak trees that lined the entrance road to Shadow Oaks. Butterflies fluttered from flower to flower and hovering hummingbirds sounded like bees. The little white flowers of the star jasmine scented the air. Hibiscus bloomed in bright hues of orange, pink, and red. Nina walked along the path that weaved from the front entrance around to the side of the building. In the distance, she spotted a pair of deer nibbling on the grass. Several benches provided resting spots along the walkway, so she sat for a few minutes to enjoy the surroundings.

After ambling in the garden for forty-five minutes, Nina wandered into the gathering room. Mike, the only other person in the room, sat at a card table assembling a puzzle. She scanned the colorful pieces spread across the table.

"What are you working on, Mike?"

He lifted the puzzle box lid to show her a picture of two antique cars and a row of motorcycles in front of a diner. "I've got most of the border done, except for the sky. The vehicles and diner are easy, but all those blue sky and cloud pieces . . ." He shook his head, pushing back his cap with its embroidered US Army lettering.

"Would you like some help?" *I hope he won't be offended.*

He laughed and pushed his cap farther back on his head. "You don't need to ask. Pick your pieces."

Nina reached for the pieces with blue and white. *The sky's all about different shades of blue.* Patiently, she pieced together the gradations of blue and assembled sections of the sky. "I'm getting there, Mike."

"Roger that."

"I haven't heard that phrase in a long time." She recalled her father's voice on the phone long ago.

Mike stopped placing a puzzle piece. "Are you former military?"

"My dad was army. I grew up on bases around the world. Did most of our shopping at the BX. Mom and I traveled all over the countries where Dad was stationed."

"Miss Liz, who sits by the window a lot, was a WASP pilot in World War II. As for me, I did my 365 in 'Nam, but didn't make it to 365 there."

"If you don't mind me asking, what happened?"

"I was on patrol. Our unit was moving slow. We knew the enemy was in the jungle. I heard a click. Too late. I tripped a land mine. When I woke up at the field hospital, my leg was gone."

Nina sighed. "I'm sorry."

"Hey. Got out of 'Nam alive. Lots of guys didn't."

"I know." Nina looked away.

"Your father?"

Nina nodded. "He was a lieutenant colonel. He died in an artillery barrage."

"Lots of deaths," Mike said.

They continued working on the puzzle in silence. Nina connected two sections of the cloudy sky, and Mike finished the yellow car.

He scratched his beard. "Don't know how you got those sky pieces together. They all look the same to me."

"The blue is deeper, darker at the top, and gets lighter as the pieces go lower. And the bottoms of the clouds have shadows."

"Your eyes are better than mine. Glad you joined us here at Shadow Oaks," Mike said. "What's your story?"

Nina gave a faint smile. "I had the same apartment for thirty years, actually longer. I used to ride my bicycle to the high school where I taught. The school district had mandatory retirement at seventy. I had to stop teaching. Then the apartment building where I lived was being converted to a condominium complex, and I had to move. I don't have any family. I thought an assisted living facility might be a wonderful choice for me."

"It's an okay place," Mike said. "Once you get to know folks, you'll fit right in. Anyone who can put a sky together like that can do a puzzle with me anytime."

"Roger that." Nina grinned. *I need to give this place more time.*

* * *

WITH PENNY AT SCHOOL, JODY AT DAYCARE, AND STEVE AT work, Megan stood in the kitchen and sighed. The house was quiet, peacefully quiet. Going back to bed was tempting. Instead, she pulled out the bottle of spray cleaner and a rag. The routine of spraying and wiping the granite countertops grew rhythmic.

"I can't believe they let me go." She rubbed the granite harder, and her voice rose. "I gave them so much of my life. Eighteen years of professional work. All the extra hours." She threw the rag across the kitchen.

"It must have been Bradley's fault. Young ingrate!" She retrieved the cloth and sprayed the cleaner on the front of the microwave. "He probably took the credit for all my work." As she cleaned, her reflection on the microwave glass glared back at her. "It's not fair."

Megan dragged the trash can over to the refrigerator. She tossed an expired bottle of Caesar salad dressing in the garbage and said, "Here's to the Golden Ad Award." A moldy package of cheese joined it. "Here's to the Best-in-Class Marketing Program." With each discarded item, she named another award the company had won because of her efforts. When the last item was thrown in the trash can, she lifted her chin. "I'm damn good, and they couldn't see it."

When she finished polishing the stovetop, she admired all the gleaming kitchen surfaces. *It hasn't been this clean since we moved in.* Megan put the cleaner away and grabbed a package of chocolate chip cookies to reward herself. As she munched on a cookie, she retrieved her phone from the bedroom, where she had left it in silent mode. The screen displayed ten voicemail messages. She groaned and clicked on the earliest message.

Abbie's familiar voice filled the air. "Answer the phone, Megs. Are you doing okay? Call me."

Megan smiled at Abbie's anxious tone and played the next message. She nibbled on another cookie.

"Hey there. It's Rob. I was shocked to hear they let you go. If I can do anything, let me know."

Since when did Rob give two cents about what happened to me? She deleted the message.

"Hello, Megan. It's Annalee. I'm sorry I didn't get to say goodbye, but I wanted you to know . . . well, to tell you how much I enjoyed working with you. You are a talented professional. Take care of yourself. I'll miss you."

Megan sniffled and wiped a tear from the corner of her eye. *Annalee was the sweetest person in the office. She always baked a cake for the monthly birthday celebrations. I'll miss you, too.*

A few messages later, another one from Abbie played. "Megs. Call me."

Abbie will not stop. Megan laughed and returned the call.

On the first ring, Abbie's voice burst through the phone. "Megs. Are you okay? I was worried. I thought something else might have happened."

"Abbie, relax. I was cleaning the kitchen and left the phone in the bedroom." Megan laughed at Abbie's audible gasp.

"I thought I might have to come to your house. You have the suicide prevention number. Right?"

"Stop it. I'm fine." *Sort of fine, I guess.* "I was thinking, though, someone needs to call Doug over in media and make sure the Pinnacle ads are starting today."

"I can't believe you, Megs. They fire you and you're worried about a client's ad."

"You know me—ever the perfectionist. I still need to file for unemployment and update my resume."

"If you need anything, anything at all, call me."

"Thanks, Abbie. And don't forget about contacting Doug."

Megan set the phone by her bedside lamp. *No point in calling anyone else back. Abbie was the exception.* Megan had admired Abbie's artistic free spirit the first time they met, close to ten years ago. *We worked well together.* With a twinge of anger, Megan's pulse increased. *Their decision ended the dynamic duo of marketing.*

She trudged into the spare bedroom, which doubled as the home office. Once at the computer, she pulled up her resume. A few quick updates, and it was ready to go. Then she searched for the unemployment site and spent the better part of an hour applying for benefits. With a sense of accomplishment, Megan searched for project management positions. She scanned through the resulting shortlist. Nothing interested her. *Perhaps tomorrow.*

The front door opening startled her. She checked the time. *That must be Penny.* Megan went into the kitchen, pleased with the sparkling appearance of the place. Penny was rummaging in the refrigerator.

"What happened in here?" Penny asked.

"It's called cleaning. How was school?"

Penny's scowl answered that question.

"You should start writing more letters to the senior center. I'll get you extra envelopes and stamps."

When Megan returned to the kitchen with the stationery, Penny was gone. Megan shook her head. *What am I going to do with her?*

Megan climbed the stairs to the second floor and tapped on Penny's door beside the off-limits sign. "Can I come in?"

At the muffled sound that she interpreted as approval, Megan entered the bedroom. "Here they are, honey."

Penny lay sprawled across her bed, staring at the ceiling, with Goku curled up beside her. Penny had removed her boots, and the mismatched socks caught Megan's attention.

"Why are you wearing two different socks?"

"Because I want to."

To control her annoyance, Megan examined the poster over Penny's bed. Two wide-eyed animated characters with open mouths and spiked hair appeared to be running away from a column of smoke. She glanced at the other posters tacked to the walls. "You like these cartoon characters?"

Penny stared at her like she had crawled out from

under a rock or had two heads. "They're manga."

I'm in no mood to start a debate with her. Who am I kidding? It's not a debate; it's a fight. Megan placed the paper, envelopes, and a book of stamps on Penny's bed and left.

With tears threatening to tumble down her cheeks, Megan returned to the kitchen. *How did everything go wrong?* She reached into the package for another chocolate chip cookie, but they were all gone.

Two hours later, Megan warmed a tray of leftover lasagna in the microwave and poured herself a glass of red wine. For once, Penny set the table without being asked to do it. Steve read a storybook to Jody. On any other night, she would have been overjoyed at this tableau of family harmony, but tonight was not a normal night. A faint smile crossed her face. *They're trying to make me feel better. And I sure do need that.*

At dinner, Steve shared a funny story about a customer who could not decide between two items in the store. Megan laughed when the others laughed, but her thoughts wandered repeatedly.

Steve reached over and took her hand. "It'll be alright."

Megan tilted her head toward him. "Thank you, sweetie."

She studied Penny, silent and sullen, and Jody, bubbling with happiness and covered with tomato sauce. "I want you all to know that the firm was fair to me. They gave me what's called a severance package, a generous amount of money to carry us over while I search for a new job."

She squeezed Steve's hand. "We'll have to be careful about how we spend money. I've already started job hunting, and hopefully, I'll find a well-paying job right away. Until then . . ." She waited to catch Penny's eye. "I'll be home most of the time to help with schoolwork and other home projects. Jody will spend less time in daycare." *That was a difficult decision, but if I have job interviews, I need to have a place for Jody to go during the day.* She took a sip of wine. *Here's to a better tomorrow.*

CHAPTER 7

Friday, September 8, 2023

As Nina walked into the gathering room, Rosemary waved frantically at her. "Nina!"

"What's going on?" Nina asked.

"Our outing today is a trip to Rippling Waters Park. You have to come with us. It has a pretty lake with benches along the shore."

Nina stalled, delaying a decision. "Who else is going?"

Rosemary counted on her fingers. "Mike, Emmett, the Trents, the Knights, and me. Perhaps a few others."

Nina glanced at Liz in her wheelchair by the window. "I'll stay here with Liz."

Mike limped into the gathering room, followed by Emily with the red bag. "Mail call," he announced.

Mail was distributed as usual, until Emily held one last envelope and looked at Nina. "Miss Nina, would you mind taking this one? It wasn't written to anyone in particular." With an apologetic smile, Emily handed her the small white envelope.

"Thank you," Nina said. *Probably another Dear Occupant flyer.*

The activity director folded the mailbag and placed it

under her arm. "Now, everyone going to the park needs to be in the lobby in about ten minutes. Andy will have the shuttle out front. Our nutritionist has prepared a lovely picnic lunch for us."

"Count me in," Mike said.

Nina glanced at the envelope Emily had given her. *The handwriting is childish. Shadow Oaks Old Person—what a way to address an envelope.*

"Are you going, Miss Nina?" Emmett asked.

"No. I think I'll read my letter and then sit with Liz. Have fun." She hurried out of the gathering room, carrying the letter with her.

Once settled in the recliner in her room, she read the return address. *Bridgewater, that's not too far from here.* Careful to keep the return address intact, she opened the envelope and pulled out a heavily wrinkled piece of paper. Unfolding it, she frowned at the tiny pieces of paper still clinging to the side of the page torn from a spiral notebook. *Someone was too lazy to take off these bits.*

The letter was written in red ink. She read the words out loud. "Hey Boomer." She stopped. "What a rude opening." She continued reading. "How RU?" Rubbing her forehead, she put the letter down. "What are English teachers doing these days? The spelling and punctuation are awful."

Nina closed her eyes and put her head against the recliner's back. *Why would someone send a letter like this? There has to be a reason. Kids don't write letters to strangers without having a reason.*

She returned to reading the entire letter.

Hey Boomer,

How RU? Got any good tea?
I need community service hours. Write back. And
soon so I can get out of being grounded.

Signed,
Poison Pen

After shaking her head, Nina stared at the letter. "Poison Pen?" Below the signature was a hand-drawn outline of a skull and crossbones. She studied the line drawing. "The basic components are not bad. The skull openings are a little low on the right side. Poison Pen—whoever you are—you have some artistic potential."

She reread the letter. *What have you done to get grounded? And who thought writing a sloppy letter like this is community service?* Nina folded the letter and stuffed it back in the envelope.

Returning to the gathering room, she spotted Liz still sitting by the window in her wheelchair. Nina approached slowly and asked, "May I join you?"

Liz nodded and a slight smile crossed her face.

Nina pulled a chair over to sit beside the centenarian. She followed Liz's gaze out the window to the garden. With a flash of red wings, a cardinal flew from a bush to a nearby tree branch.

"I hear you were a pilot in the WASPs," Nina said.

Liz sat up taller and her smile grew wider.

"I bet when you see the bird flying, you're thinking about your days in the air."

With a trembling hand, Liz pointed to the sky and nodded.

They sat together and watched the cardinal and its mate fly from one tree to another. In the distance, Nina heard the television in the media center but was content to sit with Liz in the solitude of the gathering room.

Nina glanced at Liz. *She won't respond, but she'll listen to my dilemma.* "I taught high school students for a long time, and I'm sure I helped some of them. Today, I received a letter from someone I think is a high school girl. She seems to have gotten herself in some trouble."

Liz gave no reaction.

"I'm not sure what she's done, but she wants me to write back to her. I'm not looking to get in the middle of her problem." Nina's voice trailed off, and she sighed. "But I can't help thinking that she might need me."

With a small sweep of her hand, Liz gestured toward Nina.

"When I was a new teacher, still learning the ins and outs of teaching, I had a young boy in my class. He had the saddest eyes, like a puppy dog that had been abandoned." *His eyes haunt me even now.* "His name was Carl, and he was in my fourth-period class. He didn't say much, and his drawings had a melancholy feeling. They were dark and moody."

Nina closed her eyes, and his thin, pinched face appeared in her mind. *So sad.* "I should have seen the signs that there was a problem there, but I didn't." She took a deep breath. "Two months into the school year, he took his own life."

Liz made a garbled sound and lowered her head.

"I often wonder if I could have . . . should have done

something." Nina searched for the cardinals outside the window, but they were gone. "So, now I have this letter, and I don't know what to do. Should I respond to her? Ignore her nasty little note and go on with my life? And I'm not even sure anymore what the point of my life is."

A young aide hurried into the gathering room. "I'm sorry, Miss Liz. This schedule says you should be in the media room now, not sitting here doing nothing." She released the brake from the wheelchair and backed it away from the window.

As the chair moved past Nina, Liz reached with a shaky hand and touched Nina's arm. Nina took hold of Liz's hand. The old woman squeezed Nina's fingers, and her eyes went from Nina to the window, up toward the sky.

"Is something wrong?" the aide asked.

"No," Nina said. "I think Liz is telling me I should fly like a bird."

"That's strange." The young woman pushed Liz's wheelchair out of the gathering room.

Nina sat and gazed out the window. *Fly like a bird. Be the teacher I've always been. Is that the message?*

She returned to her room and read the Poison Pen letter again. Carl's eyes stayed with her for the rest of the day.

AT DINNER, ROSEMARY RAMBLED ON ABOUT HOW WONDERFUL the field trip was. "We even saw deer. Wasn't that a treat, Emmett?"

"Indeed, as close as I could spit a watermelon seed."

Nina smiled. Emmett's descriptions were so visual. *Maybe I should go on one of these field trips, but I don't see the point.*

Rosemary set her fork down. "And what did you do today, Nina?"

For a moment, she froze. *Nothing, I did nothing.* Then the Poison Pen letter popped into her mind. "I received the oddest letter."

"Odd in what way, dear lady," Emmett said.

Nina glanced from one of her dinner companions to the next. "Don't laugh, but it was a letter from Poison Pen."

"A poison pen letter!" Rosemary exclaimed. "How awful can a person be?"

"What's a poison pen letter?" Mike's eyes wandered from Nina to Rosemary.

Emmett cleared his throat. "It's an unsolicited communication, typically written anonymously, that sends threats or abusive messages to a victim."

Mike thumped his fist on the table. "That's not right."

"No. It isn't a poison pen letter like that. It was from a young person who signed it as Poison Pen. From the handwriting, I'm guessing it was a female."

Rosemary leaned forward. "What did the letter say?"

"It was short. The writer must have been given the task of writing letters to seniors as a community service project."

Rosemary chuckled. "It is a charming idea. I wouldn't mind getting some unexpected mail."

"The letter writer was grounded. I wonder what the infraction was."

"Nothin' bad enough to be sent to jail," Mike said.

"The writer wants me to write back." Nina moved several green beans around her plate.

"You should," Rosemary said. "You could be pen pals."

"No way. Don't get involved with jailbait," Mike said.

"It could be a scam to get your money."

Nina fixed her gaze on Emmett. He had freely shared his legal opinion on many subjects over the last few days. "What do you say, counselor?"

"Mike has a point that you need to be careful in case the author of the letter is checking you out and intends to empty your bank account. On the other hand, I can imagine an authority figure assigning a letter-writing task as community service for a young person." Emmett put his hands together in a prayer position and placed them in front of his mouth. "What does your intuition tell you?"

"I've been wrestling with this all afternoon. If the child has been grounded and needs to correspond with someone, I could be that person. However, I feel conflicted. I don't need to get involved with someone else's problem. But I spent years teaching, and perhaps I can bring a third-party perspective to the situation."

"You should talk it over with Emily," Rosemary suggested. "She's the one who gave you the letter. She's gone for the day, but you can talk to her tomorrow."

"I'll sleep on the idea. My thinking may be clearer in the morning."

"Sounds like a good plan," Emmett said. "Anyone want more coffee?"

SLEEP ELUDED NINA THAT NIGHT. SHE TOSSED AND TURNED FOR hours. *How can a silly scrap of a letter bother me so much?* Finally, she got up and turned the bedside lamp on. She retrieved the letter and settled back into bed. Studying the envelope, she hoped to get more information. *Just a standard white envelope with an American flag forever stamp.*

The return address was handwritten but without a name. Nina didn't know the street name. *Bridgewater is an upscale community. Not too far from here.*

Pulling the letter out of the envelope again, she turned it over several times. *What in the world am I hoping to find? It's just a piece of spiral notebook paper.* She sniffed the paper. A faint whiff of berries. *Probably some strawberry gel ink. It's definitely written by a girl. Grounding seems like a high school–level punishment. Who are you, Poison Pen?*

Nina placed the letter on the nightstand beside her bed and shut the light off. A few minutes later, she drifted into a fitful sleep.

In the morning, Nina selected a bright red scarf to finish her outfit. *Red is a power color, and I bought this one in Spain.* She had refused to go to the bullfight but admired the matador's red cape. She wore the scarf now, more like the bull than the matador. *Going to breakfast is like entering the bullring and all eyes will be on me. Why did I ever tell them about that blasted letter?*

Nina joined the usual trio for breakfast. Rosemary started talking about the letter as soon as Nina sat down at the table.

"There's Emily," Rosemary said, waving to the activity director. "Be sure to tell her all about the letter."

"Good morning, everyone," Emily said. "You're a lively group this morning, which is good because we have a physical therapist coming today to lead us through some exercises."

"Will we have some exercises for hands?" Nina asked. "My fingers are feeling stiff lately."

"Nina, tell her." Rosemary's foot nudged her under the table.

"I'm sure we can ask for some hand exercises," Emily said. "Is there something else you want to tell me?"

Nina explained about the Poison Pen letter. She had read it so many times, she could repeat it by heart.

"Very strange," Emily said. "Would you like to give me the letter and I'll take care of it?"

Nina considered the offer. "No, I was a teacher for forty-eight years. I'm sure I can handle a child's note. But I don't have any writing paper." *Did I just commit to answering that letter?* "There's one line of the letter I don't understand." Nina swallowed. "What does 'got any good tea' mean? I doubt she's asking about hot tea or iced tea."

Emily laughed. "It's a slang expression. Like gossip or the latest update."

"I thought she wanted to know if we had good tea here," Rosemary said. Everyone at the table nodded.

Nurse Bridger stopped by the table. "Everything okay here? Is there anything you need?"

"How about some tea?" Mike's delivery was straight-faced, but everyone, including Emily, started laughing.

Nurse Bridger frowned. "You want more hot tea?"

"They're fine," Emily said. "They are in a playful mood today. I'll fill you in later."

The nurse left without smiling.

"I believe we have offended her," Emmett said.

"She'll get over it." Mike was still chuckling.

Emily laughed. "Remember, I want to see all of you in the gathering room at ten o'clock for the exercise program. Even you, Mr. Mike."

"Yes, ma'am." Mike saluted.

"Nina, if you need writing paper, stop by the office and

I'll get you some. I'm heading there now if you want to join me."

"Thank you, Emily." Nina rose and followed the activity director.

The office was near the front door, and the waiting area had comfortable armchairs. *The colors here are much brighter than in the rest of the place.*

"Have a seat here, Nina, and I'll get you some writing materials," Emily said before disappearing into another doorway.

Nina admired the painting on the wall, a landscape with a bright sunlit sky. The sky was the same shade she remembered from Galway. She closed her eyes and remembered that summer in Ireland so long ago.

"Here you go." Emily returned with a folder. "There's paper, envelopes, and a pen. When you're done writing, bring the envelopes here. We have stamps you can buy."

Nina thought about the picture of the skull and crossbones. "Can I get a pencil, too?"

"Of course." Emily handed her the folder and disappeared into the other room. She returned with three pencils. "When you need them sharpened, bring them back here. We have a sharpener to put a point back on them."

Nina clutched her new supplies and ambled back to her room. *I'm still not sure if I should get involved with little Miss Poison Pen. She obviously has problems.*

Every year, there was at least one student who struggled with some issue or dilemma. I tried to help them as best I could. Ultimately, they had to decide whether they wanted to change. How about you, Poison Pen? Are you open to change? Maybe I can show you how change can make things better. I'll start with that skull and crossbones.

In her room, Nina opened the folder and took out a piece of paper. *Emily was generous with the paper, over a dozen sheets and envelopes.* She clicked the pen with "Shadow Oaks" printed on the barrel and scribbled a few lines on the folder. *Black ink.* Then she picked up a pencil. Her fingers slid along the wooden length, and she held the point up to her eye. *It's been so long since I've sketched. A pencil in my hand feels like coming home.*

Nina pressed Poison Pen's letter flat and placed the pencil point at the top of the skull. She envisioned a face and hair. Slowly at first, she added a line and then some shading. As the image developed, she worked faster. Soon the skull and crossbones drawing was changed into a portrait of a young girl with long hair.

It was eleven o'clock by the time she was done with the sketch. *Where did the time go?* She chuckled. *I was in the zone.* Her fingers ached and her neck muscles were stiff. Carefully, she tore the sketch from the notebook paper. *I guess I better write a letter to go along with the sketch.*

Before she picked up the pen, she stretched her fingers and moved her head from side to side. *Probably should have gone to the exercise program. I'm in worse pain now than I was at breakfast.* With the pen in her hand, she bent over the paper and wrote, "Dear Poison Pen Pal." When she was done with the letter, she signed it with her full name: *Kanina Koscielniak.*

She hesitated before addressing the envelope. *Who should I make this out to?* Finally, she used the initials "P. P." for Poison Pen and hoped it would get to the right person. The folded letter and the sketch were inserted into the envelope.

Before going to lunch, she dropped it off at the office and paid for a stamp.

Now we'll see if you respond, Poison Pen.

Chapter 8

Monday, September 11, 2023

As he was leaving for work, Steve pulled Megan into his arms. "What do you have planned for today?"

"Decluttering the house is my new mission. I finished the family room yesterday. Today I tackle our closet."

Steve's mischievous grin exposed his front teeth. "Does that mean I might get to put some clothes in there?"

"I'll consider it." Megan kissed him and watched him leave the house. She wrapped her arms around herself. *He's not the least bit like Peter. Marrying Steve was the best thing I've ever done.*

With positive thoughts, she entered the master bedroom and went straight to the massive walk-in closet. *This may be a bigger project than I expected.* Besides rows of clothes, the closet held a collection of plastic storage containers and some worn cardboard boxes full of memorabilia. She pulled outdated clothes off hangers and piled them on the king-sized bed. *Growing up poor, I never had extra of anything. Now look at all this.*

The cat slunk into the closet and disappeared behind a stack of boxes.

"Goku, what are you doing back there?"

A loud meow emerged from the far rear corner of the closet, followed by scratching.

"Don't be ruining anything." Megan lifted the top cardboard box from a stack of containers and took it out to the bed. Opening it, she wrinkled her nose. The smell brought back memories of baby formula and spit-up. *Penny's old baby clothes. Why didn't I use any of these for Jody?* She held up a yellow and stained onesie. *I guess this is why. But how come I kept them all these years?*

She jumped at the sound of a crash. While Goku dashed out of the closet and into the hallway, Megan ran into the closet to assess the damage. A stack of storage containers lay in a heap. The lid had fallen off one container and its contents spread across the floor. *High school stuff.*

Megan sat in the closet and picked up her yearbook— class of 2001. She flipped through the pages and stopped at the autographs and comments written by her friends. When she found her senior photo, she laughed at her hairstyle. She continued leafing through the pages until she reached the faculty. *I don't remember Miss K signing my book.* But there were the words written in neat calligraphy handwriting.

To Megan,

Never give up on yourself. One day, you will make beautiful art.

Miss K.

Megan pondered the words. *Did I give up on myself?*
Below the yearbook, she found a program from the

Christmas musical she had helped with during her soph-omore year. She painted the background and props for the production. She chuckled, remembering the giant candy canes that used all the red paint, so she had to add some green stripes. *Sophomore year. The same grade Penny is in now. I was painting scenery for a school play and she's vandalizing the school mascot.*

Picking up the rest of the high school mementos, Megan put them back in the storage container. The last item on the floor was a sketchbook. She examined the cover. Her sloppy handwritten name sagged across the top of the pad: *Megan Brown.*

Why did I save this? I should never have been in art class. She set the sketchbook aside to take out to the trash and put the lid on the storage container, then restacked the boxes and containers.

Goku appeared at the doorway, purring and butting his head against Megan's leg. She shooed the cat out of the closet before closing the door. "Let's not have any more disasters right now." Then she bagged the clothes she had removed from the closet and took them to a donation drop-off site. The rest of the day, she applied for jobs online.

THE NEXT MORNING, MEGAN ROLLED OVER IN BED AND stretched. Steve had an early training class at work and was already getting dressed.

"Hey, Megan." Steve's voice came from the closet. "I didn't know you're an artist." He emerged with her sketch-book in his hands and came over to the bed.

Megan reached to snatch it away from him. "I meant to throw that out."

With the book in hand, he sat on the edge of the bed. He laughed and flipped through the pages. "Not so fast. I want to see what's in here."

Megan watched over his shoulder. *I barely remember doing these drawings.*

"This is wonderful. Especially this one." He held the book so she could see the page better.

"I wasn't much of an art student. My teacher said I was terrible."

Steve turned the book and studied the back of a page. "Your teacher wrote, 'Fine effort on the line work. Add more shading to create more dimension.' That's not negative."

It doesn't sound as bad as I thought it was. "What else did she write?"

He flipped another page to a drawing of her left hand. On the back of the page, in neat handwriting, was another note. "Work on getting proportions right. Keep going."

"That isn't as bad as I remember," Megan said. She took the sketchbook from Steve and started on the first page. "I was a junior and had moved into a more advanced art class. She had us keep a sketchbook. We drew or painted every day and then on Friday she collected the sketchbooks and graded them over the weekend. Come Monday, we got our sketchbooks back and started another week of drawings. I died each Monday waiting to get my sketches back."

Steve pointed at a still life pencil drawing of apples and oranges. "I'm no artist, but these are fantastic."

Megan grinned. "I remember that day. Miss K brought a ceramic bowl to class and filled it with fruit. She told us the story about how she had fallen in love with the bowl's bright colors. She bought the bowl in Poland and carried it all over Europe in her backpack, afraid it was going to be broken before she got home. Miss K said every piece of art has a story to tell. We spent the class drawing the arrangement. She stopped and helped each of us. My drawing was awful. See." She turned back a page to a misshapen bunch of circles. "The teacher turned to the next page and in less than five minutes did this sketch. She told me to practice copying it."

"That doesn't sound like she thought you were terrible." Steve stood up. "We should have some of these framed and hang them on the walls."

"No way." Megan closed the sketchbook and held it against her chest. "I don't want anyone seeing these."

"You're being way too hard on yourself. What was your final grade?"

Megan lowered her gaze. "I transferred out of the class and took an accounting class instead."

"You're kidding. Your parents let you do that?"

"They agreed there were more job opportunities for accountants than for artists."

Steve frowned. "If Penny wanted to drop art, would you let her?"

"I . . . I don't know."

He leaned over and kissed her. "I'll see you tonight."

After he left, Megan lay back down and closed her eyes. *Penny doesn't talk much about her classes. Does she like her art class? Is her teacher encouraging?*

* * *

NINA SAT AT THE CARD TABLE WITH A CHECKERBOARD IN FRONT of her. Emmett and Mike were playing against each other.

She would compete against the winner. While Nina waited, she watched the activity director place a crocheted throw over Liz's lap.

"Emily is so thoughtful," Nina said quietly.

"Yes, she is," Rosemary replied. "Such a pleasant individual. Too bad she hasn't fallen in love yet. Perhaps we can help her."

Emmett laughed. "You're not trying to match her with one of us."

"I was thinking of Andy," Rosemary said.

"Who's Andy?" Nina asked, turning her gaze back to the checkerboard.

"You've seen him. He drives the shuttle bus and does handyman jobs around here."

Nina pictured the polite young man who had helped her move into Shadow Oaks. "The one with the wolf tattoo on his forearm."

"That's him," Rosemary said. "I think he and Emily would be a cute couple."

Mike slapped his hand against his forehead. "Rosemary's playing matchmaker. Run Andy."

Nina chuckled. "Or Cupid."

"We need to bring them together more," Rosemary said.

After moving his checker and taking one of Emmett's pieces, Mike cocked his head. "How do we do that?"

All eyes turned to Nina.

She drummed her fingers on the table. "We could go to a restaurant for lunch and have them sit together."

"That's an excellent idea," Rosemary said. "Quiet, everyone. She's coming over here."

Nina studied Emily as she walked toward their table. *Yes, an intimate lunch place can be romantic.* Her mind took her back to the sidewalk café in Paris where she first met André. His soulful brown eyes had invited her to join him at his table for two. Her heart beat faster at the memory.

* * *

WHEN PENNY CAME HOME FROM SCHOOL ON TUESDAY AFTER-noon, she found an envelope propped up on the kitchen countertop. It was addressed to P. P. The upper left corner of the envelope had the logo, name, and address of the Shadow Oaks Senior Living Home. She grabbed the envelope and ran upstairs to her room.

Lying across her bed, Penny opened the envelope and removed a carefully folded piece of stationery. A faint hint of lavender clung to the paper. The handwriting was cursive, each word neatly written with little flourishes on some letters. The lines of writing were straight, even without lines on the paper. She read the letter with some difficulty, struggling to decipher a few of the cursive letters.

Dear Poison Pen Pal,

I see the educational system has severely declined since I left teaching. Since when has the letter "R" taken the place of the word "are" or the letter "U" taken the place of the word "you"?

Community service is a noble undertaking, but it should be done with care and respect. The idea of service is to benefit others. Check it in a dictionary and perform it with that meaning in mind.

Why are you grounded? Since writing to me is getting you released from this punishment, I believe I have a right to know what you did to cause grounding.

You had a doodle in your letter. I took the liberty of modifying it. Do you draw or paint?

Very truly yours,
Kanina Koscielniak

"Great. I got an English teacher to lecture me as part of my community service." Penny sighed, then picked up the envelope and peeked inside. She found a small slip of lined notebook paper. The skull and crossbones image she had drawn in red ink was now the portrait of a young girl with long hair. The lines and shading were in pencil with the red ink lines of the skull barely visible. *Wow, that is awesome. I wish I could draw like that.*

Penny reread the letter. *Pen Pal. I like the sound of that. Penny's Pen Pal.*

She sat at her desk and wrote a quick response. She glanced at the calendar hanging on her wall. *It will be October soon and that means Halloween.* She added a doodle to the letter—a tree with bare branches.

THE NEXT DAY, PENNY WAITED OUTSIDE THE PRINCIPAL'S office, shifting her weight from foot to foot. She clutched the letter from Shadow Oaks in her hand. *The last time I was here, I was in trouble. Now I can show the principal I'm working on my community service.*

Principal Nelson stepped out of the office. "Come in, Penny."

She followed him and placed the Shadow Oaks envelope on his desk.

"What's this?" Principal Nelson asked.

"It's the first response from an old lady at Shadow Oaks. That means I completed one hour of community service."

"I see." Principal Nelson examined the return address on the envelope and nodded in approval. "My mother is a resident there, and I recognize their logo." He pushed the envelope toward Penny.

"Aren't you going to read it?" Penny picked up the correspondence.

"That won't be necessary. If you're getting a response from a senior, that tells me you're writing a decent letter. I'm not interested in invading your communication."

Thank goodness. Penny smiled and put the letter in her backpack.

"I don't think you need to bring me each letter you receive when you get it. Let's get together at the end of each month. Bring the letters you received for that month. I want to make sure you're continuing this effort. If I don't see progress each month, I'll have to reconsider going to the officials. Do you understand?"

Penny nodded. *I get it.* She left the office with a sense of satisfaction. *One hour of community service done. Thirty-nine more to go.*

Chapter 9

Megan put on her jeans and an old T-shirt. *It's Friday, and the house is clean. The decluttering is done. Now what?* She paced around the bedroom. *I could do some networking.* She picked up her phone and selected her contact list. She clicked on Abbie's name and typed a message to her.

Do you have time for lunch today? She hit send and stared at the screen, waiting for a reply.

How about next week? Thursday?

Megan tapped the thumbs-up emoji. Papa Luigi's Ristorante?

See you at noon. Got to go.

Megan missed her daily workplace chats with Abbie. *Unemployment is like an isolation cell, but we can catch up on Thursday.*

Avoiding the bathroom scale, Megan walked past it twice, then came back. She stripped out of her clothes. *I don't need any extra weight.* She stepped onto the scale and closed her eyes. Slowly, she opened them to peek at the digital display. *Shit!*

She hopped off the scale and peered at herself in the mirror. *I never lost the baby weight I gained with Jody, and now I'm snacking too much.* She stepped back on the scale again and the digits returned to the same figure. She put her clothes back on and went to find her old exercise DVDs.

Jody was playing in her room, pretending her bed was an island and the cat was shipwrecked. Goku seemed content to sleep on the bed as the survivor of a sunken ship.

"Jody, want to join me in some exercise?"

"What's that?" Jody jumped up with her tutu around her neck.

"We can walk in place or stretch a little."

Jody bounced up and down. "Like this?"

"Yes, like that." Megan headed downstairs, with Jody right behind her. Goku jumped off the bed and followed them.

In the family room, Megan rummaged through the case of ancient DVDs. She found one of her old favorites and put it in the player. The rhythmic music started, and Megan repeated the instructor's movements. Jody mimicked the moves amid bursts of giggles, while Goku curled up on the sofa and slept.

"That's silly," Jody said, pointing at the exercise people and then Megan.

With her breath coming in bursts, Megan said, "You're right." *Boy, am I out of shape, and these videos are dated.* Fifteen minutes into the routine, she turned the DVD off. *That's enough for now.*

Panting, Megan trudged into the office and sat down to enter the monthly bills in the spreadsheet she had created for the family finances. The severance check in the bank gave her some peace, but it would not last forever. *Job hunting is slower than I expected, and things will bog down even more by the end of the year.* She studied the entries to find where they could make some cuts. *Daycare costs are down, with*

Jody only going three times a week. Having her stay home all the time may not be too far in the future. She had cut back on extras at the grocery store. Never having been a coupon clipper, she now searched for sale items and discounts. *It's pennies sometimes, but it adds up.*

Megan considered selling the house, but Steve had been adamant that it was too soon to do anything that drastic. *Steve seems so calm, and I'm a nervous wreck. Some nights, I can't even get to sleep because of worrying about money.*

* * *

ON SATURDAY MORNING, NINA ROSE EARLY AND WENT FOR a walk in the garden. The scent of jasmine and gardenias mingled in the air. She strolled along the pathway past the arbor and birdbath. *As pretty as this place is, I miss my travels around the world. So many summer vacations were spent in different countries.*

She stopped at the bleeding-heart vines entwined in the trellis. With an artist's eyes, she followed the curves and lines of the cascading pink flowers. *Where have I seen this before? I think it was Cameroon or Senegal.*

"Good morning, ma'am."

Nina gasped. "Oh, Andy, I didn't see you coming."

Andy carried pruning clippers and a bucket. "Would you like some of those flowers for your room?"

"They are lovely, but let's leave them here for others to enjoy."

"Glad you like them, ma'am."

"Please, it's Nina."

"Yes, Miss Nina."

"You do such a beautiful job with the garden." She gestured to the expanse of the grounds.

"It is peaceful here. Flowers bring happiness."

Nina nodded. "That's why I spend so much time in the garden."

"Miss Liz likes it, too. Now, if you don't mind, I have to trim some brown leaves and older flowers."

Nina watched him carefully prune the weathered branches and faded flowers from the hibiscus bush. *He seems like a kind man. I can see why Rosemary is trying to get him and Emily together.*

After mail call, Nina took a new letter into her room. It had the same Bridgewater address as the previous Poison Pen letter.

"Let's see what my young pen pal has to say today." She opened the envelope and eased the letter out. *Another torn spiral notebook page with fringe.*

Dear K2,

what is it like where tt r you are? I mean, do they let tt you go outside?

I got in trouble at school. Now I have to write letters to old people. How old are you? 40–50–60

I hate my stepfather. He is mean. why does Mom like him?

Good by
Poison Pen

Nina closed her eyes. *This child needs help. Help with more than spelling and punctuation.*

At the bottom of the letter was a line drawing of a tree trunk with bare branches radiating out in all directions. *The drawing itself isn't bad. The tree feels melancholy. Lonely. Are you sad, Poison Pen?*

Nina reached for the pencil on the side table and added foliage to the branches. She sketched a hillside to place the tree in a setting. Then she added a swing suspended from the tree with a little girl on it, her hair streaming behind her. Carefully, Nina tore the picture from Poison Pen's letter.

She spent the next half hour writing a response. With the tree sketch tucked inside the folded letter, she put them in an envelope and took it to the office.

After leaving the letter at the office, Nina walked into the gathering room. Rosemary and Emmett sat on one of the two striped sofas. Nina had yet to sit on either one. *That fabric color is hideous.*

"Oh, Nina. Come join us," Rosemary said. "Emmett and I were discussing our families."

That's not a conversation I want to be part of, especially since I don't have any family. Nina put her hand up. "Not sure I can add anything to that discussion."

"I was just telling Emmett that my son is coming to take me to a doctor's appointment on Monday. I thought he could come along."

Emmett shifted uncomfortably on the sofa. "I don't want to be a long-tailed dog in a room full of rocking chairs. I'm not sure that I should be in the way during something as personal as a doctor's appointment."

"I told him it wouldn't be a problem. What do you think?"

Nina put her hands together and shifted her gaze from one to the other. "It depends on what you want to accomplish."

They both stared at her like she had two heads. *I knew I shouldn't have gotten involved.*

"What does that mean?" Rosemary asked.

"Rosemary, if you want Emmett to meet your son, it is a convenient opportunity, but it is also an awkward opportunity. What are they supposed to do while you're in with the doctor? Emmett, if you don't want to go, why don't you want to go? Are you concerned Rosemary's son will interpret your presence as something it's not? Or is it?" Nina raised an eyebrow and smiled.

Rosemary reached over and patted Emmett's hand. "We're friends; only friends."

Emmett squeezed her hand. "Good friends."

I have a feeling there's more than that going on. "A popular philosopher once said, 'You are braver than you believe, stronger than you seem, and smarter than you think, but the most important thing is, even if we're apart . . . I'll always be with you.' Consider that."

"Who was that philosopher, dear lady?" Emmett asked.

Nina grinned. "Winnie the Pooh." She left while they were both laughing.

* * *

THE HOUSE WAS QUIET ON MONDAY MORNING. MEGAN SAT AT the kitchen table with a cup of coffee and fingered the cover of her old sketchbook. *High school was so long ago.* She took a sip and pushed the sketchbook away. *I need to go online and research some more job openings.* Drumming her fingers against the coffee mug, Megan seized the sketchbook and flipped the cover open.

The first page was covered with pencil lines, cross-hatching, and shading. On the reverse side of the page were the teacher's neatly written notes. Megan read the words out loud. "Let your pencil roam free." She smiled, remembering the enthusiastic art teacher with the single long braid.

Megan turned the page and laughed at the swirls of circles, ovals, and curvy lines. On the back of the page, the handwritten comment said, "A curve is not a straight line. It bends and spirals with grace."

She leafed through the pages, reading the teacher's observations on each page. Halfway through the sketchbook, she stopped. *These have all been positive notes. Why do I remember lots of negative comments?*

At the pencil sketch of a sunflower, Megan touched the paper. *I did this? It looks so real.* Turning the page, she gasped at the comment. "You have a gift for art." *This can't be right. She told me I was wasting my time.* Megan read the comment again. "You have a gift for art."

She got up and walked around the house. Her thoughts traveled back to junior year of high school. She wore her hair in a French braid then. Her clothes were thrift shop finds because her family couldn't afford much, but she decorated them with sequins and beads to make a fashion statement. Art class was the last period of the day. She chuckled. *How I looked forward to the end of the day. Not because it was the last period, but because it was art.*

It was a Friday afternoon in December. Halfway through the school year. Her thoughts took her back to that art class.

October 2000

MEGAN HAD HER SKETCHBOOK OPEN ON THE TILTED DESKTOP and studied the art teacher's face. The assignment was to do a facial portrait, and the art teacher was the model.

"I want you to focus on facial details. It's fine to do an eye or an ear, but if you feel confident about drawing my entire face, go ahead. Don't worry about hurting my feelings. I do this exercise every year and I always survive."

The class erupted in laughter. Megan relaxed and let her graphite pencil slide across the paper, capturing the intricacies of the braid, the thin line of the mouth, the spacing of the eyes, and the slight irregularity of the nose.

"That's all for today," the teacher announced. "Remember to leave your sketchbooks so I can review them over the weekend."

Megan leaned back, shocked at the likeness on her page. *It looks like the teacher.*

The teacher moved around the room, and Megan waited for her to arrive to see the portrait.

"Decent effort, Megan."

"Is that it?" Megan put her hands on her hips. "That's all you can say? It's a great picture of you. Look. I got all the twists in your braid; the eyes are spaced properly. I even got your crooked nose right."

The teacher smiled and waited for Megan's rant to

end. "Megan, art is made by the artist but appreciated by the viewer. What you think you have created and what I see are two different things. You have created an excellent reproduction of my face, but what you have missed is the personality of your subject. The assignment was to capture the personality of a subject through a portrait. Tell me, when you study this sketch, do you get a sense of my emotion? Did you notice my face changed from time to time as I thought of different things?"

Megan ripped the page out of her sketchbook and tossed it on the floor. "Obviously, I'm not meant to be an artist. Besides, there's no money to be made drawing pictures that people don't like."

She stormed out of the art room with the sketchbook under her arm and went straight to the office to transfer out of art. An accounting class met at the same time. *There, at least I can have a career.*

MEGAN SHIFTED IN HER SEAT AT THE KITCHEN TABLE AND TOOK a sip of her coffee, but it was cold. *Did I misunderstand her comment? Was she trying to teach me a lesson, and I was too stubborn to see it? She didn't say my sketch was bad. Just that I didn't show her emotion.* She turned the pages to the back of the sketchbook. Right before the start of the blank pages was the ragged edge where she had torn out the teacher's portrait.

A blank page lay before her, an off-white sheet of open space inviting her to make a mark. Megan went to the office and rummaged through the collection of pens and pencils. She selected a yellow No. 2 pencil with a sharp point.

Returning to the kitchen table, she repeated the exercises at the front of her sketchbook.

As time slipped away, she covered three full pages with doodles and marks before the point of the pencil ground down and she stopped.

AT NOON ON THURSDAY, MEGAN SAT AT A TABLE FOR TWO IN Papa Luigi's Ristorante, Abbie's favorite downtown lunch place. She ordered an iced tea with lemon. While she waited for Abbie, Megan scrolled through the emails and messages on her phone, hoping one of her job applications might lead to an interview. *Nothing.*

Five minutes later, Abbie breezed through the front door and headed straight to Megan's table. "Ciao!" She removed her beret and ran her fingers through her bright orange hair.

Megan laughed. "You've changed your hair color again."

"Do you like it? I thought it was a splendid choice for October."

"It certainly is. You won't even need a pumpkin this year."

"Is that any way to speak to a bearer of greetings and good news?" Abbie pouted.

"I stand corrected. I bet it shocked the new management."

Abbie giggled. "They haven't figured out what to do with me yet. They seem afraid to tell me what to do, so I do what I want."

The waitress interrupted their conversation to take their order. After ordering lunch, Abbie leaned closer to

Megan. "How's the job hunt going?"

"Slow. I've applied for about a dozen project manager jobs."

"And?"

"Only two interviews so far. I think I'm overqualified for what they want."

"Keep at it. You'll find something soon. Brad did."

"Brad? You mean Bradley? You've been in touch with him?"

"Yes. We're seeing each other." Abbie's cheeks flushed to a bright pink.

Megan's mouth flew open. "Since when?"

"We went out for a drink the evening of the announcement."

"Abbie, how could you!"

"It's not like that, Megs. He was hurting. He needed someone to talk to."

"But he fired me."

"It wasn't his decision. Senior management pulled the plug. They let him go, too. They told him and then made him tell you. It sucked."

The server brought their lunch orders over and refilled the beverages. The smell of marinara sauce and garlic filled the air.

"Megs, Brad and I are complete opposites." Abbie sprinkled Parmesan cheese on her pasta.

"I'm trying to picture the two of you together."

"I know. It's crazy. The unconventional design chick and the traditional business dude. Who would expect that?"

"It's going to take me a while to get used to that idea."

"Thanks, Megs."

They ate in silence for several minutes.

"Did you say Bradley landed another job?"

"Yeah. It was really quick. He's heading up a new graphic design branch for BR Vels Corp."

"Tell him I wish him well. If he needs a project manager, I'm available."

"I know of an opening, but . . ."

Megan put her fork down. "But?"

"It's a nonprofit. They can't pay what you've been making."

"Aren't you the one who said I worry too much about money?"

"I did and you do, which is why I'm not sure I should tell you about this job. But you would be a terrific fit."

"Okay. Tell me more." Megan bit into a breadstick.

"You know the downtown Community Art Center? They lost their executive director. Actually, they fired her and had her arrested."

Megan frowned. "For what?"

"Embezzling funds."

"That's awful for a nonprofit."

Abbie nodded. "I know. Several donors have stepped away. The Center may have to close."

"And you want me to work there?" *This isn't making any sense.*

"Megs, they need help. You have the financial smarts, the experience, and the determination to save them. I know the president of their board of directors and sort of suggested you might be available."

"You suggested me without talking to me?"

"You know me. Spur of the moment. Ask for forgiveness,

rather than permission."

Megan laughed. "Bradley is going to have his hands full with you."

"Give the Center a call. Tell me you'll try. Please." Abbie's eyes pleaded with her.

"Okay. What's the name of the person I need to speak with?"

"The president is Matt Greer." Abbie picked up her purse and fished for her wallet. She pulled out two twenty-dollar bills and tossed them on the table. "Lunch is on me. Look at the time. I have to go."

Megan glanced at the money on the table. "That's too much."

"See, you're worrying about money." Abbie jumped up and headed to the door. "Good luck, Megs. Keep me posted." Before she left, Abbie waved at the restaurant owner. "Arrivederci, Luigi."

With a smile, Megan shook her head. *Lunch with Abbie was just what I needed. The Art Center job never could pay what I'm worth, but Abbie begged me to try. Maybe I should.*

CHAPTER 10

AT HER SCHOOL LOCKER, PENNY LEFT THE BOOKS SHE didn't need to bring home over the weekend. She closed the locker and spotted Lacey hurrying in her direction.

"Hey, Penny, want to go to the Founder's Day Parade next weekend?"

Heartbroken, Penny glanced down. *I would love to go, but . . .* "I'm grounded. No weekend activities for me."

"That's got to be boring."

"Yeah. Tell me about it. All I can do is stay at home." Penny lifted her backpack onto her shoulder and walked toward the school exit.

Lacey followed her. "How long are you grounded?"

"I'm not sure. They tied it to finishing the community service hours."

"All those boomers need to write you letters, so we can go back to having fun."

Penny pushed the exit door open and headed toward the bus. "I'm doing okay so far. There's one old lady who's writing to me regularly."

"How many letters do you need to get?"

"Forty."

"OMG. Even if she wrote to you every day, that's well over a month."

Penny sighed. "It's probably going to be close to two or three months."

"Can you go to the Christmas Lights Festival?"

"I don't know." Penny boarded their bus.

Lacey climbed the steps behind her. "That stinks."

"Sure does. All this over some paint." *I made a stupid decision and I'm paying for it now.*

"I'll miss you at the parade."

"Well, text me pictures. I can be there via your phone."

Lacey laughed. "That's a great idea. We'll be together virtually. But when I eat the popcorn, you'll have to imagine how it tastes."

"That's a plan!" *Not the same as being there, but it's better than nothing.*

When Penny got home from school, Mom met her at the door and said, "You got a letter from Shadow Oaks. That makes another one you can show the principal."

"I wasn't expecting a response so soon." Penny grabbed the letter and ran to her room. With the door closed, she jumped onto her bed and ripped the envelope open. The same fancy handwriting spread across the folded page. A slip of paper fluttered out of the letter. Penny picked it up and recognized the ink sketch she had done of a barren tree, but now it was a beautiful scene. *Wow! K2 sure knows how to draw.*

Slowly, she deciphered the letter.

Dear Pen Pal,

You keep signing your letters as "Poison Pen." I'm sure that's not the name your parents gave you. What do your friends call you?

What kind of trouble did you get into at school? I was a teacher for almost fifty years. There's probably nothing you could have done that I haven't seen before.

Didn't your parents teach you it's not polite to ask someone's age? If you must know, I'm seventy-four. Before you say that is really old, you should meet Miss Liz here at Shadow Oaks. She's one hundred and two and likes to watch the birds visit the bird feeder outside the window. It is a lovely garden full of colorful flowers. Miss Liz was a WASP pilot in World War II. You should research the WASP pilots.

I'm sorry to hear you and your stepfather are having trouble. Have you talked to your mother about it?

You still haven't told me what you did at school that got you grounded.

Yours truly,
Kanina

Penny rolled off her bed and went to the computer. She spent the next hour watching videos about WASP pilots during World War II. *I didn't know anything about those pilots. That lady at Shadow Oaks must be ancient. Maybe when I'm not grounded anymore, I can meet her.*

* * *

Seated at a card table after breakfast on Tuesday, Emmett leaned over a word search puzzle. "Dazzle. Two *z*'s in a row should be easier to find than a tick on a dog's nose. Why can't I find it?"

"Let me have that," Mike said, sliding the puzzle book away from Emmett. A minute later, Mike tapped a gnarled finger at the puzzle. "You need your eyes checked. It's right here."

Emmett handed Mike a pen. "Circle it. You're a splendid man, even if you can't play cribbage well."

"We'll see who doesn't know how to play cribbage when we have a rematch tonight." Mike circled the word and shoved the book and pen across the table.

"Aren't you tired of being skunked?"

Rosemary leaned close to Nina. "Listen to those two old geezers. Going at it like a married couple. My Walt and I went at each other like that."

"Any man who could put up with your prattling musta been a saint," Mike said.

The banter among the trio continued for minutes until Rosemary pulled Nina into the conversation. "Nina, since you don't want to go to the library with us today, is there a book you want me to get for you?"

"I can recommend a good murder mystery," Emmett said.

"How about an action-adventure?" Mike suggested.

Nina ran her fingers along her upper lip. She had donated all her art books to the high school when she downsized to move into Shadow Oaks. *I do miss looking at other artists' work.* "An art book, if you can find one," Nina said.

"Consider it done." Rosemary lifted her teacup in a toast.

THAT AFTERNOON, NINA SAT ALONE AT A CARD TABLE IN THE gathering room and signed another letter to Poison Pen, then placed it in an envelope. At the sound of the shuttle bus arriving at the front door, she sealed the envelope. *Done just in time.*

Laughter and loud voices filled the lobby and spread into the gathering room. Nina laughed at the sight of Emmett with a balloon hat on his head. Mike brandished a balloon sword, and Rosemary carried a pink balloon animal on top of an armload of books.

"Nina, you should have come," Rosemary said. "The library had a clown entertaining the children during the reading hour. When we arrived, they invited us to join them. The clown made each of us something from balloons. I got a dog."

"Sounds like it was fun," Nina said.

Rosemary placed two oversized books on the card table. "I hope these are okay."

Nina read both titles. One book was a collection of folk art by Grandma Moses. The other was a coffee table book of seasonal watercolor paintings by various artists. She flipped through the pages of the paintings.

"Thank you, Rosemary. These are perfect." *I feel like a kid who got a birthday present. Maybe next time I should go to the library and see for myself what art books they have.*

* * *

"PENNY," MOM CALLED FROM DOWNSTAIRS. "STEVE AND I ARE going grocery shopping. Please keep an eye on Jody. She's in her room playing. We'll be back in about an hour and a half."

The words were muffled, so Penny took off her headphones. "What?"

"Watch Jody while we're grocery shopping."

"Okay." She put her headphones back on and tapped her foot to the beat of the Cosmic Dreams. Penny's fingers slid over the letters on the phone in response to a text from Lacey. The messages flew back and forth until Penny's phone went into low-power mode.

"Need to charge," Penny typed. After hitting send, she plugged the phone in and went to check on Jody.

As Penny walked down the hallway, she hoped Jody had taken a nap. *No sounds coming out of the munchkin's room.*

When Penny entered Jody's bedroom, her half sister jumped up and hid her hands behind her back. Penny narrowed her eyes. "What are you up to?"

Jody shrugged with her hands still behind her back.

"Let me see your hands."

Reluctantly, the little girl held them out. They were covered with ink. Her right hand clutched three markers.

Penny took the markers and read the labels. "These are permanent markers. Where did you use them?"

Jody moved away from the wall, and Penny gasped. A combination of Jody's handprints and squiggles that vaguely resembled flowers and birds sprawled across the wall.

Penny put her hand over her mouth to keep from laughing. *Should I scold her or praise her?*

"My drawing," Jody said.

"I can see that, but you shouldn't draw on the walls. Especially with a permanent marker. Mom's going to be mad." *At least she won't have to go to the principal's office.*

Penny inspected the wall more closely. "Let me try to clean this up." She grabbed the bleach cleaner from the bathroom and sprayed the wall, but the marks remained. "I'll try some nail polish remover."

On her hands and knees, Penny applied the pungent solution. It faded the permanent marker, but when Penny scrubbed harder, it started taking the paint off the wall. "Oh no, this is getting worse."

Jody whimpered. Goku paraded into the room and meowed loudly.

"Don't cry, Jody." Penny sat back on her heels. "I have an idea. How about if I paint something over the marker? What would you like?"

Jody pulled a picture book off her shelf and brought it to Penny. She opened the book and pointed to a page filled with black cats. "Lots of Gokus."

Penny nodded. "I can do that." She hurried into her room and scrounged around the bottom drawer of her desk. She located a handful of acrylic paints. Most containers were nearly empty, except for the black.

With a pencil, Penny sketched the outlines of the cats. The acrylic paint covered the permanent markers, and the cats took shape. When she was done, Penny stood back and admired the work.

"It looks better. What do you think, Jody?"

When there was no response, Penny went searching for the little girl. She found her napping on Penny's bed, with Goku curled beside her.

I hope Mom doesn't get upset with all the black cats.

THE FAMILY ATE DINNER WITHOUT TALKING. *Guess I should have left Jody's drawing alone. Mom hated the cats.* Penny twirled spaghetti on her fork. *This weird silence is getting to be the norm.*

Steve cleared his throat. "Penny, tomorrow afternoon we're taking Jody to see the new animated movie that came out last week. Would you like to go with us?"

Jody bounced up and down in her chair. "Come with us."

Penny stared at Steve in surprise. *It's not my first choice in movies, but it would be terrific to get out of the house.*

Mom put her fork down with a sharp clatter. "Penny is grounded. She can't go."

"Isn't that a little harsh, Megan? I mean, she would be with us, not her friends. She isn't going to get in trouble."

"A punishment is only a punishment if it hurts."

Steve took a deep breath. "She's following through on her community service. You told me she's getting letters back from the senior place. And she hasn't been out with her friends in weeks."

Penny watched the exchange between her mother and Steve. *He's standing up for me, but Mom's getting mad. Her mouth gets tight and thin when she's angry.*

"That's okay," Penny said. "I don't want to go to a kiddie movie."

"There. That's settled," Mom said.

Jody pouted. "Penny, come with us."

Penny locked eyes with Steve and shook her head. His face displayed his puzzlement. *No sense having them fight over a movie I don't care about.*

"So she'll be home alone?" Steve asked.

Let it go, Steve. Please!

"She said she doesn't want to go. If she breaks the rules while we're gone, there will be worse consequences."

What could be worse than what I'm going through right now?

After dinner, Penny pulled the chair closer to the desk in the family office. Her fingers rested on the computer keyboard. She began typing, at first slowly.

Dear KK,

Surprise! I'm typing today's letter. The computer helps me find spelling mistakes.

She picked up the last letter she had received from Shadow Oaks and reread it. She wrote a response to the first question her pen pal had asked. The words flowed across the screen. Soon she had filled an entire page. She pressed print and retrieved the finished document from the printer.

"Look at this, Goku. She won't believe I wrote all this."

Penny turned the letter over to fold it but stopped. "Seems like a shame to have a whole side with nothing on it."

She took the paper into her bedroom and picked up a black pen. Looking at the manga poster over her bed, she copied the image onto the back of the letter. She smiled at the finished picture. *Years of drawing the same figures over and over gave me lots of practice.* With a frown, she had to decide which way to fold the letter. *Should the drawing be on the inside or outside?* She settled on the drawing on the inside. *It will be an extra surprise.*

* * *

"It's a glorious October day," Nina said to herself. The humid Florida summer heat had been replaced with a cooler autumn breeze. "I'm glad the others went to a Friday matinee, so I can enjoy the grounds here by myself." She chuckled. "Papa always said if you talk to yourself, you have money in the bank. But I don't think that's true. At least my bank account doesn't agree."

She scanned the azure sky with the golden glow of sunlight edging the clouds. "Reminds me of the summer in Japan by the Seto Inland Sea."

Nina strolled along a wide path that meandered through the butterfly garden and watched a hummingbird flit from one hibiscus flower to another. The profusion of colors made her think of a Monet painting. She tucked the folder of writing materials under her arm. She had intended to write a letter to Poison Pen about keeping a positive outlook during troubling times. As Nina wandered through the garden, she noticed Liz sitting in her wheelchair under a crape myrtle tree. Nina walked to a bench near Liz and put the folder down. Then she approached Liz.

"It is beautiful here."

Liz nodded and stretched her shaky arm toward the driveway.

Nina gazed at the row of live oaks arching over the driveway leading to the center. "It's peaceful, too."

A yellow-and-black butterfly fluttered past Liz's head and settled on her outstretched arm. Another one circled her head and landed in her soft white hair.

"Liz, you're a butterfly whisperer," Nina said. *This is*

a memory to cherish. I could sketch Liz with the butterflies.

Without a word, she returned to the bench and pulled out a plain piece of paper and a pencil. For the next hour, she drew and shaded an image of Liz with butterflies perched on her shoulder and in her hair. She softened the centenarian's wrinkles and imagined her as a WASP pilot, young and strong. Nina had to stop several times to massage the fingers of her right hand.

When the drawing was done, Nina dated it and took it over to Liz, but the older woman had fallen asleep. Nina rested the drawing on Liz's lap and returned to her room.

OVER DINNER, THE TRIO OF SENIORS DEBATED THE MOVIE'S plot and the main actor's ability. Nina listened with little interest. *I prefer live performances.*

"Nina," Rosemary said. "Did you see the wonderful portrait Liz received today? One of her family members must have visited her while we were at the movies. Someone in her family is artistic. You should see it. I think Emily hung it on the bulletin board. Although, honestly, I think it should be framed and hung on the wall."

While Rosemary rambled on, Nina reveled in the reaction her sketch was receiving. *I should practice on a few more pieces.* She flexed her fingers. *I'll see how my hand feels tomorrow.*

"You have such a good eye for art, Nina. You should go see it." Rosemary lifted her teacup to her lips. After a sip, she continued, "I'd love to have a portrait done like that."

Nina smiled with secret pleasure. *That can be arranged.*

Chapter 11

Saturday, October 7, 2023

Mail call!" Mike's voice carried across the gathering room.

Emily distributed the mail and handed Nina a letter. "You're getting popular, Miss Nina. You get a letter almost every day."

Nina shrugged. "I write one almost every day."

"True. One must write letters to get letters." Emily walked across the room to deliver a piece of mail to another resident.

After leaving the card table, Nina took a seat on the sofa. *This fabric is the worst combination of colors I've ever seen.* She opened the envelope with careful fingers. Instead of the usual spiral notebook page, the letter was printed on crisp white paper. The typed message covered most of one side, with a black-and-white ink drawing on the back. *And it's signed Penny. No Poison Pen this time.*

Nina settled into the sofa cushion and read the entire letter.

Dear KK,

Surprise! I'm typing today's letter. The computer helps me find spelling mistakes. Do you have a computer?

In your letter, you asked me what I did to get community service and grounded. They are punishment for something stupid I did at school.

Our school mascot is a polar bear. Why a school in Florida has a polar bear as a mascot makes no sense. Anyway, the bear is boring and very white. It seemed so sad.

Some of my so-called "friends" thought it would be a good idea to decorate the bear for Soph Fun Day. I listened to them.

We skipped our first-period class, and one kid brought cans of paint from home. We had one paintbrush and I'm the tallest, so I started. I was painting some makeup on the bear's face when the coach found us. The other kids saw him coming and yelled, but I didn't hear them. I got caught.

I still don't understand why I didn't hear them.

The principal gave me community service, and my parents grounded me. I can't get out of being grounded until the community service is done. Please keep writing me letters.

As always,
Penny

Nina folded the letter and knew the response she wanted to send Penny. She walked over to Emily. "Is there a computer I can use to type a letter?"

"Certainly, Miss Nina. There's a computer in the media room. It's hooked to a printer. We just ask that you only print a page or two."

"That sounds perfect."

Wandering into the media room, Nina composed in her mind how she was going to answer Penny. By the time she figured out how to use the software, typing the letter took most of the afternoon. She paused many times to stretch her fingers.

* * *

LATER THAT WEEK, PENNY COLLECTED THE MAIL FROM THE mailbox and flipped through the catalogs, bills, and advertisements. At the sight of the Shadow Oaks envelope, she grinned. *These letters are coming so quickly.* She carried the mail into the house and dropped it on the kitchen counter near her mother.

"Got another Shadow Oaks letter," Penny said.

"How many does that make?"

Penny ticked off the letters on her fingers. "This is number nine."

"Be sure to let the principal know."

"Mom." Penny held the unopened letter. "The old lady who's writing these letters is pretty cool."

"In what way?"

"She's not treating me like a kid. She's writing to me as

if I'm an adult."

"Is that supposed to mean I don't?"

Penny sighed. "That's not what I said." She tapped the envelope against her leg. *We never agree on anything.* "I better read her letter and answer her."

Once upstairs in her bedroom, Penny ripped the envelope open and pulled out the typed letter. *She knows how to use a computer.* Penny scanned the note and then read it slowly.

Dear Penny,

I enjoyed receiving your typed letter. It was free of spelling errors, which is something I appreciate.

Your drawing of the manga character was a decent representation. Try adding color to make the figure more like the original. I was fortunate to have spent some time in Japan with a mangaka. If you like drawing manga, perhaps you could start a manga club at your school.

Copying is a reasonable learning technique. Many of the old masters did that when training. The test of a true artist is to stop copying and create original work.

The garden here at Shadow Oaks is in bloom with Gerbera daisies, now that the weather is cooler. The hibiscus is in bloom, too. I've enclosed a sketch of a pink hibiscus. Unfortunately, I don't have any paints, so all I can do is a pencil sketch.

One lady here recently borrowed a book about the artist known as Grandma Moses. She was a self-taught folk artist who started painting at seventy-eight. She lived to be one hundred and one.

I believe I previously mentioned Liz, another resident here. She is one hundred and two. I frequently sit with her in the garden.

I hope school is going well for you.

Your friend,
Kanina

Penny lay back on her bed and stared at the ceiling. *Form a manga club? How would I do that?*

THE NEXT DAY, AFTER PENNY LEFT THE SCHOOL BUS, SHE RACED down the hallway to the art classroom. "Mrs. Silsbury." Her breathing came in gasps.

The art teacher stopped cleaning paintbrushes and dried her hands. "Is something wrong, Penny?"

"No, I just need to talk to you about an idea."

The teacher laughed. "You had me worried. What's the idea?"

"Can we form a manga club?" Penny watched Mrs. Silsbury's face, trying to read her reaction.

"Certainly. There would have to be several other students interested in participating. There's a form we have to fill out and get Principal Nelson's approval. The club needs a sponsor. I would be glad to do that unless you had someone else in mind."

Penny's smile grew. "You would be perfect."

"Do you think other students would be interested?"

"I don't know, but I've seen some lockers with manga drawings taped inside the door."

Mrs. Silsbury went to her desk. "I'll request the form from the office. You'll need to write a summary of what the purpose of the club is. I'll contact some art teachers at other schools to see if they have something similar."

"That would be fantastic." *I can't believe this is going to happen.*

"Something you might consider, Penny, is expanding the idea."

"What do you mean?"

"Well, manga is incredibly specific. It could be an art club. That would allow the club to cover other types of artwork and subjects. It might attract more students."

Penny tilted her head. "I hadn't thought about that."

"Well, take some time to consider it. I'll still get the form, and you write the purpose for whatever you want to propose."

Other students entered the classroom, and Mrs. Silsbury glanced at her watch. "I need to get ready for class."

"Thanks so much." *I have to write to Kanina about this. It's so exciting!*

* * *

THE FAN ON THE HEATING AND COOLING SYSTEM MADE A buzzing sound, followed by a loud bang and a long hiss. The system was original to the house, and the last service call had warned the system might not last long. Megan and Steve stood outside, looking at the failing equipment in the back-yard.

"I'm afraid it's time to replace it," Steve said. "At least it didn't fail during the summer heat."

"How much is that going to cost?" Megan twisted her hands together.

Steve appeared thoughtful. "A house this size, I'm guessing, in the ten- to twelve-thousand-dollar range."

"Oh, no." Megan's stomach tightened. *We don't need another problem right now.*

"We'll know when we get the HVAC company out here." He put his arm around Megan. "We knew that system was going to need to be replaced."

"But the cost . . ."

"I bet they do financing. It'll be okay."

Megan pulled away from Steve. "You keep saying that, but it's not going to be okay. It's never going to be okay."

"Megan, listen to yourself."

She took a deep breath and stepped back into Steve's arms. "You keep me from going overboard."

"That's what I'm here for. Of course, we could *not* fix it, and when it gets cold, you could snuggle close to me." He kissed the top of her head. "You are such a worrier, Megan. We will get through this."

"I wish I had the confidence you have."

"You're a smart, talented woman. The right opportunity will come along."

She wanted to believe him. *But when?*

* * *

"Okay, I did it," Mike said during breakfast on Monday morning.

Nina, Rosemary, and Emmett gave him a questioning look.

"What did you do?" Nina asked.

"I unscrewed all the light bulbs in the gathering room lamps. When the knitting ladies go to turn on the lamps, they won't light up. Emily will be called. Then she'll get Andy to change the bulbs." Mike beamed at his ingenuity.

Rosemary put her cup of tea down. "I hope this works. We'll need to be in the gathering room to make sure Emily and Andy talk about something other than light bulbs."

"When do the ladies usually get together to knit?" Nina asked.

"Ten o'clock precisely every morning, sure as the cake comes out of the oven," Emmett said.

Nina chuckled. *I love his sayings.*

"We could play a game of cribbage at one of the card tables," Emmett said.

Nina frowned. "What's that?"

"That, dear lady, is a card game of numbers and skill."

"He likes it because he always wins," Mike said.

"I'll teach you," Rosemary said. "Emmett and I will be partners. You and Mike can team up together."

"Good luck, Miss Nina," Emmett said. "Mike always loses."

The army veteran snorted. "Not this time. With a teacher as my partner, at least she'll be able to count."

They moved into the gathering room fifteen minutes before the knitting ladies arrived. Nina learned the basic rules of the game and completed a practice hand by the time the ladies had settled on the sofas and pulled out their yarn.

"Here we go," Mike said.

One lady with a bag of knitting supplies tried to turn on the lamp beside the sofa. The *click-click* of the switch did not turn on the light. She moved to another lamp with the same result.

"Emily!"

The activity director hurried in. "What is it, Mrs. Henderson?"

"The lights won't work. None of them."

Emily tried turning on the lamps without success. "Let me call Andy. He can change the bulbs."

With a chuckle, Mike hid his mouth behind a hand of cards. Nina could see the corners of his mouth and imagined a broad smile behind the playing cards.

Emily hurried to the office, and a few minutes later, Andy showed up with a toolbox and a collection of light bulbs. He tried the first lamp. When the light didn't function, he removed the lampshade and grasped the light bulb to unscrew it.

Nina and the rest of the cribbage players kept playing cards but continued to glance over at Andy.

"He'll know it just needs to be tightened when he feels how loose it is," Mike said in a whisper.

Andy twisted the light bulb tighter, and the light blazed on. "It only needed to be tightened."

Emily pointed to another lamp. "See if this one needs tightening, too?"

At the second lamp, Andy made the same discovery. "Someone's been playing with the bulbs."

"Why would someone do that?" Emily asked.

"I don't know, but in the future, check that the bulb isn't loose." He winked at Emily, then picked up his toolbox. He gathered the spare light bulbs he had brought in and headed toward the doorway.

"Oh, Andy," Rosemary called, waving her hand at him.

The handyman stopped and turned around. "Is there something I can do for you?"

Emily came over to the card table. "Is there a problem?"

Rosemary smiled sweetly. "I was wondering when your birthday is?"

Andy put his toolbox down. "January fourth."

"And Emily, when is your birthday?" Emily asked.

"December eleventh."

"That's interesting," Rosemary said. "Andy, you're a Capricorn, the goat. Capricorns are detail-oriented, like to start new projects, and can be shy."

"Andy, that sounds like you," Emily said. "You're so good at your job because you pay attention to details."

"And I agree he's shy," Emmett added.

"Emily, you're a Sagittarius, the Archer," Rosemary said. "The bow and arrow is your sign. You jump right into things."

"I agree with that assessment, dear lady," Emmett said with a nod.

"You're easy-going, with a thirst for learning new things." Rosemary rubbed her hands together. "Sagittarius and Capricorn are like opposites, and you know opposites attract."

"How do you know so much about astrology?" Nina asked.

"It's a hobby. It's useful at parties when you're meeting

people. See what we just learned. They both have birthdays coming up within a month of each other. We need to plan a birthday party for them."

"There's no need for that," Andy said.

"And that is a typical Capricorn. You're being shy, Andy." Rosemary shook her finger at the handyman. "The two of you should go out. Go to a concert together."

"We'll think about it," Emily said. "Please tell whoever loosened the light bulbs to leave them alone." She eyed everyone sitting at the card table. "The knitting ladies need the light, and Andy has other things to do." She smiled at Andy.

He picked up his toolbox and winked at Emily. "I'll see you later."

When Emily and Andy were gone, Nina gave Rosemary a high five. "Well done."

They all burst into laughter.

* * *

C U TOMORROW.

Penny sent her last message to Lacey on Sunday evening. Then she dropped the phone on her bed and ran downstairs.

Mom and Steve relaxed on the couch watching a reality show. Penny went to her mom's side. "Mom, tomorrow is school photo day. Lacey and I are going to add some wow to our photos."

Mom turned away from the show. "What does that mean?"

Steve reduced the TV volume.

"We're going to add some extra accessories. Lacey's

older sister has a tiara from her prom, and she's letting us both use it."

"You'll look like a princess," Steve said.

Penny focused on him and remembered him calling Jody a princess. *Does he think of me that way, too?*

"What other accessories are you planning?" Mom asked.

"I was hoping we could use your pearls."

Mom shook her head. "No. Absolutely not."

"I promise I'll be careful with them."

"I'm sorry, Penny. They're too expensive for you to wear to school or give to Lacey."

She clasped her hands together. "Please, Mom. You can trust me."

"I said no. Discussion closed."

"What time is the photo session?" Steve asked. "We have some imitation pearls in the store that look real. They don't cost much. I could buy two and bring them to school for you and Lacey."

Mom's lips tightened. "That's not necessary, Steve. This is only a school picture."

Penny sighed. *That's right. It's only a school picture, and I'm just not important. She even rejected Steve's offer to help me.*

"We may not buy any photos this year," Mom said.

"Then, I guess it doesn't matter what I wear," Penny said and went back upstairs, fighting back tears.

CHAPTER 12

Tuesday, October 24, 2023

PENNY OPENED THE ENVELOPE FROM SHADOW OAKS AND removed the letter printed on Shadow Oaks stationery. She carried it to her room and plopped down on the floor. Goku soon joined her.

"We got a long letter today, Goku. Listen to this."

Dear Penny,

It is nice to have your proper name to use. Thank you for answering my question about why you were grounded. At some point in all our lives, we each do something stupid. The important thing is not to let that stupid thing define us for the rest of our life.

What you described in your letter about not hearing your "so-called friends" yell a warning is called being in the zone. This means that when you are being creative, your mind becomes focused on what you're doing and goes into a special zone. We tune out voices and other sounds.

Being in the zone is a creative space. The next time you are drawing, pay attention to how it feels when you become totally immersed in your artwork. You will lose track of time.

I will keep writing because you recognize you made a mistake. We should learn from our mistakes and not make them again.

As always,
Kanina

Penny flipped the letter over. On the back of the paper was a detailed pencil sketch of a hummingbird at a hibiscus flower. In small letters at the bottom of the page were the words "Try copying this drawing."

"Goku, she wants me to draw a bird. I never drew a bird or a flower. Should I try it?"

The cat yawned and stretched.

"I'll take that as a yes." Penny grabbed her sketchbook and stared at the hummingbird. She began to draw and realized she was slipping into the zone. *It feels so peaceful.*

It was late on Wednesday night and Penny was almost asleep when her phone chirped with a message from Lacey.

Have extra ticket for the Cosmic Dreams concert on Friday. Can U go?

I would love to go! With a sigh, she typed, "I'm still grounded."

I know but ask ur mom.

Penny glanced at her alarm clock. It's late. Will ask her tomorrow.

The Cosmic Dreams concert was sold out the last time I checked. I wonder how Lacey got tickets. Penny typed her question.

My sister won them from a radio station contest, but her boyfriend has other plans. She gave them to me. If U can't go, I'll ask Glenda.

I would love to see them in person, especially Jupiter.

Will ask at breakfast. She typed a moon emoji and put the phone down.

The next morning, at breakfast, Penny waited until after her mother was sitting down and drinking her coffee. "Lacey's sister won tickets to the Cosmic Dreams concert."

"What are the Cosmic Dreams?"

"A new band. They're fire. I have a whole playlist of their songs. Their concert is sold out."

"I've never heard of them." Mom took a sip of her coffee.

That's because you listen to all that old stuff. Penny ate a spoonful of cereal. "Lacey's sister can't go, so she gave the tickets to Lacey. And she invited me. It's tomorrow night."

"Of course, you told her you can't go."

"I did, but I was hoping you might let me go. I've been writing letters and getting letters back." She raced into her next argument. "Besides, Lacey needs someone to go with her."

Mom put her coffee cup down and locked eyes with Penny. "The answer is no."

Steve walked into the kitchen, adjusting his tie. "The answer to what?"

"Penny wants to go to a concert Friday, but she can't

because she's grounded."

Steve poured himself a cup of coffee. "Who's playing?"

"It doesn't matter," Mom said.

"Cosmic Dreams." Penny glanced from her mother to Steve.

"Isn't that the group with the members who are named after planets?" Steve sat at the table.

Penny stared at him in surprise. *I didn't realize Steve knew about them.* "Yes. Jupiter is cute."

Mom gaped at Steve with a shocked expression. "How did you know that?"

Steve laughed. "I'm in retail, remember? We have T-shirts for each band member."

"Do you have one for Jupiter?" Penny asked eagerly.

"I'm sure we do. What size do you want?"

"She doesn't need a T-shirt since she's not going to the concert." Mom rose from the table. "You better hurry, Penny, or you'll miss the bus."

Steve looked at Penny and shrugged.

She finished the rest of her breakfast in silence, fuming over Mom's stubbornness and puzzling over her stepfather's willingness to get involved.

On her way to the bus stop, she sent Lacey a message.

I CAN'T GO. WICKED WITCH SAID NO.

Lacey responded with a crying face emoji.

Penny boarded the school bus and waited for her friend to join at the next stop.

Lacey entered the bus with a big smile on her face and jumped into the seat beside Penny. "Glenda can go with me."

I should be going with her. Penny nodded and held back tears.

* * *

WITH PENNY GONE, MEGAN POURED HERSELF ANOTHER CUP OF coffee and sat back down with Steve. "Do you think I'm being too strict with Penny?"

"Megan, she's your daughter. She made a mistake, but she hadn't been in trouble before or since then. Is she doing her community service project?"

"Yes. I'm actually surprised and happy that she's writing letters without me having to nag her about it."

"You could relax the restrictions a little to show her you appreciate what she's doing."

Megan watched Steve eat his breakfast. *How did I get so lucky to find him?*

Steve finished the last of his coffee. "How about I bring home that Jupiter T-shirt? What size does she wear?"

"She's a medium. I'd love to see her in something other than black."

"Bring her into the store sometime and go shopping together. We're having a big sale right now, and I get an employee discount."

Megan rubbed her forehead. "I'll think about it." *The last time I took Penny shopping, we didn't talk to each other for days afterward.*

LATER THAT DAY, MEGAN SAT AT THE KITCHEN TABLE WITH HER sketchbook open before her. She held her pencil and studied the photograph she wanted to recreate on the blank page. *Penny and Jody together. This was when we went to Disney last year.*

Jody's face glowed with happiness. Her light-colored

curls curved around her face. *She takes after her father. Good-natured and easy-going, just like Steve.* Megan's focus shifted to Penny's image. Her short, dark hair was so severe. *And she takes after her father. Moody, challenging, sometimes unpredictable, just like Peter. My two daughters.*

Megan sketched an oval for each face and added marks for facial features. As she studied each face, she recognized some of her own features. *They both have my upturned nose.* She shaded their hair and added shadows for depth. Finally, she put the pencil down. *Not bad. I need to practice a little more, but it's not bad.*

When Penny came home from school, Megan met her at the front door with a smile and a plastic bag with a Jupiter T-shirt inside. *She's going to be thrilled.*

"Steve got you the Cosmic shirt you wanted. We discussed it and decided you can go to the concert because you've been doing great with your letter writing."

Penny's lips quivered. "It's too late. Glenda's going with Lacey."

"I'm sorry."

"No, you're not. You want to make my life miserable." Penny ran past her and up the stairs.

Megan stood at the bottom of the steps with the plastic bag in her hand. *Oh, Penny. I really am sorry.*

* * *

LATER THAT WEEK, NINA OPENED THE ENVELOPE FROM PENNY and unfolded the drawing it contained. The pencil drawing of the hummingbird was remarkably like the one she had sent with her last letter. *Excellent job, Penny. This is an accurate reproduction.*

She read the letter that accompanied the drawing. Then she sat back and pondered how she should respond. She reread the letter.

Dear Kanina,

My mom was fired from her job. She calls it down-sized. Whatever you want to call it, we have less money these days. My mom thinks we may need to sell our house. Depending on where we move, I might have to change to a different school. I'm worried about that. I don't have a lot of friends and I don't want to lose the few I have.

Do you have a lot of friends where you live?

Your pen pal,
Penny

Nina's thoughts traveled back to her childhood. *Military life meant lots of school changes. How did I deal with that? My mother always made it seem like a new adventure. We explored the places we moved to, visiting museums and markets, meeting local artists and artisans. It was not easy, but there were always other army brats in the same situation.*

She closed her eyes. *Friends? I guess the people here are my friends now. I always felt that my art was my best friend. It was always there for me. When I was sad or happy, art was there.*

Nina took the hummingbird drawing and tacked it

to the bulletin board beside the superheroes drawing by Rosemary's grandson. She stood back and admired Penny's artwork. Then she went into the media room to type her response letter. *This may take a while.*

THE NEXT DAY, DURING THE MORNING MAIL CALL, EMILY arrived with a handful of mail. The top one was an envelope decorated with black doodles. "Someone has an artist soul," she said, handing the envelope to Nina.

Nina chuckled. "Yes, I think so." She ran her finger along the doodle. *Like a Celtic knot.* She took the correspondence to her room and settled into her comfortable chair. *I wasn't expecting another note this soon.* She opened the envelope and pulled the letter out. A piece of paper fluttered to the floor. She let it stay there while she read the letter.

Dear Kanina,

I'm sending you a photo of me so you know what I look like. This is a selfie I took during our summer vacation to the lake. I'd like to have a photo of you. Please send one.

The vacation at the lake is fine, but it's kind of boring. I hope one day to go to interesting places all around the world.

Keep writing to me. I like getting your letters.

Coming to you with a smile,
Penny

Nina bent forward to retrieve the fallen photo, but she couldn't reach it while seated. She stood up and, using the arm of the chair for support, got down on her knees and reached for the photo. Once she had it, she struggled to get up. *Getting old is a royal pain.* She sat in the chair again and examined Penny's image.

"Why, you're a pretty young thing. Almost like a pixie fairy with that short hairstyle. And you want a photo of me? Why would you want to see my wrinkles and brown spots?"

Nina rose and walked to the mirror over her chest of drawers. She examined the wrinkles and lines that crossed her face. *When did I get so old?*

Her eyes wandered to the sketch on the nightstand by her bed. She ambled over to it and removed the sketch from the frame.

"You can have this one, Penny. One of my exceptionally talented students did it years ago. A little more practice, and it would have been perfect."

Before going to bed, Nina sat in her recliner and thought back to her students over the years. *So many students. Some made me smile. Some made me sigh. A few even made me cry.*

Gloria had an attitude the size of the Alps. Cold, icy, and rocky. She came into class with a chip on her shoulder. She didn't want to be there and didn't want to do the work. But one day, while I was showing slides of artwork by the masters, one picture must have reached her. I never knew which painting it was that triggered her emotions but suspected it was Michelangelo's "The Creation of Adam." Gloria started crying. I heard her soft sobs and, without making a fuss, handed her a tissue. We discussed how art affected people in different ways. After that class, Gloria was different. She still had an attitude, but the ice on the mountaintop had melted a little.

Megan had talent. It was always a pleasure to work with a student who had a natural talent. The initial classes had gone well. Then we arrived at the annual portrait class for advanced art students. Megan did a proper rendition of my face. Actually, quite good. However, when I tried to encourage her to go deeper into the emotion, she rebelled. She ripped the drawing from her sketchbook and threw it on the floor. I'm glad I kept it. She changed classes and never returned. I called her mother but was told she had transferred to accounting, where there were better chances for employment. So sad. She had so much natural ability. That drawing was the best portrait any student had produced. And now my young pen pal will have it.

William came to class because girls seemed to take art classes. He wasn't talented at art, but I helped him refine the precision of his lines and angles. The last I heard, he had landed a job doing auto detailing. His line work on pinstripes was excellent. I like to take credit for that.

Claude attended my class and went into architecture. He enjoyed the lessons on perspective. He loved drawing buildings. Every assignment I gave him had to have a building in it.

Francine was in the same class as Claude. She had an excellent eye for color. She figured out the importance of the color wheel, complementary colors, patterns, and quick sketching.

All those students and so many more. I hope I made

a difference in their lives. I learned so much from them. I learned to always treat each student as an individual, each with his or her own needs. Perhaps I helped shape the future of some students.

* * *

ON FRIDAY AFTERNOON, PENNY SAT AT THE COMPUTER AND played her video game. *At least Mom hasn't taken away my computer privileges.* She scored double points and opened a new door in the kingdom. *Wow! Lots of weird creatures in here.* She moved her character to the left and lifted her right shoulder as she swung an axe at a three-headed beast.

Jody wandered into the room. "Penny." She tugged Penny's arm.

"Not now. I'm trying to clear this room to get to the throne."

"Come play with me." Jody came closer to the computer screen and her head got in Penny's way.

"Jody, you need to move."

"Play with me." Jody stamped her foot.

Penny kept moving the controls. "Gotcha." When she had cleared the room of the beasts, she looked around. *Jody's gone. Guess she found something better to do.*

The game played a repeated tune. *On to the next level. I haven't gotten this far before.* She continued playing until Mom called her for dinner.

A FEW DAYS LATER, PENNY SCRATCHED GOKU'S FURRY NECK with one hand and texted Lacey with the other.

Jody ran down the hallway and into Penny's bedroom.

128

"Look! I'm a ballerina. What are you going to be for Halloween?"

With a yawn, Penny said, "I'm not dressing up this year."

"Why not?" Jody twirled around on her tiptoes. "It's fun."

"I don't feel like it."

Jody skipped out of the room with Goku running after her. "Mommy, when are we going trick-or-treating?"

Penny returned to texting Lacey. "Halloween is lame."

A minute later, Mom's voice called from downstairs. "Penny, can you take Jody trick-or-treating tonight?"

"I thought you grounded me," Penny shouted.

Her mother's footsteps thumped up the stairs and stopped outside Penny's doorway. "Steve has to work tonight, and I have to get ready for an interview first thing tomorrow morning. I'd appreciate it if you'd take Jody to a few houses in the neighborhood."

Jody jumped around in her ballet costume. "Please, Penny."

Penny opened her mouth to complain but took a deep breath. "Alright."

"We're trick-or-treating! We're trick-or-treating!" Jody danced down the hallway.

"Thanks," Mom said.

"Whatever." Penny picked up her phone and read the latest message from Lacey.

After an early dinner, Penny took Jody by the hand and visited several of the neighborhood houses. Jody's Halloween bag was soon filled with candy. They reached the end of the street and stopped outside the fence of the corner residence.

The lights were off.

"Doesn't seem like they're home," Penny said.

"My friend lives here." Jody yanked Penny's hand.

"Their lights are off. That means they don't want trick-or-treaters. Besides, it's dark now and time to go home."

Jody ran to the gate and pulled it open. "Trick or treat!"

"Wait, Jody!" Penny hurried after her. "They have a big dog." *Donovan's a German shepherd and always looks mean.*

Barking from the back of the yard grew louder. The jingle of metal tags increased.

"Jody, get out of there!" Penny ran through the gate and picked Jody up. The bag of candy dropped and spilled across the ground.

"My candy!" Jody screamed.

The dog gave a deep growl, the sound vibrating in his throat. The dog's breathing was close, too close. Penny raced through the gate and slammed it shut. The metal fence rattled as Donovan leaped against it. The dog howled, then turned to sniff the pile of candy strewn across the grass.

Jody whimpered. "My candy."

"We better go home," Penny said. Her heart raced and her knees shook. "I'm sorry about your candy, Jody, but we had to get out of there."

When they entered their front door, Jody ran straight to their mom. "Mommy, Mommy!"

"What happened?" Mom's eyes fixed on Penny.

"She went into the Beckers' yard, and Donovan was loose."

Mom's hand covered her mouth. "You shouldn't have let her go in there."

"I told her not to, but she didn't listen to me."

With an expression that changed from shock to annoyance, Mom put her hands on her hips. "What am I going to do with the both of you?"

"You could thank me for possibly saving her life." Penny stormed up the stairs to her bedroom. *I didn't want to take her trick-or-treating. This is why Halloween is lame.*

Chapter 13

Wednesday, November 1, 2023

MEGAN TOOK A DEEP BREATH, SMILED, AND OPENED THE front door to the Community Art Center. *Right on time for the interview.* She tucked the leather portfolio under her arm. It held samples of her work and a list of the marketing awards she had earned.

She entered the exhibit room. A collection of framed art covered all the white walls, and a cluttered desk sat in the center of the open space. Except for the desk chair, there was no other seating. Megan walked around the perimeter of the room, examining the paintings and drawings. Her heels clicked against the tile floor, echoing across the room.

Checking her watch, Megan pursed her lips. *We're not getting off to the right start. Where's the receptionist? Anyone could walk in here and steal a painting. Although, I don't know why they would want to. Most of these are awful. Jody's finger paintings are better than many of these.*

"Mr. Greer," Megan called in a loud voice.

When there was no answer, she walked to the rear of the Art Center and knocked on a closed door. She called Mr. Greer's name again. Then she tested the doorknob. The door swung open, exposing a dark room with rows of tables. *A classroom.* She wrinkled her nose. *But it smells musty.*

At the sound of the front door opening, Megan spun around and dropped her portfolio.

"Ah, you must be Megan Hinson," the short man with glasses said. "I'm Matt Greer, the president of the board of directors for the Center."

Megan retrieved her portfolio and hurried across the room to shake hands with Mr. Greer.

"Sorry I wasn't here to greet you." He pushed the glasses closer to his eyes. "I had to visit the shop next door. They unlock the front door for us and keep an eye on who enters."

Megan blinked. "Are you saying there's no one here to meet people?"

"There's not much foot traffic. Let's go into the class-room." He gestured for Megan to follow him.

Mr. Greer turned on the lights and led Megan into the dimly lit classroom. A lighting tube flickered overhead. They settled into plastic seats at a paint-splattered table.

"I received the resume you emailed. You have quite an impressive background."

"Thank you. I advanced from accounting through marketing and into project management. I also brought along some samples of my work and awards." Megan slid her port-folio across the table.

Mr. Greer studied the contents and nodded. "I have a few questions for you."

"Certainly."

"You're no longer employed. Why?" Mr. Greer's glasses had slid down his nose and he pushed them back into place.

"They let me go due to a business acquisition.

Unfortunately, it's getting to be more common in corporations these days."

Mr. Greer jotted down some notes on a piece of paper. "Do you have any criminal history?"

Megan chuckled. *I guess since they fired someone for embezzlement, they would want to know that.* "No, except for a speeding ticket several years ago."

After scribbling a few more notes, Mr. Greer peered at Megan over the top of his glasses. "What is art?"

What kind of interview question is that? Megan's heart beat faster and she licked her lips. Her mind flashed back to high school art class with Miss K. The words slipped out of her mouth easily, exactly as Miss K had told them years ago. "Art is the expression of love, happiness, pain, and loss by an individual, shown in a way that can be shared with others."

"Well stated," Mr. Greer said. "That sounds vaguely familiar." He wrote Megan's words down and rose. "The board of directors will make the hiring decision. We'll let you know soon."

Megan left the Art Center, certain she had aced the interview but unsure if she was interested in the job. *There's still the matter of salary, but we can discuss that when they offer me the position.*

THAT EVENING, STEVE PULLED MEGAN ASIDE BEFORE DINNER. The look on his face worried her.

"Megan," he said. "I don't want to upset you, but my store is on a list of locations that the chain may close."

Megan clutched her throat. "They're going to close your store?"

"Now, slow down. I didn't say that." Steve's hands

rested on her shoulders. "Management is looking at stores that are not as profitable as they would like. My store is on that list. They may make some changes to make us more profitable."

"Could you lose your job?" Megan's voice rose. *How will we survive if Steve's fired, too?*

"I don't know yet. There's a meeting next week with the team to review cost-cutting options."

"But you could lose your job."

"Megan, let's not jump to that conclusion."

"I can't help it. I'm afraid we're going to lose everything."

Steve pulled her close. "That's not going to happen. We have equity in the house. We can downsize the cars if necessary. And if I need to, I know I can find another store manager job."

Megan nestled against Steve's chest. "I thought I would find a job without any trouble, but that hasn't happened."

"You'll land a good position soon," Steve said. "You need the right situation for your talents and that's going to take some time, but it will happen."

"I hope so." *If I don't get a job soon, I hate to think about what will happen.*

THE PLATES AND SILVERWARE LAY ON THE DINNER TABLE. Megan carried the casserole from the kitchen and set it in the middle of the table. Taking off her oven mitts, she called, "Dinner's ready." She heard Steve's recliner move and the sound of the kids' footsteps coming down from upstairs.

"Smells, um . . . nourishing," Steve said.

Penny and Jody frowned at the lumpy gravy covering

the top of the casserole and each wrinkled her nose. Megan almost laughed. *Years apart and two different fathers, but they are definitely my kids.*

"What is it?" Penny asked.

"It's a new recipe I found online. It's a healthy one-dish dinner."

"Let's try it," Steve said and placed a heaping spoonful on his plate.

"Why is it green?" Penny leaned closer to study the casserole.

Megan scooped a portion onto Jody's plate. "It has pureed peas."

"Yuck." Jody stuck out her tongue and pinched her nose.

"Like baby food?" Penny took a tiny portion and spread it around her plate.

Steve ate a forkful and chewed it slowly. "Is there any meat in it?"

"It's a meatless meal," Megan said. Her shoulders sagged. "I wanted to try something different."

Steve's gaze went from Penny to Jody. "How was everyone's day today?"

"I made a paper bag turkey," Jody said. "It's stuffed full of paper."

"Can we eat it for Thanksgiving?" Steve held his fork and knife like he was ready to eat.

"No, Daddy. It's a dec . . . decoration." Jody wagged her index finger at her father.

Steve laughed and turned to Penny. "And how was your day today?"

Megan braced herself. *There's no telling what might come out of Penny's mouth.*

"We have a field trip coming up. I need twenty-five dollars."

Megan frowned. "That sounds like a lot."

"It covers the bus, lunch, and the art museum ticket."

"Not this year," Megan said. "Money is tight right now."

"But, Mom. It's the sophomore trip for the year."

Steve cleared his throat. "I think we can swing twenty-five dollars."

"Thanks, Steve," Penny said.

Megan fumed. *We could use that money toward our bills.* She put her fork into the contents of her plate and slid it into her mouth. She chewed and swallowed.

Slowly, she pushed her plate away and gazed at the faces around the table. *They're right. It's awful.* "I have some leftover chicken pot pie if anyone wants that."

There were positive answers from all around the table. Everyone started laughing at once.

THE NEXT DAY, MEGAN WALKED THROUGH THE JOB FAIR, A stack of resumes in her portfolio. She studied the displays set up around the room. *Fast-food restaurants. Construction companies. Temp services. Few are likely to be looking for my skill set.*

The display for Enterprise University included large panels of professionals working at computers. She scanned the messages on the display.

"Hi. May I help you with some information about Enterprise University?" A bright young man with a welcoming smile extended a brochure in Megan's direction.

"Thanks," Megan said. "What sort of openings do you have?"

The young man picked up a folder. "We're here for those who want to get retrained for a new career. Are you interested in a career change?"

"Not really. I was hoping to find a position based on my years of experience."

With a swift move, the young man opened the folder and pointed to a chart. "Most job hunters discover that years of experience mean little these days. Employers are looking for employees with current technology skills."

"My years of experience tell me that your spiel is not appealing. Telling experienced professionals that their experience is not what employers want is very negative. Negative messaging discourages action, rather than creating a call to action."

The young man looked at her with wide eyes. "And how is your job search going?"

Megan walked away without answering. *I will not argue with him. Although I'm thinking he might have a point.*

She was halfway through the exhibit space when her phone vibrated. She glanced at the screen and her heart beat faster. Bright Beginnings Day Care flashed across the screen. She answered the call immediately.

"Mrs. Hinson, this is Beverly at Bright Beginnings Day Care. Jody is fine, but I need to talk to you about some recent behavioral changes that we're noticing."

"What sort of changes?" Megan headed to a quiet spot in the corner of the exhibit hall.

"Jody has always been a happy, pleasant child. We love having her here. But over the last few weeks, we've observed some changes in her behavior. She's become more aggressive with other children. Yesterday, she hit another child when he ran past her on the playground. Today, she got into a tug-of-war over a toy and wound up biting the other child."

"Oh, my Lord. That doesn't sound like Jody."

"That's why I'm calling. I wanted to make you aware of what we're noticing. This is a change for her."

"Do you think it's because she's not going there every day?"

"Mrs. Hinson . . ." Beverly's voice trailed off.

"Yes?"

"I don't think it's the change in the number of days she attends Bright Beginnings. Have there been other changes at home? Perhaps some tension or difficulty?"

Megan closed her eyes. *Of course, there have been changes.* "We are going through some challenges."

"Perhaps you need to spend more time making sure Jody feels loved."

Megan bristled. *First, I have a kid tell me my experience doesn't count. Now, I have another kid telling me I need to love my child more.*

"Mrs. Hinson, Bright Beginnings has a nonviolence policy. We rarely have to use it, but it requires that if a solution to a child's violent behavior isn't found, that child will not be welcome at Bright Beginnings. Do you understand?"

With a sigh, Megan relaxed her shoulders. "Yes, I understand. I'll talk with Jody about what's going on."

"Thank you, Mrs. Hinson." The relief in Beverly's voice was clear.

"I appreciate you letting me know. Please give me some time to work on this."

"Of course. I'll let you know at the end of the week if

we're seeing the return of her happy, bubbly personality."

When the call ended, Megan put the phone away and left the job fair. *I hadn't even noticed that what's been going on at home was affecting Jody. I've been so focused on finding a job and dealing with Penny. Have I been neglecting Steve, too?*

After Megan picked up Jody from daycare, they drove home and she asked, "How was your day today?"

"We made sock puppets," Jody replied from the back seat.

"That sounds like fun."

"I wanted the green sock to make a frog, but Jeffrey took it."

Megan glanced in the rear-view mirror to see Jody's face. "How did that make you feel?"

"Mad. He wouldn't give it back to me." Her face puckered into a pout.

"What did you do?" Megan glanced in the rear-view mirror again.

Jody looked out the car window. "I took it from him."

"That wasn't a nice thing to do. You could have made something else."

"I wanted to make a frog. I needed a green sock for a frog." Jody kicked the seatback in front of her. "Miss Beverly gave my sock to Jeffrey."

"Jody, stop kicking the seat."

"I don't wanna."

Megan steered the car into their driveway and pulled into the garage. "Sometimes we don't get what we want."

Jody screamed, "No! No!" Tears ran down her cheeks.

Unfastening her seat belt, Megan twisted around to

look directly at Jody. "Did Jeffrey make a frog?"

Jody whimpered. "No. He made a monster."

"Well, a green monster does sound scary. What color sock did you get?"

"A brown sock."

"What did you make?"

"A frog."

Megan smiled. "There are brown frogs. Did you give him a name?"

"Froggie Friend."

"That's a happy name. Did Jeffrey give his puppet a name?"

"He called it Meanie Monster. He said I was mean, just like his puppet."

Megan reached back to touch Jody's leg. "That's because you were mean to him."

Jody stared at her.

"Trying to take the sock away from him because you wanted it was mean. Tomorrow, I want you to tell Jeffrey you're sorry. Can you do that for me?"

Her lower lip quivered. "I guess so."

"It's better to make people happy than to make them sad or angry."

"But Jeffrey made me sad."

"Did he take the sock before you?"

"Yes."

"You should have been happy for him. Instead, you were sad for yourself and then you were mean to him. Let's go inside and see if we can practice being happy."

"How do we do that?"

Megan opened the driver's door. "I'll show you when

we get inside." *Who knew being a mother meant being a part-time psychologist? If I can figure this out with Jody, maybe I can work on it with Penny, too.*

CHAPTER 14

Friday, November 3, 2023

WHEN PENNY RETURNED HOME FROM SCHOOL, MOM STOOD waiting for her in the kitchen with an oversized manila envelope. "Penny, you got something special from Shadow Oaks. There's even extra postage on it. You should show that to the principal. He might count that as two letters."

Penny smiled and took the envelope. "I showed him the first couple of letters, and he said to wait until the end of the grading period to show him all I received."

"How many have you gotten?"

"I don't know. I've lost count. She's writing almost every day." Penny's fingers edged along the envelope. *What I want to do is go to my room and open this.*

"What do you write about?" Mom eyed the manila envelope.

"Nothing in particular. Just little bits about what's going on. She told me about some of the people at Shadow Oaks. They're playing matchmaker with two of the workers there."

"I'm glad you're taking this community service seriously. I bet your pen pal is happy to receive your letters."

"It's fun getting hers. Do you think I could get some

fancy note cards to send?"

Her mother's expression darkened. "We're watching our budget right now. Keep using the printer paper."

Penny sighed. "Okay." *She's so worried about how much everything costs.*

Penny left her mother and hurried upstairs. In her room, she ripped open the manila envelope and found a letter on Shadow Oaks stationery and a piece of heavier paper. When she pulled them out, she held a slightly yellowed sketch of a woman with a long braid over her shoulder. *So this is what you look like. You drew me a picture of yourself. You are a talented artist and much younger than I expected.*

Penny propped the portrait against the wall at her desk. *Now I don't have to imagine who you are.*

* * *

ON MONDAY MORNING, MEGAN OPENED THE DOOR AND INVITED the realtor into the house.

"You have a lovely home," the realtor said.

"Thank you. It has a brand-new heating and cooling system."

The realtor typed into her tablet. "Any other improvements?"

Megan mentioned the professional landscaping that had been done last year.

The realtor nodded. "Good for curb appeal."

They walked through the house with Megan pointing out features. When they got to Penny's closed door, Megan paused. "This is my teenage daughter's room. It's a mess right now, but it will be neat for any showings." Without stepping into the room, Megan let the realtor scan the space.

"Yes, that would need a good bit of work before I could take a photograph for the listing."

After touring the entire house, Megan led the realtor back to the kitchen table.

"I've pulled some comps for the area," the realtor said. "I believe we should go out at $399,000."

"That's all?" Megan had expected a much higher price.

The realtor pulled out an agreement. "It's a buyer's market right now. Lots of quality houses are available, so prices are low. And selling a home during the holiday season can be challenging. If you want a quick sale, I recommend you stay below $400,000."

"But we thought we had more equity . . ."

"In the past, you might have, but not in today's market. You said you wanted a quick sale. Shall I list your home?"

Megan closed her eyes and shook her head. *This is the third realtor who's told me the same thing.* "I guess I'll wait until the market improves." She showed the realtor to the door. *If Steve loses his job, at least we know how much this house might go for. By the time we pay off the mortgage, there isn't much left.*

The next day, Megan stroked the pearl necklace resting against her silk top. She studied her reflection in the bedroom mirror. *Hair is a little longer than I'm used to, but it's neat. My outfit is classic. Overall impression is polished. You're as prepared for this interview as you can be. Let's do it.* She picked up her portfolio from the bed and headed to the garage.

She slid into the driver's seat and turned the key in the

ignition. The starter made a grinding sound. She tried again, with the same result. *Not now, car. I have to get to this interview on time.* She leaned forward and turned the key again. The grinding sounded weaker this time. She drummed her fingers against the steering wheel.

Picking up her phone, Megan called Steve, but the call went to voicemail. "I'm having car trouble and I need to get to an interview. Please call me as soon as possible."

Once again, she tried to start the car. The check engine light flashed in bright red. This time, the engine was silent. Megan sat back and placed her hands over her face. *Think.*

She picked up her phone again and called a rideshare. The dispatcher reported a fifteen-minute wait time. *We're going to be cutting it close.* She returned inside the house to wait for her ride.

When the vehicle arrived, Megan dashed outside and into the back seat. "Commerce Center, Grand and Main."

The cost of this trip is one more unwelcome expense. And how much is the car repair going to cost?

The car pulled up to the Commerce Center with minutes to spare. Megan hurried into the lobby and checked the directory for Bennington and Richards. Riding the elevator to the seventh floor, she calmed her breathing and lifted her head. *I'm the best candidate for this job.*

The interview lasted two hours. When it ended, Megan congratulated herself that she had stayed relaxed the entire time. On the return ride to her house, she closed her eyes and imagined receiving the job offer.

The garage door was open when she arrived home. Steve's car sat alone in the driveway. Her disabled car was gone.

Megan spotted Steve in the garage. "Where's my car?"

With a rag, he wiped grease from his hands. "I tried to jump-start the battery, and that didn't work, so I had it towed to the service shop. They'll put it on the computer and find out what's wrong."

"It's one thing after another," Megan said. *I wonder how much this is going to cost.*

"Depending what the problem is, it may be covered under the warranty." Steve tossed the rag onto his tool chest. "You look fabulous. I'd hug you, but my coveralls are filthy. How did the interview go?"

Megan smiled at him. *He has such a way of knowing what I'm worried about and trying to distract me.* "It went well. I should hear something in a few weeks." *The sooner I land a job, the sooner I can unwind.*

* * *

EMILY STOPPED NINA IN THE HALLWAY AFTER BREAKFAST. "Nina, I heard you're not joining us today on the shopping trip. I've noticed you haven't gone on any of our outings."

"Shopping is not my idea of a fun time, and I don't need anything," Nina said.

"Is there a place or an activity that you would enjoy? Miniature golf? Opera?"

"Heavens, no." Nina shuddered.

"Well, if you think of anything, let me know. As the activity director, I want to plan trips for everyone. I want you to enjoy your Shadow Oaks experience."

Nina watched Emily walk away. *A visit to the art museum would be delightful. Why didn't I suggest it?*

Probably no one else would want to do that.

LATER THAT DAY, NINA SAT WITH LIZ IN THE GARDEN. WHEN the shuttle bus returned from the shopping excursion, the residents emerged with boxes and bundles.

Rosemary hurried over to them with two bags full of items. She handed one bag to Nina. "I bought you a few things."

Nina's eyebrows lifted. "You shouldn't have." She peered into the shopping bag and gasped.

"The salesperson at the arts and crafts store was extremely helpful. She told me this is everything you need to do watercolor painting. There's paper, a palette, paints, brushes, pens, and even a how-to-paint book."

Nina's eyes darted from the art supplies to Rosemary. "Why did you do this?"

"I saw your eyes light up when you opened that library book with the watercolor paintings. I have a feeling you could be a wonderful artist. You always wear such pretty scarves that go beautifully with your outfit. Having an eye for color is a gift, and I think you have that gift."

Nina blushed and stammered for words to express how she felt. "Thanks so much. I don't know what to say." Tears welled in her eyes, and she blinked them away. *Why did I get rid of all my art supplies when I moved? I've missed them so much.*

"Now, now," Rosemary said. "There's no need to cry. I bought lots of things for myself, too. Walt left me plenty of money, and I can't take it with me." She picked up her bag and left.

Nina clutched the art supplies. "Liz, I don't understand

how she knew or why she did it."

Liz reached a thin finger and pointed to Nina's chest.

"You think she knows what's in my heart?"

The old woman nodded.

In her room, Nina opened the bag. In the bottom was a set of fine-tipped ink pens. She opened the package and tested each pen to learn the line widths. Once she was satisfied, she took a piece of paper and drew a few tentative black lines. With each stroke, her pen moved faster.

The Paris sidewalk café with the table for two filled the right side of the scene. The Eiffel Tower rose in the distance. On the left, window boxes of flowers appeared on the page. Piece by piece, she added to the scene—a bottle of wine on the table, two glasses, the café sign hanging over the narrow street, a girl on a bicycle, and clouds in the sky.

The ache in her hand changed to a nagging pain. Finally, she stopped and sat back. With a critical eye, she examined the pen-and-ink drawing. *Not bad for working from memory. This should show Penny how compelling black and white can be.*

Nina flexed her fingers and massaged her palm. *I used to draw for hours without stopping.* She glanced at the clock by her bed. *Goodness, I* have *been drawing for hours! It's dinnertime already.*

After dinner, Nina went to the media room and typed a letter to Penny. Returning to her room, she folded the letter and the drawing in thirds and placed them in an envelope. *I hope my young pen pal finds that helpful.*

Chapter 15

Wednesday, November 8, 2023

THE LAST BELL RANG FOR THE END OF THE SCHOOL DAY, AND Penny hurried to the art classroom. *Don't want to be late for the first Art Club meeting.* When she arrived, half the seats were already filled. She recognized a few sophomores, but the rest were freshman or upper-class students who she didn't know. Penny took an open seat near the door.

Mrs. Silsbury stood at the front of the room. "Welcome to the Art Club of Bridgewater High School. I'm your sponsor, but this is your club. You all will decide what activities or events to do. I'll help you get approvals, but you need to do the work. Does anyone want to suggest some things the club could consider?"

Students shouted ideas, and Mrs. Silsbury wrote them on the board.

"Painted rocks," someone offered.

"How about a poster contest?" a voice from the back of the room asked.

"New signs for the pep rallies," Penny said.

When the suggestions stopped coming, Mrs. Silsbury asked one more time. "Any other ideas?"

Penny hesitated. *Jody's mural was small but made*

such a difference to her bedroom. "A mural for the cafeteria."

"Yeah!" One student cheered.

"Let's do that," another student said.

"Fab idea!"

"I want to do that!" A chorus of students shouted their approval.

Wow! I didn't think my idea would get this kind of reaction.

Mrs. Silsbury added Penny's suggestion to the list on the board. "This is a great starting point. Some of these activities are easy to do. Others cost money, so we might need to do some fundraising or apply for a grant. Let me run this list by the principal to see which of these require approval. For example, painting a mural in the cafeteria may need approvals from Food Services and Facilities."

A collective grumble spread through the room.

"Don't worry. These are just the steps we need to go through to get approval. At our next meeting, I'll let you know what we would have to do."

Penny and the other students cheered. *We are so lucky to have such a great art teacher.*

* * *

MEGAN PULLED THE STORAGE CONTAINER OUT OF JODY'S closet. "Let's play dress-up."

Jody jumped up and down. "Princess. Princess."

With the top popped off the container, Megan and Jody removed the tutus, dresses, and wigs. Jody grabbed a crown from the bottom of the box and placed it on her head.

"You are lovely, Your Highness." Megan curtsied.

Giggling, Jody put on a sparkly blue dress. "Lipstick, Mommy."

Megan led her daughter into the master bathroom and opened her makeup drawer. With a few quick strokes, she added pink lipstick to Jody's mouth. Then Megan dusted a touch of blush to both Jody's round cheeks.

"You are so pretty. Let me get my phone to take a picture." She passed her jewelry box on the way to retrieve her phone. *I bet the pearls would finish the princess's fashion.* She lifted the pearl necklace from its velvet-lined case and placed it around Jody's neck.

Her daughter's fingers played with the pearls. "I'm a pretty princess."

Megan clicked photographs, taking close-ups of Jody's laughing expression. "Daddy will be home soon. He's going to be thrilled to see you all dressed up."

Megan's phone chirped, and she read the screen, not recognizing the number. "Mommy has to take this call. Please go play princess in your room."

Jody ran off with a wave of her arms.

"Hello, this is Megan Hinson." She headed toward where she had left her portfolio.

"Good afternoon. This is the HR Department at McNully and Wilton. We've reviewed your application and have a few questions."

Megan beamed. *At last, my job hunting may be paying off.* "Of course." She grabbed her portfolio and went down to the kitchen table. For the next twenty minutes, she answered questions about her background and experience.

"Thank you. We will be back in touch if we decide to hold an in-person interview."

Megan sat back, deflated. *I thought after all that, I was going to have an interview scheduled.*

The door to the garage opened, and Steve came through. "Hello, beautiful."

"You're in a cheerful mood," Megan said, her spirits lifting.

"Of course, I'm home early and get to see my lovely ladies."

The front door swung open, and Penny shouted, "I'm home! I got the mail."

"We're in the kitchen," Steve called out.

Penny wandered in and dropped her backpack. "What's for dinner?"

"I'll have to pull something out of the freezer. I was playing with Jody and then I got a call about a job."

"Daddy." Jody ran into the kitchen with her crown tilted to one side.

"There's my littlest princess," Steve said. He picked Jody up. "You are so fancy today."

Megan saw Penny's mouth drop open and followed her gaze to the pearl necklace around Jody's neck.

"Mom," Penny said. "How come she can wear your pearls for dress-up, but I couldn't wear them for school photos?"

"That's different. Jody wasn't leaving the house. I was with her almost the whole time she had them on."

"I see how it is. Jody is your favorite." Penny stomped out of the room. Her footsteps resounded through the house, ending with the loud slam of her bedroom door.

Steve put Jody down. "Mommy probably wants her necklace back now."

The little girl pouted but came over to Megan.

"You look wonderful," Megan said. "But it's time to take off the necklace." She undid the clasp and held the pearls in her hand.

Steve bent down to Jody's level and said, "Why don't you put your crown away and get ready for dinner?"

"Yes, Daddy." Jody ran up the stairs while singing a silly song.

Megan met Steve's gaze. "Do you think Penny's right? Am I favoring Jody over her?"

"I think you know the answer to that question," Steve said gently.

"Penny is such a challenging child."

"That statement shows part of the problem. She's not a child, yet you still treat her like one."

"She's only sixteen." Megan frowned. *When I was sixteen . . . When I was sixteen, I was working a part-time job to help pay the rent.*

"She asked you to let her wear your pearls for a school photo, and you said no. Yet you let Jody wear them to play princess. Don't you see something not right about that?"

"The daycare said Jody needs more positive experiences." Megan stiffened her posture.

"Yes, and so does Penny."

"You're sticking up for Penny?" *He's taking sides against me.*

Steve put his hands on her shoulders. "I'm saying that both girls need positive experiences. We all do. Penny made a mistake, and you lost your job, but we need to get past all that."

"I didn't lose my job." Megan's voice rose. "I was

downsized!" She stood up and stormed out of the kitchen. "I'm going for a walk. Dinner is in the freezer."

SITTING IN HER BACKYARD A FEW DAYS LATER, MEGAN LAID THE sketchbook on her lap and watched the birds fly by. Billowy clouds drifted across the horizon. Squirrels ran up and down the laurel oaks, jumping from one branch to another. *Everything's in motion. How am I going to draw things that don't stand still?*

She tapped her pencil against her upper lip. She studied the tree. *Ah! It's not moving.* The trunk was gray with a dark knot halfway up the left side. Full clumps of leaves hid part of the slender branches. Through the leaves, she could still see portions of the trunk and the larger branches. A bird flew into an opening in the leaves. A gentle breeze shifted the leaves slightly, exposing a few of the lighter undersides.

Her breathing slowed as she noted more details. A shadow cast by the tree weaved across the ground. Bits of blue sky were visible through the tree. The upper branches poked skyward. She had never looked at a tree this closely before. *Amazing!*

Megan put her pencil tip on the paper and sketched the general outline of the tree. Her eyes followed the lines of the tree and she transferred them to the paper. She turned the pencil point on its side, shading the shadows and clumps of leaves. She added more details until she was satisfied. Then she held the sketchpad up to compare it to the tree. *Wow! I can't believe I did that.* She couldn't stop the smile that spread across her face.

* * *

"Nina," Rosemary said after lunch. "My son is coming to take me for a ride in the country tomorrow afternoon. Would you like to come along?"

"Thanks, but I think I'll pass."

The corners of Rosemary's mouth drooped. "I thought you might like to meet him. He's in education."

Nina gave a wicked smile. "How about having Emmett join you? I bet he would enjoy a ride with you."

"If I invite him, my son will think there's something serious between us."

Nina chuckled. "Well, isn't there?"

"No. Whatever would give you that idea?"

"The way you bat your eyelashes at him," Nina said.

"I do not."

Nina looked at her from an angle. "I know better. And I've seen the way he offers you his arm."

"He's just being a gentleman," Rosemary said.

"Is there some reason you don't want your son to meet him?"

Rosemary hesitated. "His father was the love of my life. Walt was all I could have ever dreamed of for a husband. We had forty-five wonderful years together. I'm not sure any other man could take his place. I don't want my son thinking I'm trying to replace his father."

"Your son wants you to be happy. If Emmett makes you happy, wouldn't your son approve?"

"I'm afraid to find out."

"Don't make the mistake of missing out on love." Nina's thoughts went into her past.

"You never married?" Rosemary asked gently.

"No. My life was focused on teaching and traveling."

After André, there was no one else. I tried to find someone, but no one came close to him.

"There's still time."

Nina chuckled. "Sounds like you're talking about you and Emmett." *I'll have to find opportunities to help their romance along. They are meant for each other.*

Chapter 16

Monday, November 13, 2023

After breakfast, Andy moved the card tables in the gathering room and arranged the chairs in a circle.

"What's going on?" Nina asked.

With a chuckle, Andy kept moving the chairs. "Emily's directions were to pull the chairs together for a fun activity. I don't know what she has planned."

"Neither do I." *This is when I escape to my room.*

Emily breezed into the room with a box and observed the circle of chairs. "Very nice, Andy. That's perfect." She placed the box under a chair and hurried over to Nina. "I'm so glad you're here. Pick any seat you want."

Nina stood still. "What is this for?"

"It's an enjoyable little activity. Oh, look, here come some more people." She welcomed the other residents and gestured toward the chairs.

Organized fun is not my idea of how to spend a quiet morning. Nina backed toward the hallway.

"Nina," Rosemary called from her place inside the circle. "Sit here near me."

Too late. I guess I'm going to have some fun. Nina followed Rosemary's directions and looked around at the residents filling the chairs.

"There's still one empty chair," Emily said from where she sat. "Right next to me. I promise I won't bite."

Andy pushed the card tables along the wall to clear a path for Liz's wheelchair.

"Andy could join us," Rosemary said.

His head jerked around at the mention of his name. "What do you need done?"

"Take a seat." Rosemary pointed at the empty chair beside Emily.

"Take it away?" Andy reached for the back of the seat.

"No. Sit in it."

"Me?" He gave Emily a questioning look.

"They want you to join the game," Emily said.

Andy squirmed with all eyes on him. "There are things to do in the garden."

From her seat, Emily reached for his arm and pulled the reluctant Andy into the circle. "This will only take a few minutes."

Poor Andy. He looks like a kid transferring into a new school.

"We call this the Get to Know Me game," Emily said. She pulled an orange foam ball and a paper bag from the box near her chair. "We're going to throw the ball around the circle, and whoever gets the ball has to answer a question pulled from this bag. The person who threw the ball gets to pick a question from the bag. If you don't want to answer a specific question, you don't have to, but then you have to answer two more questions. I'll get us started." She tossed the ball to Mike.

Reaching in the bag, Emily pulled out a slip of paper

and read, "Are you right-handed or left-handed?" She dropped the paper back into the bag.

Mike showed the ball in his right hand. "That's easy. I'm right-handed." He threw the ball to Nina.

She used both hands to catch it. Then she waited for a question. Mike made a big production out of reaching into the bag.

"Name one thing still on your bucket list," Mike said.

I don't have a bucket list. Nina found her voice saying words before she could still it. "Another trip to Paris."

Mike laughed. "Sounds like you've been there before."

"Yes, a few times." Nina tossed the ball to Rosemary, then pulled a paper from the bag. "What's your favorite color?" *Why couldn't I have gotten a simple question like that?*

"Pink." Rosemary tossed the ball back to Nina.

Surprised, Nina caught it. "I've already had it."

"That's fine," Emily said. "New people often get more questions because everyone is curious about them."

"What's the name of your first love?" Rosemary put the slip of paper back in the bag.

Nina blushed. *It was so long ago.* "André Ritchie," she said with her best French accent.

"Oh là là." Rosemary clapped her hands. "We'll have to hear more about this over dinner."

Nina quickly threw the ball toward Emily, but it flew past her, and Andy caught it. She pulled a paper from the bag and scanned the question. She looked at Andy and the women on either side of him. Miss Liz sat on his left and Emily was to his right. She changed the question slightly. "Andy, use one word to describe the person sitting to your right."

Andy looked closely at Emily, while her face reddened. "Angel."

Good answer! Nina chuckled to herself and watched Emily lean a little closer to Andy.

Rosemary clapped her hands. "That's true."

The game continued with laughter and cheers. Nina caught the ball repeatedly. *I think they're ganging up on me!*

"Where were you born?" Emmett asked her.

"Japan. My dad was in the military, and I was born while he was stationed in Japan."

"When is your birthday?" Andy read from the slip of paper.

"June."

Rosemary smiled at her. "You're a Gemini—the sign of the twins. Creative, intelligent, adaptable."

"The artist Paul Gauguin and I share a birthday," Nina said. "About a hundred years apart."

Everyone laughed. Nina relaxed and enjoyed the game as she learned more about the other residents.

Mike was asked "What's your favorite food?"

"Whatever's for dinner tonight." His answer set everyone clapping and stamping their feet.

"On that cheerful note, we're going to end the game," Emily said. "Thank you to everyone for playing and to Andy for helping with the chairs." She smiled at Andy a little longer than Nina expected.

Musing over this new development, Nina returned to her room with a sense of satisfaction. *I think my question helped Andy score a few points with Emily. This was a fun activity.*

AT DINNER, EMILY ANNOUNCED AN OUTING FOR THE NEXT DAY. "We planned an extra activity for this week. For those who are interested, we'll visit the local art museum. The shuttle will leave at ten o'clock, so meet in the lobby before then. We'll have lunch at the restaurant next to the museum."

Nina grinned. *This is the outing I've been waiting for.* "Who's going tomorrow?"

A trio of eyes fixed on Nina. Rosemary put her teacup down and blinked a half dozen times. "Are you going?"

"Yes, I'm looking forward to it."

"Nina, if you're going, I'm going," Rosemary said. "And it may be our chance to bring Emily and Andy together during lunch."

Mike kept eating and shook his head. "That's not my kind of place."

"Why not? Art is for everyone." The words came out of Nina's mouth automatically. *How many times did I explain to high school students why it was important to study art?*

"I received a new word search book from my son, and I think I'll start working on it tomorrow," Emmett said.

"You should come to the museum," Nina said. "The word search will still be here when you get back. Art holds something for everyone. You'll see tomorrow."

Emmett glanced over at Rosemary, who batted her eyelashes. "Since Rosemary's going, I guess I'll go along, too. You can teach this old dog some new tricks."

"I'll certainly try," Rosemary said.

Besides enjoying the art, we may have two romances to tend to tomorrow. Nina's excitement grew. *I hope I can get to sleep tonight.*

THE NEXT DAY, THE MUSEUM STAFF MEMBER PLACED AN orange band around Nina's wrist. "That provides admission to all exhibits. There's a traveling exhibit in the Marlboro Room. It's quite exceptional and includes a Vincent van Gogh painting. Enjoy your visit."

"I will," Nina said. *I feel like a giddy schoolgirl.*

While all the Shadow Oaks residents were together in the museum lobby, Emily gave a final set of directions. "Lunch will be at noon in the restaurant right next door. Meet here in the lobby at eleven forty-five if you want to join us. We'll come back to the museum after lunch or you can visit other shops nearby, but be back here in the lobby by three o'clock. We won't leave without you, but we want to be on the road before the rush hour traffic starts. You're free to visit the exhibits on your own or with a buddy. If anyone needs assistance, I'm here to help."

"Oh look," Rosemary said. "There's a gift shop over there. I love museum gift shops. They have the most unusual things. Want to come with me, Nina?"

Nina smiled but shook her head. "I think I'll find the Marlboro Room. I'd like to see the van Gogh. Emmett could go with you."

"My pleasure." Emmett held his arm out and escorted Rosemary across the lobby.

With a sense of satisfaction, Nina set off to explore the museum. Historic oil paintings in gilded frames lined the gallery walls. Nina paused at a landscape by Eugene Boudin. She studied the sweep of sky across the canvas. *The King of the Sky.* She recalled the lesson she had taught all her classes on Claude Monet and impressionism. *It was Boudin who encouraged Monet to paint outdoors.* She wandered through the museum and felt inner peace and tranquility. *I've been missing this feeling since I retired.*

A museum docent in a navy-blue blazer approached. "Can I help you?"

"I'm looking for the Marlboro Room," Nina said to the young man.

"Right this way. You're in for a real treat there."

Nina followed the docent into an expansive room with benches before each group of paintings. She spotted the van Gogh from across the room. *Such beautiful work.* She walked slowly, studying the painting from different angles. Finally, she settled on the bench and admired the sunflowers captured on canvas before her.

The painting took her back to Paris and the memory of André. As they had sipped wine at the sidewalk café, the scent of the brilliantly colored flowers cascading from the window boxes overhead surrounded them. André had leaned close, inhaling deeply. The tip of his nose had glided along her neck. She closed her eyes, reliving the moment he had whispered, "Magnifique."

When she opened her eyes, the van Gogh sunflowers shimmered before her gaze.

* * *

PENNY SAT ON THE END OF A BENCH WITH AN OLD LADY AT THE other end. Tugging the black hoodie closer to her face, Penny sank lower on the bench, hiding behind the elderly woman. *A stuffy art museum is an awful field trip. I was expecting it to be more fun than this. If Mrs. Silsbury doesn't miss me, I can just hang out on my own without the boring lecture.*

"This way," the docent said, leading Penny's classmates into the next gallery.

Penny watched them go and exhaled. *Free at last.*

"It's beautiful," the old lady beside her whispered.

Penny glanced at her bench companion. "What?"

"The van Gogh." She gestured toward the framed artwork before them. "He painted sunflowers so lovingly."

Penny studied the painting hanging in front of them—two cut sunflowers against an abstract blue background. Vincent '87 scrawled across the bottom corner.

"He painted that one in Paris. Such a romantic city." The old lady sighed.

"They look dead." *All dried up and tired.*

"They probably wilted while he painted. In his later paintings, he kept them in a vase. He loved yellow." The old lady's voice was mesmerizing.

Penny looked at the woman's profile more closely. She wore a bright scarf around her neck. Her hands were thin and wrinkled, as was her face, but she had a pleasant expression. Penny stood up and approached the painting, leaning closer. The flowers were vibrant, the brush strokes strong and bold.

"I bet I could do that."

The old lady chuckled. "You should try."

Penny looked at the black skull and crossbones drawn on her wrist. "I don't do color." *Except for my socks.*

"Vincent said, 'The sunflower is mine in a way.' You should make it yours, too."

Mrs. Silsbury hurried over. "Come along now. You need to stay with our group."

Penny winked at the old lady. "I will."

The old lady called after her, "And go to Paris."

"Someday I will!"

** * **

NINA RETURNED TO THE MUSEUM LOBBY AT THE DESIGNATED time to join those going to lunch at the restaurant next door. Rosemary and Emmett were arm-in-arm. The Denzel couple stood together. Emily and Andy rounded out the group. Nina did a quick count and realized she was the odd-numbered person.

"Everyone ready?" Emily looked around. "We don't want to leave anyone behind."

As a group, they walked to La Crepe Cellar a few yards beyond the museum entrance. Emily led the way, and Andy held the restaurant door open.

"Table for seven," Emily told the server.

"Right this way. We were expecting your group."

The interior of the restaurant resembled an evening along a Paris sidewalk with small café tables and twinkling lights overhead. French music played in the background. Scents of croissants and baguettes filled the room.

"How romantic," Rosemary said, leaning closer to Emmett.

The server with a white apron around his waist led them into a small room. The Denzel couple sat across from each other. Emmett held a chair out for Rosemary and then sat beside her. Nina looked at the remaining three chairs. *Where I sit will determine whether Emily and Andy sit together.* She waited for Emily to select a chair. With a smile, Nina sat in one of the empty seats, leaving an unfilled chair beside Emily. When Andy joined the group, he had no choice but to sit beside Emily. Nina winked at Rosemary, who returned a wink.

The waiter distributed menus. "Bonjour mesdames et messieurs!"

"What did he say?" Andy asked.

Nina smiled. *It's been a long time since I spoke French, but I recognize that phrase.* "He said, 'Hello ladies and gentlemen.'"

The waiter continued, "Welcome to La Crepe Cellar. Je m'appelle Jacques. My name is Jacques."

As he spoke, his accent took Nina back to France. She recalled that summer with André and the sidewalk café where they met. He had spoken to her in French, explaining in English when she didn't understand. Their conversations had been long and focused on painting, especially when he told her about his friend who had an art gallery.

The waiter worked his way around the table, taking orders and explaining items on the menu. When he moved close to Nina, she closed her menu and spoke in French. "Crêpes suzette, s'il vous plaît." *I'll skip lunch and go straight to dessert.*

The waiter smiled and launched into a conversation with her in French. *Oh my. My French is rusty, but this is fun.*

When the waiter left, everyone spoke to Nina at once. "That was lovely to listen to," Rosemary said.

"Did you grow up in France?" Emily asked.

"No, but I traveled quite a bit. I speak several languages."

Rosemary waved her hands together. *I think that means I'm supposed to bring Emily and Andy together. Get them talking about themselves.* "Andy, I've been meaning to ask you about your tattoo. Why a wolf?"

"You ever hear of Duran Duran? My dad listened to them and I grew up singing 'Hungry Like a Wolf' with him. When he died, I had the tattoo done."

"I like 'Ordinary World,'" Emily said.

Andy closed his eyes. "'And as I try to make my way to the ordinary world, I will learn to survive.'"

"You know it." Emily clapped and gave Andy a broad smile.

He nodded, and the corners of his mouth turned upward.

I have no clue what they're talking about, but at least they're talking. Nina listened to their exchange of musical favorites until the waiter brought their lunch orders. Jacques prepared her crêpes suzette beside the table, and everyone gasped at the burst of flames when the Grand Marnier was added. At the taste of her decadent dessert, Nina's thoughts returned to a certain Parisian café and her Frenchman.

Chapter 17

Tuesday, November 14, 2023

MEGAN GOT OUT OF THE SHOWER TO FIND A VOICEMAIL message on her phone. With her hair still dripping, she pressed the play button.

"Mrs. Hinson, this is Matt Greer from the Community Art Center. The board of directors considered your application for the executive director position and has decided to continue searching for the ideal candidate. Thank you for your interest."

She replayed the message. *You've got to be kidding. They're not hiring me—with all my years of experience. Obviously, they don't know what they're doing.*

She gazed at her hazy image in the steamy fog on the bathroom mirror. *If I can't get a job like that, I might not be able to get anything. Without a decent-paying job, we'll lose the cars or the house, or both.*

She knew the anxiety of losing everything. She was eleven when her parents were evicted from the apartment above the music store. The apartment was part of her father's pay for working in the store, but when he was fired for being drunk on the job, they had to leave. For a week, they stayed in a cheap motel. The sights and smells of the run-down place still haunted her.

If Steve loses his job, we'll lose everything.

* * *

THE NEXT DAY, ON THE MORNING SCHOOL BUS, PENNY WROTE a letter to Kanina. Her hand jiggled with each bump the bus rumbled across. As her pen jumped across the paper again, she frowned. *I may have to rewrite this.*

Lacey got on the bus at the next stop. "Hi, Penny. You still doing homework?"

"No. I'm writing to my pen pal."

Lacey leaned over to look at the page, but Penny pulled it away, suddenly feeling protective of her correspondence with Kanina.

"How many more of these letters do you have to do?" Lacey asked.

"I think I still need her to answer about twelve more."

Lacey studied her fingernails. "It must be boring writing to a boomer. What do you have to say to each other?"

Penny closed her notebook and put it in her backpack. "It's working out okay. She's got a lot of interesting stories and does cool art."

"What do you write to her?"

"I tell her about things."

Lacey raised an eyebrow. "What kind of things? Do you write about me?"

"Never. I told her how I felt about Steve."

"That seems kinda personal."

Penny laughed. "What's she going to do with it? She's not posting on social media or sharing it with the world."

"Still, I'd only tell her what I had for dinner or ask her about the weather."

With a shrug, Penny looked out the window. "I need her to keep writing letters. If all I write is that I had pizza for lunch, she'll stop writing. Besides, she writes really interesting stuff. She used to be a teacher."

"Boring!"

Penny crossed her arms. *Kanina is writing to me like I'm an adult. I wouldn't mind writing letters to her after the community service part is done.*

IN ART CLASS, MRS. SILSBURY ADVANCED THE IMAGE PROJECTED on the classroom screen to a new painting. "Anyone recognize the subject in this painting?"

Several students shouted out, "Eiffel Tower."

"That's right. It's called 'The Eiffel Tower' and was painted by George Seurat in 1889, the year the Eiffel Tower opened. Seurat was born in Paris, France, and painted in a style called neo-impressionism. The term *pointillism* describes his art." Mrs. Silsbury enlarged the image. "Notice the dots of color."

Penny studied the painting effect. "It's not very precise."

"Exactly," Mrs. Silsbury said. "This style relies on the mind and eye to blend the color dots into a larger image. Seurat believed the use of color could create emotion. When you view a work of art, pay attention to the emotion it creates in you."

Penny thought about her black-and-white manga drawings. *That's what's missing in my drawings. Emotion.*

"Tomorrow we'll talk more about color theory," Mrs.

Silsbury said as the bell rang. "Penny, I'd like to see you for a few minutes."

Penny went over to the teacher's desk. *I wonder what this is about.*

"I've submitted the list of possible Art Club projects. While we wait for approval, we can continue to plan activities we'd like to undertake."

Penny shifted her backpack to a more comfortable position. "Do you have some more ideas?"

"I was thinking we could plan an art festival here at the school. I bet if we approach Mr. Edwards, the music teacher, we could hold a joint music and art event. Or we can investigate local art contests and encourage club members to create pieces for shows. We could invite a professional artist to speak to the club."

"Wow. Those are all awesome ideas." Penny brightened at the thought of doing any of those activities.

"Of course, we still need to receive the principal's approval on the list of what we submitted, but I wanted to get you thinking about how we might proceed."

With a big smile, Penny nodded. "I'll ask around and see what other kids may be interested in doing. There's a comic con in a few months. We could dress as our favorite characters and go as a group."

"You'll have to fill me in on that one, but it sounds like fun. Now, you better get going or you'll miss your next class."

"Thanks, Mrs. Silsbury." Penny's feet barely touched the ground as she left the art room.

* * *

TODAY IS JODY'S DAY FOR DAYCARE. MEGAN AND STEVE HAD agreed three days a week of daycare would be good for Jody and allow Megan time for job interviews and networking. *If this job hunt takes much longer, we'll be cutting back to two days a week.*

Megan dropped Jody off and chatted with the daycare staff before heading to visit the local community college. She had an appointment to talk to the dean about a potential adjunct professor position. *I'm reaching for anything, but there's no telling what they may need. I have had so many job experiences.*

The meeting began on time and progressed well until the dean asked about her education. When she explained that she never completed her master's degree, the conversation came to an abrupt halt.

"I'm sorry, Mrs. Hinson," the dean said. "I thought you understood that adjunct professors here are required to have completed a master's program. We owe it to our students to have credentialed staff."

"I completed all the coursework, but I was expecting a baby and didn't finish my thesis."

The dean glanced at his watch. "That's unfortunate. Perhaps you should finish your degree requirements. Please come back when you do." He stood up.

I'm being dismissed. "Thank you for your time." She shook the dean's hand and left with less energy than she had when she entered.

Another dead end.

* * *

173

"Emily," Nina called down the Shadow Oaks hallway.

The activity director turned. "What can I do for you, Miss Nina?"

"I wanted to tell you how much I enjoyed the trip to the art museum."

"I'm so glad you joined us and hope you'll come on other outings."

Nina smiled. "Can we go to your office? I need to talk to you."

"Of course." Emily led the way through the administrative area to her office and gestured for Nina to sit in the chair by her desk. "Is something wrong?"

"Not at all," Nina said. "I had an idea while we were at the museum. I was a high school art teacher for forty-eight years and selected Teacher of the Year three times."

"Very impressive! I didn't know all that."

Nina picked at a loose thread in her scarf. "Would you be interested in holding art classes here? I'd be glad to teach anyone who wants to learn to draw or paint."

Emily's face lit up with a broad smile. "Why, Miss Nina, that's a wonderful idea."

"We wouldn't need much in the way of supplies. Some paper and pencils to get started. We can use the card tables in the gathering room."

Emily clapped her hands. "That's simple stuff. When would you like to start?"

That was easier than I expected. "We could start Monday of next week."

"Next week is Thanksgiving," Emily said. "Many residents will be away visiting with family."

Nina rolled her eyes. "I totally forgot." *With no family,*

Thanksgiving is just another day.

"The Monday after Thanksgiving would be a good choice. I'll make an announcement this afternoon before dinner. But Miss Nina, don't be disappointed if no one wants to take part."

"I hadn't even considered that." Nina frowned. *Why would she even think that? Art lessons will be fun for everyone.*

"When I first arrived here, I set up some chair yoga classes with a certified instructor. The chairs were all set up and no one came. I tried several times but couldn't get anyone to attend."

"Even if only one person comes, I'll be glad to teach the class."

Emily stood up. "Let's try it."

Nina sauntered back to her room to plan an introductory lesson. *I always enjoyed putting lesson plans together.*

LATER THAT DAY, VOICES FILLED THE GATHERING ROOM. TWO people occupied a card table assembling a puzzle, while a rowdy game of cards was underway at another table. On the couch, a pair of knitters chatted while their needles clicked together. Across from them, two couples talked about their grandchildren.

Nina carried the Grandma Moses library book into the room. She took a deep breath and straightened her shoulders.

Emily rang a handbell. "Hear ye, hear ye."

Laughter and cheers followed before the residents settled down.

"We have a wonderful event planned for the Monday after Thanksgiving," Emily announced. She glanced at Nina.

"Our own Miss Nina, who was an art teacher for almost fifty years, has offered to hold an art class for us right here in the gathering room."

The knitters returned to knitting.

"Miss Nina, would you like to say a few words about the class?"

Nina went to the center of the room. "You all have artistic talent. You may not have explored it before. This class will be a fun way to get in touch with your creative side."

"And what side would that be?" Mike shouted out. He rocked back in his chair with laughter.

"Everyone can draw," Nina said. "If you can hold a pencil, you can use it to express your feelings or share your experiences." Nina opened the library book to a two-page color spread of a landscape painting. "Grandma Moses was a famous folk artist. She was self-taught and started painting when she was seventy-eight. Her paintings showed what life was like when she was a young girl. She lived to be 101."

Rosemary raised her hand. "I'm not seventy-eight yet, but I doubt there's much hope of me being an artist."

"This class will be easy. You might be surprised at what you can draw." Nina closed the book.

The two couples on the sofa returned to sharing pictures of their grandchildren.

Emily came over to Nina's side and announced to the room in a loud voice, "Classes will be here in the gathering room a week from Monday at ten o'clock in the morning for anyone interested." She turned to Nina and whispered, "That's all we can do."

With a sigh, Nina tucked the library book under her arm and took it back to her room. *I didn't expect everyone to be excited, but they didn't even seem interested.*

* * *

ON FRIDAY, MEGAN WAS DRESSED FOR A JOB INTERVIEW AND had the car keys in her hand when her phone rang. She continued into the garage and glanced at the phone screen when she reached the car but did not recognize the caller's number. *Could let it go to voicemail. Probably a spam call, but it could be a potential employer.* Standing beside the car, she accepted the call and brought the phone to her ear.

"Babe, it's Peter."

Megan gasped. *Peter!* She sputtered, unable to get a word out.

"It's been a long time, babe."

It sure has, you SOB. "What do you want?"

"Is that any way to talk to your high school sweetheart?"

"You mean my ex-husband."

"That's cold, babe."

"Stop calling me that." Megan's heart pounded faster.

"I still get to you?" Peter's laughter vibrated the phone in her hand.

Megan clenched her open hand into a fist. "You owe years of child support."

"Babe—"

"I said don't call me that." She paced across the garage, fighting to control her anger.

"How's the little one?"

"The little one is named Penny, and she's sixteen." Her jaw tightened and her shoulders tensed.

"I'd like to see her."

"Since when? You can't just pop into her life after all these years." Megan's voice rose in volume.

"Don't get all huffy."

"You were never there for her or me. You don't have a place in our lives." She closed her eyes and took a deep breath. Memories of being a struggling single mom flashed through her mind.

"You pushed me away."

"You were cheating on me with another woman." The memory of that dark time still hurt.

"Look. I want to see Penny. I'm her father."

"Her father wasn't here when she learned to ride a bike. Her father wasn't here when she fell and needed stitches. Her father wasn't here when she became a teenager. Her father wasn't here when she got into trouble at school."

"So I missed some things."

Megan's temper flared. "Some things? Those things are her life."

"Are you going to let me see her?"

"No!" *I won't let that happen.*

"I found your phone number. I can find her."

"Don't you dare."

"Tell Penny I'll be in touch with her."

The call disconnected. Megan stared at the phone in her trembling hand. *I can't believe he's back.*

THE NEXT DAY, MEGAN TIGHTENED THE LACES ON HER WALKING shoes and marched down the tree-lined street at a brisk pace. With a water bottle strapped across her body, she set a goal to walk down to Cypress Creek Park, a two-mile hike.

A mile into the walk, she slowed and considered

turning back. Her shins were throbbing, and her breathing came in ragged bursts. *I'm so out of shape.*

She kept walking, but slower. She mulled over the mess her life had become. *Lost my job, Penny vandalizing others' property, Jody misbehaving at daycare, the car and AC breaking down, bills and more bills, no new job in sight. And now Peter barges back into my life.* With each step, the list got longer.

Do we sell the house? Send Penny to a tough-love program? Get a job flipping burgers? Take Jody out of daycare? Her mind swirled with options and alternatives, each one bleaker than the one before.

She stepped off the curb, right into the path of a vehicle turning left. The blare of the car horn made her head jerk skyward. She lurched backward and landed on her rear. The car swept by and someone shouted out the window, "Watch the light!"

Megan sat on the ground. *I was lucky. One second earlier and I could've been under that car.* She brushed off her hands and climbed to her feet. *No damage was done, except for my pride. I should've been paying more attention to where I was going.*

No matter what she did for the rest of the day, disturbing thoughts of Peter, financial ruin, and Penny in jail interrupted her activities. *It's probably good I don't have an interview today. I'd be a wreck.*

Megan straightened the comforter on the bed and smoothed the wrinkles. *How did my relationship with Penny go so wrong? It's just like me and my mother. Once she pawned Grandma's pearls, we never got along.*

After Megan collected the dirty laundry, she went down

to the laundry room. As she loaded the washer, she recalled the last argument she had with her mother six years ago. *Never dreamed it would be the last time I would see her. She died without seeing how well things turned out with Steve.*

March 2017

MEGAN SAT ON HER MOTHER'S TATTERED COUCH IN THE STUDIO apartment in the run-down part of town. The place had a sickening smell. The blare of a television from another apartment filled the room. Her mother did not look well.

"Mom," Megan said. "I've met someone special. We're going to get married."

"Hope he's better than the last deadbeat you married." Her mother lit a cigarette and coughed.

"That's not fair, Mom. Peter—"

"Is he paying child support for Penny?"

"No," Megan said. "But—"

"Did he cheat on you?"

"Yes." Megan lowered her head.

"Then he's a deadbeat. Is this new man making good money?"

"He's an assistant store manager and hopes to be a store manager soon."

Her mother frowned. "Hope doesn't pay the bills."

Megan took a deep breath. "His name is Steve Hinson. I'd like you to meet him."

"If I don't like him, are you going to walk away from him?" She puffed on her cigarette and blew a cloud of smoke into the air.

"Mom, that's a ridiculous question."

"I warned you about Peter, and you didn't listen. Why is this any different?"

"I can't talk to you." Megan stormed to the door. "I'll send you a wedding invitation."

Her mother's voice called after her. "Save yourself a stamp."

Save yourself a stamp. Those are the last words I heard my mother say. Now Penny and I are going down the same path. Megan sighed.

She pulled the wheeled garbage can down to the curb. It was full. *Full of broken toys, craft supplies that had dried out, worn-out shoes, the detritus of my life. I'm done decluttering. The house is ready to go on the market. I've been fighting the need to do this. We can't continue to pay the minimum on credit cards. We're getting deeper into debt.*

After leaving the garbage can at the curb, she walked toward the house. *This place was my dream. Ever since growing up in small apartments, I wanted a house of my own. Only it's not my own. It's the bank's house, and if we can't pay the mortgage, it'll be foreclosed.*

Steve is so optimistic that I'll find a well-paying job, but it's not happening. I was on top of the world. How did it come to this?

She straightened the fall wreath hanging on the front door. *Such a pretty house.*

Where will we go from here? If we move out of the school district, Penny will have to change high schools. But that might be an improvement. Get her away from the bad influences in her life. But changing high schools is rough. I had to do it, and I don't want to put her through that.

She rubbed her forehead. There must be a solution. But what is it?

CHAPTER 18

Monday, November 20, 2023

MEGAN FOLDED THE LAST PIECE OF LAUNDRY, THEN PICKED up her ringing phone. The display flashed Abbie's name, but the call was abandoned. Megan looked at her missed calls. *Abbie didn't leave a voicemail.* She hesitated. *Maybe she hung up because she had to do something else or someone came into her workspace. It could have been a misdial.*

Curious, she returned the call. The phone rang and Abbie answered.

"Hi, Abbie. I missed your call."

"I hate to bother you." Abbie's voice sounded shaky.

"Is something wrong? Are you okay?" Megan closed her eyes. *I hope they didn't fire her, too.*

"Megs, you know the client we were working on when they let you go."

"Sure, the unusual restaurant concept. Is there a problem?"

"Remember how worried you were about the numbers?"

"I sure do." *I knew there was something wrong with the estimates.*

"They're blaming me."

"Did you tell them that Bradley came up with the figures?"

Abbie sniffled.

"You didn't tell them." Megan pictured Abbie taking the blame to protect Bradley, even though he no longer worked there.

"No."

"Are you still dating Bradley?"

"Yes."

"Have you talked to him about this?" Megan ran her fingers through her hair.

"Not yet."

"Talk to him. Have him explain to you exactly how he arrived at those numbers."

"Okay."

"I wish there was more I could do for you, but I never understood the numbers myself."

"I told them it would take time to build the customer base."

Megan smiled. "Excellent. That's the message I wanted them to hear."

"Anything else, Megs? I'm afraid they're going to let me go."

In rapid-fire succession, ideas flashed through Megan's head. "If they want to reach their customers, they need more advertising. They provided a minimal advertising budget. The budget should be doubled. They could do a vlog, which is low cost, showing how their unique dining concept works. Make it fun. It might go viral."

"I'm getting all this."

"Have them find a nonprofit that they can partner with.

Something that resonates with the owner, so it becomes a personal crusade. If I remember correctly, the owner's son had a rare condition. I don't remember the specifics, but that sort of thing shows the business has a heart."

"They never should have let you go, Megs. You're amazing."

"Thanks, Abbie. Sorry I can't do more for you. Have Bradley explain the numbers to you."

When the call was over, Megan frowned. *I feel bad for her, but there's not much I can do.*

Megan's phone rang again, and she thought it might be Abbie calling back.

"Mrs. Hinson, this is the Human Resources Department at Bennington and Richards. You interviewed this month for a project manager position at our local office."

"Yes, I met with several senior management officials." Megan recalled the details of the interview. *It went really well. I felt comfortable, and the people seemed sharp and professional.*

"You made quite a positive impression."

Her spirits rose. *Maybe they're going to offer me the position.* "Thank you."

"In fact, it was so positive that management would like to consider you for a lead role in opening a new office."

Megan sat on the family room sofa. "Where would the new office be located?"

"We have two opportunities. One in Alaska and the other in Ireland. Those are new markets for our firm. Our leadership team felt you displayed the range of experience that we would like to have as part of our team. Pay will be quite competitive for the respective markets. After an initial start-up period, you will receive annual bonuses based on revenue generated. Moving expenses will be covered. We offer spouse relocation assistance. Our medical insurance package is gold-level for the industry."

With numb emotions, Megan listened to the HR representative enumerate the positives of working for the consulting firm. *Alaska or Ireland? How could I ask Steve to leave his job? Penny's in the middle of high school. I can't move her across the country or out of the country. What happened to the job I interviewed for?*

When the representative paused for breath, Megan posed her question. "What about the local position I interviewed for?"

"That position has already been filled. The leadership team thought your experience was better suited to these new positions."

"Please thank them for the consideration. I'm not interested in relocating my family at this time."

She sat in a daze for minutes after the call ended. *Should I have talked to Steve first before deciding? No, I made the right decision. I wasn't interviewing for a position that meant moving.*

* * *

WHEN PENNY CAME HOME FROM SCHOOL, THE MAIL WAS SITTING on the kitchen counter. She grabbed the Shadow Oaks envelope and ran up the stairs to her bedroom. After throwing her backpack on the floor, she leaped on her bed and ripped open the envelope. She unfolded the two pieces of paper. The first was a typed letter. The second sheet was an ink drawing

186

of the Eiffel Tower. *How weird. We talked about the Eiffel Tower painting in art class the other day, and I had a conversation with an old lady in the art museum about Paris last week, and now this arrives.*

She lay back and read the letter, glancing at the drawing occasionally.

Dear Penny,

I can tell you like black-and-white drawing. Enclosed is a sketch I did in black ink. It shows the variety of line widths and how crosshatching can create shadows and depth.

Every picture tells a story. It is the artist's role to share that story with the viewer. Sometimes a little background on the origin of the story helps the viewer.

The enclosed sketch is a Paris street scene. The Eiffel Tower helps to set the location, since it is an iconic presence in Paris.

When I was between my freshman and sophomore years in college, I spent a summer in Europe. It was a glorious summer. I was nineteen and independent, fluent in several languages.

I don't think I shared with you that I was an army brat. My father was a career army officer, and my mother and I traveled the world with him as his assignments changed. So growing up, I was exposed to many different cultures and learned to speak multiple languages.

Anyway, in the summer of 1968, I was

traveling in Europe, staying in youth hostels, visiting many towns and villages, traveling from place to place. And then I arrived in Paris and met André.

I first saw him sitting at a table for two with a bottle of red wine and two glasses. I was passing by with my duffel bag over my shoulder. Our eyes met, and he beckoned me over.

I joined him for a glass of wine. He ordered some fruit and cheese. The sun was shining, and I fell in love.

This drawing captures what I remember of that sidewalk café. It takes me back to that day.

When you draw, always think about the story you are sharing with your viewer.

Sincerely,
Kanina Koscielniak

Penny sat up with a jerk. "But what happened? You can't stop and not tell me more." She dashed to her desk and pulled a page from her notebook. As she wrote, she glanced at the drawing and imagined herself walking past the café and a handsome Frenchman waving to her. *She was only three years older than me.*

* * *

ON TUESDAY MORNING, MEGAN TOOK A DEEP BREATH AND called the Human Resource Department for Market Biz. "Hi. This is Megan Hinson. I recently interviewed for the social

188

media marketing rep position. I haven't heard anything, so I wanted to check on the status."

Computer keys clicked in the background. "That position was filled last week."

"Oh." Megan's energy slipped away. "Was there any feedback about my interview?"

"The hiring manager didn't share any. Have a nice day."

Megan put the phone down and started crying. *I can't even find a job below my previous level.* Failure and depression closed in around her. *This shouldn't be happening.*

After drying her eyes, she put on her walking shoes. *Exercise might make me feel better.* The brisk walk recharged her energy. She studied the clouds spreading across the sky. A light breeze kept them in motion. *I've been going about this job hunt all wrong.*

Her feet continued in a steady beat against the pavement. *I need to show my ability, rather than just talk about it.* She increased her pace. *All these rejections are making me feel worthless, but I know that's not true.*

Soon she was jogging along the sidewalk. *I know how to prove my value.* A cramp in her side made her stop. Panting, she leaned over, but with a smile on her face. *I know what to do now.*

* * *

PENNY SAT NEXT TO LACEY ON THE SCHOOL BUS WITH THE afternoon sun streaming through the window and warming the side of her face.

"That pep rally was lame," Lacey said.

"In Art Club, we talked about making better signs for the rally."

"When are you going to do it?"

"Mrs. Silsbury said we have to get the principal's approval."

Lacey studied her fingernail polish. "Do it anyway!"

Penny looked out the window. *I can't get in any more trouble.*

At the next bus stop, Lacey picked up her book bag and stepped into the aisle. "Happy Turkey Day tomorrow. Text me later."

Penny watched her leave. *Ever since I've been grounded, Lacey and I haven't done anything fun together.*

One stop later, Penny exited the bus and headed home. Her phone rang steps before she got to her house. *I don't recognize the number.* She answered before it went to voicemail.

"Penny, this is your father."

Penny stopped walking. "Daddy?"

"Yes, honey. It's me." His gravelly voice was hoarse but familiar.

"Where are you?"

"I've been traveling around, but I'm missing my little girl. Thought we might get together."

Penny's heart beat faster. "Yeah! When? Where?"

"Soon. Real soon. I gotta finish some business and then we can get together. Gotta go."

"Wait . . ." The phone signaled the call had ended. *But I have his number now.* Penny quickly saved it to her contacts under the name Daddy.

Penny staggered into her house and dropped her backpack on the floor.

"Mom!" she shouted several times before running to the garage and opening the door. The spot where Mom's car normally stayed was empty.

Returning to the kitchen, Penny found a note on the refrigerator: *Gone to a job interview.*

Figures! I need to talk to her, and she's gone. Penny retrieved her backpack and trudged upstairs to her room.

She took off her boots and lay on her bed, staring at the ceiling. With a meow, Goku jumped on the bed and curled up on Penny's stomach. She rubbed the cat's furry head. "I can't believe it, Goku. My dad called me today. I recognized his voice."

The cat purred and tucked his tail around his body.

"He left a long time ago . . . because of me." She closed her eyes. *That was an awful night.*

February 2013

SIX-YEAR-OLD PENNY HAD BEEN SENT TO BED EARLY FOR dropping a glass full of milk at the dinner table. In her bed, she held her teddy bear tight and pulled the covers over her head, burrowing deeper into the bedding. She whimpered and pulled the bear close to her face. The shouting from downstairs grew louder.

"It's okay, Teddy," she whispered. "It's just Mommy and Daddy talking really loud." She knew better but didn't want to scare poor Teddy. He was already missing an eye and his stuffing was getting lumpy.

It sounded like they were moving furniture around, and then there was a crash. Penny knew that sound. It was just like when she dropped the glass on the kitchen floor tonight.

Penny scrunched her eyes closed. "They're mad because I dropped the glass and spilled the milk. Oh, Teddy, I didn't mean to do that."

Daddy's volume grew louder, but his words were garbled.

"You're a liar. Get out." Mommy's voice was almost a shriek.

The front door slammed, and the walls in Penny's bedroom vibrated with the force of it.

"Someone left, Teddy. Now don't be scared."

Quiet settled through the house, and Penny shifted the covers to look across her room. Darkness hid the stuffed animals piled in the corner and the dolls on the shelf.

"I should be asleep, Teddy, but they were so loud." She shifted the bear's position in her arm. "You stay here."

She tucked the bear into bed and tiptoed to the top of the stairs and listened to the sounds below. Her mother was mumbling and sniffling. Penny crept down the stairs on bare feet and into the kitchen. Red liquid and shattered glass covered the floor.

On her hands and knees, her mother picked up shards of glass. Tears streamed down her face and she held the bottom half of a broken bottle.

"Penny, get out of here. You'll get hurt."

"I'm sorry, Mommy. It's all my fault." Penny ran up the stairs and jumped into bed. "Teddy. Daddy left because I broke a glass."

She was almost asleep when her mother came into the bedroom and sat on her bed. "It wasn't your fault, darling."

Penny nodded but didn't believe her. And then when Daddy didn't come back, she knew it was true. It really was her fault.

ROUSING HERSELF FROM THE PAINFUL MEMORY, PENNY PRESSED start on the microwave and waited until the package of popcorn stopped popping. She was eating popcorn when Mom came home.

"You look sharp, Mom." Penny hadn't seen her mother in a professional outfit since she was let go. *And she's wearing her pearls.* "How did the interview go?"

"I did fine, but they need an IT expert, not me."

Penny held the bag of popcorn toward her mother. "Want some?"

"Thanks." Mom took a handful.

After eating a few more pieces, Penny put the bag down. "Mom."

"Yes."

Penny's insides quivered. "Daddy called me today."

Her mother's face contorted and changed color. "Shit. I told him to leave you alone."

"You what? Told him not to call me? Why?" Penny crossed her arms and stared at her mother.

"Penny, you don't understand. I'm trying to protect you."

"By keeping my dad away from me?"

"He's not what you think he is." Mom reached for her arm.

Penny pulled away. "And how would I know? I was six when he left. And it was all my fault."

"It wasn't your fault."

Penny held back a sob. "Then what happened?"

Her mother walked to the kitchen table and sat down. "Come over here, Penny."

Joining her mother, she pulled a chair out, sat down, and waited.

After a deep breath, her mother spoke slowly. "I met your father in high school. We got married when we graduated from college. A year later, you were born. Everything was going well. We both had well-paying jobs. We bought a house. But that wasn't enough for your father."

Penny leaned forward. *This is the most she's ever talked about him.*

"I loved him, but that wasn't enough for him. He . . ."

"He what?"

"He cheated on me with another woman. When I confronted him, we fought, and he left."

"I remember that night. I thought it was my fault because I spilled the milk."

Mom took Penny's hand. "No, honey. It was your father's fault. And when he left, he didn't stay in touch. I had to hire a private investigator to find him for the divorce proceeding."

Penny swallowed and looked down at her lap. "He called me today after school and wants to get together."

"He called me, too. I told him to leave you alone."

She looked up and locked eyes with her mother. "But he's my dad. Even if he cheated on you, he's still my dad."

"I know. I was wrong to tell him to stay away, but I don't want him hurting you, too."

"Who gave you the right to make that decision for me?"

Penny pulled her hand away from her mother's clasp. "I'll see him if I want to."

"But he'll hurt you," Mom said.

"I'll take my chances." Penny stormed out of the kitchen and ran to her bedroom.

CHAPTER 19

Thursday, November 23, 2023

MEGAN SURVEYED THE DINING ROOM WITH SATISFACTION. The candle in the Thanksgiving centerpiece glowed brightly. The platter of turkey, bowls of stuffing and mashed potatoes, a basket of biscuits, and green bean casserole filled the table. Jody's paper turkey decoration occupied one of the dining room chairs. Steve and the girls sat in the other seats. Megan joined them and bowed her head.

"Dear Lord," Steve said. "We thank you for this fine meal and all the blessings you have given us."

"Amen," Megan said. "Happy Thanksgiving."

Steve reached for a biscuit. "Everything smells delicious. Just like Mom's."

Megan jabbed a fork into a slice of turkey. *I haven't cooked a turkey in years, not since we started spending every Thanksgiving at the Hinson estate.* "Mother Hinson had a lot more practice."

"I'm glad to be home this year," Penny said.

"My parents are disappointed we couldn't go up to New York this time." Steve added a spoonful of potatoes to his plate.

Megan poured gravy over her serving of turkey and

frowned at the lumps in the gravy. "Airfare for the four of us isn't in our budget until I get another job. Hopefully, we'll spend Thanksgiving up there next year."

Penny rolled her eyes. "Do we have to?"

"Penny," Megan said in a stern voice.

Steve reached over and touched Megan's arm. "It's okay, Megan. Penny has a right to ask the question."

Megan nodded and cleared her throat. "Sounds like you don't want to go to Upstate New York."

"It's boring," Penny said. "There's nothing to do there."

Steve laughed. When he stopped laughing, he pointed at Penny. "You're right."

Megan stared at him, then at Penny's surprised reaction.

"I am?"

"Sure. My mother and father are ancient, and spending a long weekend listening to adults talking is no fun."

Megan's eyes darted from Penny to Steve and back to Penny. *He agrees with her. And it's true, it is boring.*

"They enjoy being grandparents and like seeing you and Jody," Steve said.

"You mean seeing just Jody." Penny put her fork down. "I'm a nobody to them. They don't want to see me."

"Penny," Megan said. "You're a step-granddaughter, and I'm sure they want to see you."

"Well, it's still boring there."

Steve nodded. "Maybe we can add a few more outings and activities when we go there next time. You like Japanese art, right?"

"Yes."

"My parents' neighbor has a Japanese garden, complete

with a teahouse and a footbridge."

"I didn't know that," Megan said. *Steve is full of surprises, even after five years.*

"The estate north of my parents' place hired a Japanese gardener, and he laid out a beautiful garden with a koi pond and pathways. Would you like to see that, Penny?"

"Of course!"

Jody tapped her fork against her empty plate. "My turkey wants a biscuit."

They all laughed, and Jody received a biscuit to share with her paper turkey. Conversation swirled around the table, broken only by the clatter of cutlery against china. Finally, Steve pushed his chair back from the table and patted his stomach. "I can't eat any more."

Megan enjoyed the satisfaction of successfully cooking a complete Thanksgiving dinner. *That went over better than I expected.*

From the family room, the persistent ringing of Steve's phone joined the din. "I better go see what that's about." He left the table and hurried to catch the call.

"Is the store open?" Penny asked.

"No," Megan said. "But there could be a problem. Anything from a fire or a broken sprinkler system." She listened to Steve's voice in the distance. *Hope he doesn't have to go into the store today.*

Steve strolled back into the dining room with the phone to his ear and a smile on his face. "I'm going to put you on speaker."

"Happy Thanksgiving, everyone," two voices crackled over the phone in unison.

Mother and Father Hinson!

"We just finished eating," Steve said. "Megan made a feast for us."

"Bet it was as delicious as mine," Mother Hinson said.

Megan forced a smile. "I'm sure it wasn't as tasty as yours."

"We were discussing that since you couldn't visit us for Thanksgiving, we'll come to you for Christmas. We can hardly wait to see how big Jody is getting."

Megan glanced over at Penny, who made a face.

"And of course, we want to catch up with Penelope and learn what she's up to these days," Mother Hinson added.

"That would be lovely," Megan said. *I wish I meant it.*

"Grandma, I made a turkey," Jody shouted.

"That's wonderful, dear."

"Dad," Steve said. "I was telling Penny about the Wesleys' Japanese garden. She'd like to see it the next time we come up."

"That's easily done," a deep baritone voice responded. "This year they added some stone garden lanterns. They're solar-powered and light the pathway to the teahouse."

Steve winked at Penny. "Sounds terrific."

"We'll let you enjoy the rest of your Thanksgiving and will be in touch to work out the details of our visit." Mother Hinson smacked her lips in a kissy sound. "We love you all."

"Thanks for calling," Steve said and ended the call. "How about that? We're going to have company this Christmas."

Under the table, Megan wrung her hands together. *How are we going to survive their visit?* "That's nice, honey. I hope they won't be disappointed with our home."

"Not to worry. If I know my parents, they'll book a suite at the best hotel in town."

"Then I won't have to give up my bedroom?" Penny asked.

"No." Steve laughed. "They're more comfortable when they're in control of their accommodations."

That's a relief! Megan smiled weakly. "Who wants pumpkin pie?"

* * *

NINA SAT ALONE AT THE DINING ROOM TABLE SHE USUALLY shared with her trio of friends. Mike had gone out with some fellow veterans for a Thanksgiving meal. To everyone's surprise, Emmett had accepted Rosemary's invitation to attend her family's holiday get-together. That left her alone at Shadow Oaks. She glanced wistfully across the room at Liz with the pair of teens who joined her for dinner. *Probably her great-grandchildren.*

The squeaky wheels of the dessert cart intruded on her thoughts. A uniformed person with a sour expression pushed the cart toward her. The lips curved in a scowl and eyebrows drawn together gave her a formidable look.

"Pumpkin pie?" Her voice mirrored her expression.

Nina folded her hands in her lap. *Thank goodness she's not the usual staff here.* "Yes, please."

The plate landed on the table with a thud, causing the dollop of whipped cream to slide off the slice of pumpkin pie. The woman and her cart were gone before Nina could thank her.

I should have scheduled a trip somewhere. Why did I think holidays would be different here? Last year, she had spent Thanksgiving at a museum in Mexico City enjoying the colors and heritage of artist Frida Kahlo. Each Thanksgiving, she indulged in a trip to a place where the holiday wasn't celebrated. Today, she was alone on Thanksgiving, a day with such a strong focus on family gatherings. A painful emptiness threatened to bring tears to her eyes. Instead, she poked her fork at the piece of pie.

THE DAY AFTER THANKSGIVING, THE SHADOW OAKS STAFF bustled around the facility, stringing garland, hanging wreaths, and decorating Christmas trees. Nina admired their attention to detail.

The twinkling lights and bright ornaments give a festive glow to the awful paint color and upholstery in the gathering room. The sing-along tonight should lift everyone's spirits.

The lights glowing on the tree in the gathering room reminded Nina of the time when her father was stationed in Germany, and her mother had taken her as a child to the Munich Christmas market. Walking through the busy rows of shops, vendors, and food stalls, the sights had dazzled her young eyes, and the smells were tantalizing. She and her mother had shared a bratwurst sandwich, finishing with warm gingerbread and candied nuts. The highlight of the trip was watching the dancing figures on the glockenspiel, while the many bells rang. The memories made her smile. *Those were good times.* She sighed. *And so long ago.*

* * *

ON SATURDAY EVENING, PENNY HEARD STEVE'S CAR PULL INTO the driveway and the front door open, followed by Steve hollering, but she couldn't understand what he was saying. She closed her social studies book and raced down the stairs.

Mom and Jody were at the window watching as Steve walked around his car. He bent over and peered under the car.

"What happened?" Penny asked.

"Jody opened the door when she saw Steve pull up, and the cat ran out. He ran under the car, but Steve doesn't see him."

Penny raced out the door. Her heart pounded faster.

"Goku! Goku!" She got down on her hands and knees and searched under the car, but there wasn't any sign of the cat.

"I've looked in the bushes," Steve said, "but I don't see him."

Penny ran back into the house. "Mom, I need some cat food."

Jody cried, "Goku ran away!" Tears trickled down her cheeks.

"We'll find him," Penny said. *But Goku is an indoor cat and hasn't ever left the house.*

Steve came in, shaking his head. "No sign of him."

With a bowl of dry cat food in her hand, Penny went back outside and shook the bowl. She walked up the street, calling the cat's name and shaking the bowl of food. It was dark and getting colder when she returned home.

"I didn't find him." Penny placed the bowl on the kitchen counter. Her throat tightened, and she blinked to fight back her tears.

"He'll probably be at the door tomorrow morning meowing to be let in," Mom said. "Now come eat."

If he doesn't get hit by a car or attacked by a dog. Without an appetite, Penny pushed her dinner around on her plate.

ALL DAY SUNDAY, PENNY WANDERED THROUGH THE NEIGHborhood searching for Goku. Disappointed that she couldn't find him, she returned home.

That evening, she blasted her music on high and danced around her bedroom to the latest Cosmic Dreams song. When her phone rang, she turned the music volume down and picked up her phone. "Daddy" flashed on the screen. Her heart thudded against her ribs. She quickly accepted the call.

"Hi, Daddy!"

"That's my girl." The voice on the phone rose above the sound of multiple voices and background noise.

"Where are you? It's really loud."

"That's Vegas for you."

"You're in Las Vegas? I thought you were coming to see me." Penny's shoulders drooped.

"Maybe in the future."

"When can we get together? I need to talk to you about something Mom told me."

"Don't believe a word your mother says. She's a money-grabbing liar."

Penny blinked and stiffened. "She said you left because of another woman."

"She's a liar. She kicked me out."

"I remember that night." Penny shuddered at the memory. "There was a lot of screaming and broken glass."

"Hey, darlin'. I gotta go."

"Wait. Can I call you sometime?"

"No. I'm really busy. I'll call you again."

The phone call ended, and Penny stared at the blank screen. *He's gone. He can't be right. Mom's not a liar. Why did he call me?*

Chapter 20

Monday, November 27, 2023

THE DIGITAL CLOCK IN THE GATHERING ROOM DISPLAYED 10:00 a.m. A stack of blank paper lay in the center of each card table. Sharpened pencils rested beside the paper. Nina looked at all the empty seats. *No one wants to even try to learn.* She paced around the room. *Even those who regularly use the room for other things are staying away.*

Emily stopped by five minutes later. "This looks wonderful, Miss Nina."

"But no one came." Nina's shoulders drooped.

"I warned you they might not."

"You did, but I hoped . . ."

"Give it time." The activity director walked away and then turned back. "I have a few minutes. How about if you give me a lesson?"

Nina brightened. "It will be a mini lesson."

"That sounds perfect." Emily pulled out a chair and grabbed a pencil and paper.

"Let's begin with the tools we'll be using." Nina launched into her lesson with enthusiasm.

Five minutes later, Emily put her pencil down. "I didn't know one pencil could do so many kinds of lines. Thank you for the lesson. I would love to stay and do more, but I have a conference call scheduled in a few minutes."

"Thank you for humoring an old lady," Nina said.

"Don't give up. We'll keep trying. Next time there should be a few more students."

"It's possible, but I doubt it." Nina collected the papers and pencils. *I can't even teach anymore.*

* * *

On Tuesday morning, the phone rang once, twice, and three times. Megan tapped her foot. *Pick up, Abbie. Come on, pick up.*

The phone stopped ringing and Abbie's voicemail message began. "Hi, fellow human being. You must need to reach me. Leave a message, and the cosmos will send it to me."

"Abbie, I can't stop thinking about the Art Center. I have an idea I want to run by you. Call me ASAP." Megan's foot tapped faster.

With a pad of paper on the kitchen countertop, Megan wrote a list of ideas to improve the financial situation at the Art Center. Her list grew longer and more detailed. Her pen flew across the paper in a crazy mind map of ideas. *This is no different from any other project I've ever done.*

All afternoon she moved her ideas from the sheets of paper onto the computer, creating detailed plans and schedules. *This is full-out project management planning.*

At four o'clock, she paused midway through the project budget to pick up Jody from daycare. Her mind bubbled with ideas throughout the drive to the daycare. *I haven't felt this excited in a long time.*

With Jody strapped in her booster seat, Megan drove to the nearest craft store. "Let's go shopping, Jody."

Jody wiggled in her seat and cheered. "A shopping we will go. A shopping we will go."

Megan laughed and joined her in the song. Her spirits soared in happiness.

"We need to get some arts and crafts supplies. This will be fun."

In the rear-view mirror, Megan saw Jody's eyes widen and her hands clap.

I should have had more moments like this with Penny. But I was busy working and worrying about how to pay the bills. I hope I can make up for the lost time with her.

Later that day while she was cooking dinner, Megan's phone rang and she answered. "Hi, Abbie."

"Your message sounded urgent. Is everything okay, Megs?"

"Everything's fine. I had a brainstorm and need to run some ideas by you."

"How 'bout a drink after work tomorrow?"

Megan paused. *I guess Penny could watch Jody until Steve gets home.* "Sounds like fun. Dizzie's at six o'clock?"

"Perfect. You mind if Bradley joins us?"

Megan smiled. "Sounds like you two are still together."

"We have some news to share," Abbie said.

"You're pregnant?"

Abbie laughed. "No, Megs. You'll find out tomorrow."

Megan returned to cutting carrots, musing over what Abbie's news might be.

At dinner, she explained her plans for tomorrow.

Penny agreed not only to watch Jody, but to prepare dinner.

ON WEDNESDAY, MEGAN ARRIVED AT DIZZIE'S JUST BEFORE SIX o'clock. The after-work crowd was boisterous and animated. At the bar, she ordered a glass of Cabernet Franc, then found a small table in a corner and put her portfolio on the table-top. *Should be a little quieter here.* She sipped her wine and waited for Abbie and Bradley, speculating about what news Abbie might have to share.

Five minutes later, Abbie breezed through the door in a floral-motif jumpsuit. Her rainbow-hued hair curled around her face, and her laughter filled the air.

Megan stood up and waved to her friend. "Abbie, over here."

Pushing her way through the crowd, Abbie joined her. "You're looking stunning, Megs."

Megan peeked at Abbie's ring finger. *No engagement ring.* After Abbie received her martini, they clinked their glasses, and Megan made a toast. "To good friends and new opportunities."

Abbie leaned forward. "Tell me more."

"I didn't get the Art Center job, but I've been thinking that I could help them by creating a fundraising plan and a marketing plan."

"That's a marvelous idea, and you're a master at developing effective plans."

"I'd offer to help them as a volunteer. If the plans work, maybe I can turn it into a paying position."

"Sounds solid, Megs."

Megan opened her portfolio. "I need some brainstorming ideas from you."

Abbie took a sip of her martini. "Sure. What are we brainstorming?"

"I need ideas of what the Art Center should offer the community. What kinds of programs would make it successful?"

"It's pretty pathetic right now," Abbie said. "It has an excellent space for displays to showcase local artists and to bring out-of-town exhibits to the community. Of course, there should be art classes, contests, and grants. Maybe an art resource library."

Megan scribbled notes as Abbie spoke. "This is why I needed you."

"We always make a powerful team," Abbie said.

As the crowd grew, the noise level rose. Megan closed her portfolio. "Thanks, Abbie. The next part is to focus on fundraising."

"You need sponsors," Abbie said in a loud voice to be heard over the bar noise. "Here comes a potential one now." She waved to Bradley working his way through the crowd.

Megan raised an eyebrow. "Bradley?"

Abbie nodded and then held her arms out to him.

He kissed Abbie and winked at Megan.

"His company, Vels Corp., might be interested in a sponsorship," Abbie said.

With raised eyebrows, Bradley snorted. "What are you two plotting? And what have I walked into now?"

They all laughed.

"I'm working on a fundraising plan for the Community Art Center," Megan said.

Bradley shrugged. "I'm not familiar with it."

"I'll fill you in tonight," Abbie said.

"There may be some naming opportunities," Megan said. "I have to finish drafting the plan and present it to the president of their board of directors."

"Let me know when you get past that point." Bradley put his arm around Abbie's waist.

"Will do," Megan said. *Now I have an incentive to finish the plan.* "Abbie, you mentioned having some news?"

With a grin, Abbie locked eyes with Bradley. "We're engaged."

"Congratulations!" Megan raised her almost-empty wineglass. *I guess opposites attract.* "Have you set a date?"

"Megs, are you kidding?" Abbie showed her bare ring finger. "We're still getting the engagement ring sized."

"A certain someone"—Bradley pointed at Abbie—"had to have a uniquely designed ring."

They laughed until Megan had tears in her eyes.

"I'm not surprised." Megan finished the last of her wine. "I have to go, but I'll stay in touch."

THE NEXT DAY, MEGAN ENTERED THE COMMUNITY ART Center with a confident stride, her portfolio in her arm. It held the detailed marketing and fundraising plans she had spent hours working on. *Some of my best work ever.* Her eyes roved around the front room with a fresh perspective. The musty smell made her shake her head. *This run-down room is going to get a thorough cleaning and a facelift. That cluttered desk will be repurposed to greet visitors and volunteers.*

"Mr. Greer," she called in a firm voice.

"Back here, in the classroom."

She marched into the classroom and extended her

hand to the president of the board of directors for the Art Center. "It's kind of you to meet with me again."

Mr. Greer shook her hand and quickly slid his glasses back into place. "Your offer sounded intriguing."

They sat at the same paint-splattered desk they had used for the interview, but now Megan was in charge.

"As you know, I have years of experience with marketing and project management. I can understand the hesitation to hire me with the Center's limited budget. Let's put the question of salary aside for the time being. I have a proposed marketing plan, which ties into a fundraising plan I would like to present to you."

"That is generous of you," Mr. Greer said.

"I will provide my services and years of experience to help the Center reestablish itself in the community, build a network of sponsors and supporters, and present a series of programs designed for various audiences."

"And you'll do all that for no charge?" He fumbled with his glasses.

"Exactly. Under the condition that if my plans are successful in six months, you will consider bringing me on as a paid employee. Until then, I will be the acting executive director not drawing a salary."

"But at the end of six months, we may not be able to pay you what you're accustomed to."

"I understand that." Megan smiled and paused. "There are more things in life than money. It's taken me a long time to figure that out."

Mr. Greer nodded.

"If I can't deliver the results presented in these plans in six months, I'll relinquish the acting executive director title and you can hire whomever you want."

"That sounds reasonable."

Megan opened her portfolio and removed both the marketing and fundraising plans. "Let me go over both of these with you."

For the next hour, she summarized the detailed plans to rebuild the role the Art Center played in the community, the services the Center would offer, and projected sources of revenue.

At the end of her presentation, Matt Greer sat back and rubbed his hands together. "I want you to start right away, but I need to call an emergency meeting of the board to get their approval."

"Certainly." Megan rose from the table. "I'll leave the plans with you. If you want me to explain them to the board, I would be glad to do that, too."

"These are excellent documents, and I believe the board will agree with my recommendation that we proceed. I'll call you as soon as the board approves your offer. How soon can you start?"

"Immediately." Megan shook his hand and left with her head held high. *If they say no, it's their loss. I hope they say yes, because I want to do this.*

An hour after getting home, Megan took a deep breath when Matt Greer's name appeared on her phone. As she accepted the call, she worried that such a quick call might be a refusal.

"I did an emergency conference call with the board," Matt Greer said.

Megan paced around the family room, wishing he would talk faster.

"They unanimously decided to accept your offer. Can you start tomorrow?"

With a big smile, Megan closed her eyes. "I certainly can."

After ending the conversation, she twirled around the room. *I'm taking a big risk, but I know I can do this.* She stopped spinning. *If I can't, my severance pay will be gone and we'll be broke. That means this has to work.*

Chapter 21

Friday, December 1, 2023

M EGAN'S FIRST ACTION AS THE ACTING EXECUTIVE DIREC-
tor of the Community Art Center was to clean the
front windows inside and out. It took a lot longer than she
expected. *There's no telling how long it's been since these
were last washed. With the grime gone, people passing by
can see into the exhibit room while walking or driving along
the street. We need to replace the paintings on display, but
we'll do that when we hold classes and encourage students
to display their work.*

After the windows, she organized the front desk in the
exhibit area by clearing off the work surface. *This is the first
thing people see when they walk in. It should be where we
display flyers for upcoming events, have sign-up sheets for
classes, and log in volunteers. It's not the holding place for
junk mail, empty lunch cartons, and soda cans.* When she
was done, she stepped back and admired her work. *Much
better!*

Then she headed into the classroom. Standing at the
open door, she assessed where she should start. *Art supplies
should be stored in bins. Reference materials and resources
belong together on bookshelves. Those aprons are disgusting*

and will be thrown out. She jumped right into sorting art supplies into categories. Along with the paint-crusted aprons, she discarded lots of nearly empty paint tubes and dried-up glue bottles. Finally, she gathered and cleaned an assortment of paintbrushes and neatly stacked pads of paper.

Megan stretched her aching back muscles. The classroom looked better, but piles of art books and magazines were scattered around the room on shelves, art desks, and in the storage closet. She checked her watch. *I'll sort the books, but that will be it for today.*

Books on drawing were piled together. Watercolor books went into another stack. Oil painting, pastels, and mixed arts each had their own pile. She placed them on shelves along one side of the room. Feeling proud of what she accomplished, she rested her hands on her hips. *Tomorrow I'll clean the tables and finish these magazines.* She eyed the tumbled stack of periodicals. *I bet I could throw those all out and no one would miss them.* She bent over and picked up an issue of *Coastal Creatives* magazine. *This one's from 1970. I wonder if a collectibles shop would be interested in these.*

She glanced at her watch again. *I have to get Jody. Maybe I can bring some of these home and see if there's anything worth saving. I can throw them out at home as easily as here.* She scooped up an armload of magazines and took them to her car, then returned to turn off the lights and lock the doors. *It looks much better. Not a bad first day.*

* * *

THE AIR HAD A CHILL TO IT, AND NINA PULLED HER SWEATER tighter. A slight breeze ruffled the flowers and whispered through the oak branches, setting the Spanish moss swaying. Nina sat in the garden with Liz.

"Maybe we should go in, Liz. It's getting cooler fast."

Liz wore a knitted hat, and a large blanket was draped over her wheelchair. She smiled but shook her head.

"You must be a Northern lady," Nina said. "This is hot chocolate weather for me."

After a few minutes of observing the tree branches sway, Nina licked her lips. "I need to talk to someone." She glanced at Liz. "I'm feeling useless these days. I don't have much reason for living. There's no purpose in my life anymore. I thought offering an art class here would give me a way to share a lifetime of experience, but no one's interested."

Nina rubbed her hands together for warmth. "Is this all life has for us? We sit in the garden and watch the wind blow?"

Liz worked a trembling hand from the blanket and gestured for Nina to come closer.

Nina rose and bent closer until her braid brushed against the old woman's arm.

Liz's lips moved, and Nina struggled to understand the garbled word.

"Courage?"

The old woman repeated the sound.

"You want me to have courage?"

The old woman's hat bobbed up and down.

"I guess I'm just feeling sorry for myself. It takes courage to go on when the way isn't clear."

The wind picked up and a flurry of leaves tumbled through the air.

"I think we better go in now." Nina pushed Liz's wheelchair into the building. She leaned close to Liz's ear and whispered, "Thank you. You have been a godsend to me."

***

AFTER JODY WAS IN BED FOR THE NIGHT, MEGAN SAT IN THE family room with a stack of art magazines beside her while Steve watched television.

"What in the world do you have there?" he asked.

"These are old art magazines from the Art Center. Someone had saved them. I thought I should do a quick review before throwing them out."

Steve gave her a puzzled look. "What are you hoping to find?"

"Some old articles about painting techniques." Megan picked up the top magazine and flipped through the pages. She sneezed at the swirl of dust.

"Don't waste your time on stuff like that. With the internet today, people can find videos about all kinds of painting stuff. Who's going to read old magazines?"

"You're probably right." She leaned over to drop the issue on top of the stack, but she accidentally kicked the pile. The magazines tumbled over and spread across the floor. She kneeled and gathered the scattered periodicals back into a pile.

Steve joined her and lifted one to examine it. "Hey, this one is from May 1969. That's twelve years before I was born. These are old." He tossed the magazine toward the pile Megan had created. It flew past the stack and the pages tumbled open.

Laughing, Megan reached for it and gasped. "Oh my God, Steve!"

"What?"

"Look. Look at this." Megan held the open page for him to see. "I know her! That's my high school art teacher. The one who wrote in my sketchbook. But she's much younger in this photo."

"Wait. This article is from 1969. When were you in her class?"

Megan thought back to high school. "I think it was 2000."

"That's over thirty years between the article and when you had her as a teacher," Steve said.

"She was older when I was in her class, so that makes sense."

"What does the article say?"

Megan got up from the floor and sat in her chair to read the article. She skimmed through it, flipping the worn pages.

"This is a review by an art critic who attended a college art exhibition for Kanina Koscielniak." She put the magazine down and glanced at Steve. "We always called her Miss K, because we couldn't pronounce her name."

Megan returned to reading. "It says the exhibition included charcoals, watercolors, pastels, and oil paintings by the college sophomore. Let me read you this part. 'Talented is too little to say about this future art superstar.' Here's a quote from her professor. 'Kanina has a rare gift for art.' He goes on to say that he wishes he had her ability. In talking about himself, he said, 'Those who can't do, teach.' He teaches, but Kanina can do."

"Is she still alive?" Steve asked. "She might like to have this article."

"I don't know. I transferred out of her class and never saw her again." Megan set the magazine aside. "I wonder if any of my classmates remember her. I'll have to search the internet and see what I can find."

* * *

DURING THE SATURDAY MAIL CALL, NINA RECEIVED A LETTER from Penny. *She wrote this in a hurry. Her handwriting is barely legible when she writes fast.* She scanned the letter, then she read through it more carefully. *So, you want to learn more about that bittersweet time in my life.*

Dear Kanina,

I loved your drawing, but your letter made me crazy with questions. I need to know more about André. Was he handsome? Did he speak English? Did you get married? Did you have children? What happened?

I NEED MORE INFO!!

Yours always,
Penny

Kanina closed her eyes. *I never should have sent her that café drawing or given her any details. For years, I've packed those memories away and now I need to revisit them and share them with someone I barely know.*

She lowered her head and raised her hands to cover her face. *Is it still that painful to think about? After all this time?* She visualized his face, the dark hank of hair that fell over his right eye. He was clean shaved. Older and wiser in the ways of the world. He loved her art, admired her talent. His hands were strong, yet gentle. His voice still rang in her ears with all his sweet words.

She took the pad of art paper outside, along with the set of ink pens, and sat where Liz liked to sit. She pulled André's face into her conscious thoughts and drew it on the page. She captured the sweep of wavy hair over his expressive eyes, the alluring curve of his lips, and the firm set of his jaw. At the bottom of the page, she wrote "André." *I can't write about him, but I can sketch him.*

On the back of the drawing, she wrote Penny's questions and her answers.

Was he handsome? Yes.
Did he speak English? Yes.
Did you get married? No.
Did you have children? No.
What happened? It is a long, sad story.

Even thinking about André gave her heart an aching hole full of yearning. *Penny, you do have a poison pen if you can make me feel such regret.*

* * *

THE NEXT DAY AT DINNER, MEGAN AND STEVE CONTINUED talking about the *Coastal Creatives* article.

"What a surprise it was," Megan said to Penny. She shared the story of finding the old magazines at the Art Center and how one of them included an article about her former high school art teacher. "I'm going to search for her online and see what I can find out about her. If she's alive, I'd love to give her this article. But she may have died by now."

"How do you know it was your teacher?" Penny asked.

"There was a photo with the article. She was a college student at the time, but even back then she wore her hair in a single, long braid that she always kept over her shoulder."

"What?" Penny jumped up from her chair. "What was your teacher's name?"

"Penny, what's wrong?"

"What was her name?"

"It was challenging to pronounce. We called her Miss K. In the article, her name was Kanina Koscielniak."

Penny ran from the table and raced up the stairs.

"What in the world is that all about?" Steve asked.

Megan shrugged. "I don't know."

A few minutes later, Penny thundered down the stairs and thrust a paper in front of Megan. "Is this her?"

Megan gasped. "Where did you get this?"

"My pen pal sent it to me. That's what was in the large envelope."

With her mouth open, Megan looked from the drawing to Penny and back to the drawing. "This is your pen pal?"

Penny nodded hastily. "Yes. She sometimes signs her name Kanina Koscielniak. She even wrote in one letter that there was a famous Polish artist with the same last name, but she wasn't related to him."

"And she sent you this drawing?" Megan examined the pencil drawing and traced her finger along the outline of the image.

"I printed a selfie and sent it to her. I asked her to send

me one of her. Instead of a photo, she drew this picture."

Megan's hands trembled. "She didn't draw this. I did."

Steve held his hand out. "Let me see it. When did you draw this?" he asked, handing the drawing back to Megan.

"She gave us the assignment in class to draw a portrait of her. I worked hard at mine and thought it was an excellent sketch. But she said I needed to practice. I got upset and ripped the drawing out of my sketchbook and threw it at her."

"Wow, Mom. You were a badass."

"Penny." Steve's head tilted toward Jody.

"Sorry. Mom, you were awesome back then."

Megan gave a half smile. "I was full of myself. I transferred out of her class and into accounting."

"That's crazy," Penny said.

Studying the portrait, Megan suddenly understood what Miss K had said all those years ago. "She was right. This is a decent picture of what she looked like, but there's no emotion in her expression."

"But Mom, she kept it. It must have been good enough for her to have kept it for all those years."

"Imagine that. She kept it."

Steve stood up. "Why don't you two go do your online research to see what you can find out about the talented Miss K? Jody and I will clean up after dinner."

"Thanks, honey," Megan said and hurried after Penny, who had already run to the office.

* * *

THAT NIGHT, NINA SLEPT FITFULLY, TOSSING IN HER BED. HER dream took her back to Paris.

Nina sat at the same table where she and André met every afternoon at the same time. She waited for him to arrive. *I'm pleased with today's watercolor painting. The view of Notre Dame along the bank of the Seine River is spellbinding.* She lifted the painting from her art portfolio and admired it. *It's my best one yet.*

She ordered a bowl of bouillabaisse and a glass of Sauvignon Blanc. As she ate, she wondered what might be delaying André. *I can hardly wait to hear what his art gallery friend thought of my paintings.* Yesterday, she had given André all the artwork she had completed over the summer. *About two dozen watercolors and a dozen graphite sketches.*

The server cleared away her empty bowl and glass.

Nina looked down the sidewalk in both directions. *Where can he be? He's never been this late before.* Darkness closed in around her, with only the warm light glowing from the windows along the street to brighten the evening.

"L'addition, s'il vous plaît," Nina said to the server.

She paid the bill and picked up her easel and art supplies. *Why isn't he here? Something must have happened.* Her heart raced. *He has all my paintings!*

"André!"

Nina bolted straight up in bed. Her heart pounded wildly, and she clutched her chest. *It was only a dream. I'm here at Shadow Oaks in my room. That happened long ago. All those paintings were lost forever. And never another word from him.*

With difficulty, she went back to sleep, until a siren woke her. *That sounds nearby.* She sat up in bed and rubbed her eyes. Carefully, she slipped one leg and then the other onto the floor. She slid her feet into her slippers and put on her robe. *An ambulance here in the middle of the night is not good.* The lighted digits of her bedside clock read 3:08 a.m.

She turned on her bedside lamp. Her room looked familiar and cozy in the warm light. Tying a knot in the belt that secured her robe, Nina walked across to her door. Sounds from the hallway grew louder. She hesitated. With shaking fingers, she opened her door and peeked into the hallway. Other bedroom doors were cracked open with faces peering out. Mike limped down the hallway, his prosthetic leg visible below his shorts.

"What is it?" Nina asked as he passed by.

"Not sure, but I'm going to check."

Other people gathered in the hallway, most with tousled hair and hands over their mouths in shock and concern. Nina stepped out of her room. She searched for familiar faces in the growing crowd. *Mike. Rosemary. Emmett. The Turners.* She recognized most of the other Shadow Oaks residents. With growing fear, she knew who was missing. Liz.

The ambulance siren stopped, and a hush fell over those in the hallway.

"They turn the siren off when there's no need to go to the hospital," someone said.

A night attendant with Mike by her side appeared at the hallway entrance. "I have some sad news. Mrs. Liz Campbell has passed away. Her family has been notified."

A muffled cry escaped Nina's lips, followed by a tear rolling down her cheek. *Such a dear, dear lady. Courage. She told me to have courage. Did she know she would be gone soon and I would be alone again?* Nina returned to her room and cried herself to sleep.

Chapter 22

Monday, December 4, 2023

A T BREAKFAST, EMILY ARRIVED DRESSED IN BLACK, LOOKING sad and red-eyed. Her usually cheerful greeting was somber. "I have heard from Liz's grandchildren. There will not be a funeral service. Because of her advanced age, she had no surviving siblings, and all her children have already passed away. Her grandchildren are scattered. They decided her remains will be cremated."

"How sad," Rosemary said.

"If you are interested, we can celebrate her life here," Emily said. "Anyone who wants to share a story about their connection with Liz is welcome to share it. We'll meet out in the garden at three o'clock this afternoon. It's getting cold, so dress warmly. Any questions?" When there were none, Emily left.

Breakfast continued, with only the sound of cutlery against plates and coffee cups being put down on tables. Nina pushed the pancakes around her plate with no desire to eat them. *This will be me in the future. I have no family to make arrangements. No friends to share stories about my life. I will just be gone.*

A SMALL GROUP GATHERED IN THE SHADOW OAKS GARDEN AT three o'clock. Andy had arranged a circle of chairs near the spot where Liz liked to sit. Nina had a tissue in her pocket, prepared for the tears she knew would come.

Emily stepped into the center of the circle. "Thank you for attending. We all knew Mrs. Liz Campbell in different ways. For me, she was the first resident I met when I arrived here five years ago. It was her birthday. She was ninety-seven, and she was wearing a red boa and a tiara. Five of her grandchildren were here, and they told me Liz had been a WASP pilot during World War II. She ferried planes from the factory to military bases.

"She loved to dance, and on that birthday when I met her, she did a swing dance with another resident. The following year, she had a stroke and became limited to a wheelchair. In all the time I knew her, she was always such a pleasant person to be around."

Nina sat in shock. *I didn't know all that.* She imagined a youthful Liz doing the jitterbug. The thought brought a smile to her lips. With a lighter heart, she listened to other stories and realized how little she knew about someone who had become very important to her.

Dabbing her eyes, Emily stepped forward again. "Anyone else want to share a few thoughts about Liz?"

Nina raised her hand tentatively. "I haven't been here long, and didn't know Liz that well, but in the short time I had with her, I discovered what a kind soul she was. We would sit here in the garden and admire the flowers and the oak trees. She loved it out here. Even when the winds grew cold, she wanted to stay out here. She was a truly beautiful person." She wiped away a tear at the end of her speech. *I will miss her so much.*

"Thank you, Miss Nina. That was lovely. Now, in memory of Liz, here's a swing dance tune she loved. 'In the Mood' by Glenn Miller."

As the music played, many residents tapped their feet and clapped to the beat. Emmett and Rosemary got up and danced on the grass. He twirled her, and she kicked her leg in the air, raising a cheer from everyone.

"Be careful," Emily shouted.

"Andy, you and Emily should join us," Rosemary called.

The music changed to "Moonlight Serenade." Andy shrugged and took Emily's hand. They did a slow, swaying dance alongside Emmett and Rosemary doing a foxtrot. When the song ended, the rest of the group whistled and applauded.

As the residents departed, Nina lingered. *Liz would have approved of the celebration.*

* * *

MEGAN LOOKED AROUND THE COMMUNITY ART CENTER classroom table at the four members of the board who had decided to attend the information meeting about the upcoming art contest. Matt Greer had briefed her on the assembled wealth of the five aged board members. *They care or they wouldn't be here, but they have to support the need for fundraising events and some new activities.*

"Megan will explain how the art contest will serve as our first fundraiser for this fiscal year." Matt sat down and nodded in her direction.

She stood and smiled, catching the eye of each board

member. "The Community Art Center has a long history in our town, but recent challenges have resulted in the loss of key sponsors." She paused as the board members murmured to each other. "The arts are important to our society and supporting local artists begins with us. I've already submitted several grant applications to generate additional funding. The next thing is to conduct an annual art show. We'll start small this first year, while we learn how to be most effective. I've done some research and determined the best practices for these types of events."

"My dear," said a white-haired matron. "Am I to understand that you have never conducted an art show before?"

"That's true."

A chorus of *tsk-tsks* erupted from the board members.

"But I have run many multi-million-dollar projects and held significant recognition events. I'm confident we can hold a successful art contest. There will be a series of entry fees with cash prizes for first and second place in three different categories: youth, amateur, and professional. The cash awards will increase as the skill level increases, with the professional winner receiving five hundred dollars."

"That sounds like a lot of money," said the matron.

"We want to attract quality artists, and to do that, we have to award prizes worthy of their attention. I'm confident the entry fees will cover the total of all prizes. This year, the contest may only break even, but we are executing a long-range plan. The schedule for the event is extremely tight, but we need to raise funds immediately."

"I've looked over Megan's projections," Matt said. "And the figures make sense."

"Thank you, Matt," the matron said. "If you're

comfortable, I concur."

"The name of the contest and theme for this year is Rebirth."

"I love that," said a diminutive lady who sat next to the matron. "I think I shall paint a phoenix."

Excited chatter spread around the table as each member discussed potential ideas.

"If I may have your attention for a few more minutes," Megan said. "I have an experienced artist in mind as the judge for our event. For the time being, I am keeping the judge's identity a secret." *Especially since I haven't spoken to her yet.*

All heads nodded in agreement.

"Every entry will be displayed in the main room. In addition to the judge's selections, there will be a people's award. Artists can send their family and friends in to vote for their artwork, which should increase foot traffic and awareness of the Center. The winner of the People's Award will receive a sizable ribbon to display and an extra cash reward. At the artist's discretion, pieces will be for sale after the judging is complete. The Community Art Center will keep half the proceeds from any sales. That's how we will generate some needed revenue. We also will host an opening reception with invitations going to the Chamber of Commerce and the Downtown Business Alliance. This will increase the Center's visibility." She distributed the draft flyer for the event.

"Excellent idea," the matron said. "My dear, you seem to have this well under control."

Megan smiled and acknowledged the applause from the board members. *This is going to work. I know it!*

* * *

After school, Penny lay on her bed and studied the flyer her mother had given her. *Rebirth Art Contest.* She read the submission guidelines. *I qualify as youth. The theme is rebirth. The art needs to be an original work. What could I enter that fits that theme?*

She got up and went to her desk. Doodling on a piece of notebook paper, she drew a familiar manga character and then another one. *They're not original.* She crumpled the sheet and threw it in the trash. She tapped her pencil on another piece of paper.

Maybe I shouldn't think about entering an art contest, even if it's one Mom is running. She got up from her desk and paced around her bedroom. *But Mrs. Silsbury said it's good practice to enter contests. Even Kanina said to practice.*

She read the flyer again. *Mom seems excited about this contest.* Returning to her desk, she thought about the sunflower at the art museum. She drew a few random lines and shaded one spot. *If van Gogh painted sunflowers multiple times, I can find something to draw and make it my own. I'm going to do it. I'll talk to Mrs. Silsbury tomorrow about the theme.*

The next day, in the art classroom, Penny unfolded the flyer and handed it to Mrs. Silsbury. "My mother gave me this."

The art teacher took the paper and nodded. "I saw that, too, on a bulletin board at the library. I'll make copies for the next Art Club meeting. You should enter."

"I am." *There, I committed. Now I have to do it.*

"Terrific. Maybe other club members will participate, too."

Penny took her backpack off and set it on the floor. "The problem is, I don't understand the rebirth thing."

"You mean the theme," Mrs. Silsbury said. "Many art contests have a theme, and your artwork needs to reflect the stated theme. For this contest, think about ways to show rebirth. How would you show a new beginning? For example, the acorn from an oak tree could be a rebirth of the tree. Or the tree is the rebirth of the acorn. Does that help?"

"I guess I'll have to think about it a little longer."

"We can talk about it some more during Art Club tomorrow."

When Penny got home, she wrote a letter to Kanina, mentioning the art contest and discussing the theme. *I can't wait for her reply, but she hasn't responded yet to my last letter.*

CHAPTER 23

Wednesday, December 6, 2023

AT THE END OF THE DAY, PENNY AND LACEY HEADED TO their school bus, working their way through the press of other students. They talked about the new boy in geometry class.

"He's cute," Lacey said.

"If you like jocks." Penny rolled her eyes.

"Penny. Penny." A man standing outside the school fence waved in her direction.

"Do you know him?" Lacey asked.

Penny squinted her eyes and peered at him. He wore blue jeans, dark glasses, and a faded leather jacket. He had thick, dark hair, and a mustache.

"I don't think so. It's not Steve."

"Maybe we should get on the bus." Lacey's voice trembled.

"Penny. It's your dad." The dark-haired man waved again.

Penny stopped moving. *My dad?*

Lacey tugged on her arm. "Let's go home."

"But it may be my dad." Penny took a step in his direction.

"He could kidnap you. Please, Penny, let's get on the bus."

"He came to see me. He was in Las Vegas when I last spoke with him, but now he's here to see me." Excited, she ran over to the fence.

"I can't believe you're here," Penny said when she reached the fence. *He looks older than I expected. Sort of worn-out-looking.* "You could have called me to let me know you were coming."

"There's my little girl," he said. "Not so little anymore."

"I'm sixteen now." She put her fingers through the fence to touch him.

"Old enough to be working a job? Bet you have some savings now, a big girl like you."

Penny blinked twice. *He wants to talk about money?* She pulled her fingers back through the fence.

His eyes darted beyond Penny, and she turned to follow his gaze.

"Is there a problem here?" the school resource officer said and stood beside Penny.

"No, officer. I was just talking to my daughter."

The officer moved between Penny and the fence, blocking her view of her father. He towered over her.

"Is he bothering you?" The officer stared right into her eyes.

Penny swallowed and shook her head. "I didn't know he was coming. He was in Las Vegas."

The officer turned back toward Penny's father. "There's an official procedure for picking up a student. Otherwise, she needs to get on the bus to go home."

"That's fine, officer. Penny, I'll see you around." He walked away.

Penny watched his old car drive away with a puff of black smoke.

"You should let your family know what happened here," the officer said.

Penny wet her lips. "Yes." In a daze, she walked back to her assigned bus. *That was my dad.*

* * *

Megan heard the front door open, followed by her daughter's rapid footsteps.

"I'm in the office, Penny," she called in a raised voice.

The refrigerator door opened, and the rustle of a bag ripped open followed. *Guess I better go see how school went today.* When Megan walked into the kitchen, Penny sat at the kitchen table, eating cookies and looking out the window.

"How was school?"

"I saw Daddy today."

Megan sat in the chair across from Penny. "He came to your school?"

"Yeah. At the end of the day."

Oh, Lord. Megan breathed slowly. *Don't panic.* "Did you talk to him?"

"Only for a few minutes. The SRO came up and Daddy left."

Megan exhaled. *Thank goodness! What might have happened if she went with him?* "What did he say to you?"

Penny focused on her, and the expression on her face made Megan cringe.

"He thought I was working and might have saved some money."

Megan closed her eyes. "Penny, when I told you your father left because he was seeing another woman, there was more."

"I don't want to hear it." Penny stood up suddenly.

Megan reached for her arm. "I know you don't, but you should let me tell you the whole story."

Penny sat back down.

"My mother tried to warn me, but I didn't listen to her. I hope you will listen to me." Her eyes searched Penny's face for any sign that she might be getting through to her. "Peter had a gambling problem. I thought I could get him past it, but I couldn't. He lost money, lots of money. He started owing bad people money. You were only a baby then. I had a decent job and made a healthy salary. We paid off his debt, and he promised he would stop gambling."

Megan sighed. "But he couldn't stop. Years went by, and the pattern kept repeating. Eventually, he got in so deep that we couldn't pay it off. He started doing jobs for some people, the wrong kind of people. That's when he started seeing other women."

"There was more than one woman?" Penny asked.

Hanging her head, Megan bit her lip. "Yes. I don't know how many. Our family was falling apart. Finally, one night I told him we had reached the end. He was mad. He threw a wine bottle at me and left."

"That was all the broken glass on the floor," Penny said quietly.

"Yes. He left and disappeared from our lives." Megan held onto Penny's arm. "I didn't want to tell you all this. If he had stayed away, I wouldn't have said a thing, but you need to know about him. Please stay away from him. If he's asking for money, it's probably because he owes someone."

Penny nodded.

"Honey, I'm sorry. I love you and don't want you hurt."

Penny stood up, slowly this time. "I'm going to go do some homework."

"Alright, honey. If you want to talk, I'm here." She watched Penny leave the kitchen. *She's like a closed book to me.*

* * *

NINA WORE HER HEAVIEST COAT AND OPENED THE FRONT DOOR to walk through the garden, even though last night's chill had killed all but the hardiest plants. She strolled along the pathway to where she and Liz had sat many times. Something rustled in the stiff stalks of the rose bushes. She approached cautiously and bent forward to get a closer look.

The rustling stopped. A small deer burst out of the foliage; its white tail flashed by Nina. In shock, she jerked back and lost her balance. She fell backward, twisting in an awkward angle and landing on her left hip. A sharp pain shot through her knee. Her head hit the ground. Flashes of light passed before her eyes.

She gasped in pain. Her breathing came in sharp spurts. She lay still, afraid to move. *Did I break anything? Stay calm.*

With the tiniest movement, Nina tested each limb. She moved her fingers. *Only the usual arthritis.* Her wrists and elbows bent like normal. She wiggled the toes on her right foot without pain. When she tried to bend her left leg, a sharp knife pain exploded in her knee.

"Help!"

She tried to sit up, but the movement took her breath away. Dizziness took over. She lay still and closed her eyes. She heard footsteps running, getting closer. A voice rang in her ears. *Liz?* The last thing she remembered was hearing an ambulance siren.

* * *

AFTER THE KIDS HAD GONE TO BED, MEGAN SAT ON THE COUCH beside Steve. She tucked her legs under her and leaned against him.

"I like this," Steve said and turned off the television. He wrapped his arm around her.

"You have no idea how safe I feel with you."

He squeezed her tighter. "I won't let anything happen to you."

Megan rested her hand on his chest. "It's not me I'm worried about. Peter showed up at Penny's school today. Nothing happened, but I'm worried."

"Would he try to kidnap her?"

Megan hesitated. "I don't think so, but she might willingly go with him."

"Do we need to get a restraining order against him?"

"It might be a good idea."

Steve shifted his position and pulled out his phone. He scrolled through names on his contact list. "There he is. Rodney West. He's an old buddy who's an attorney. I know him, but we may have to give him a retainer."

"I'm usually the one who worries about spending money, but I think we should do this."

"I'll call him tomorrow. I don't want anything to happen to Penny, and I don't want you worrying."

"You are the best thing that ever happened to me." *Now I can get to sleep tonight.*

* * *

THE NEXT DAY, NINA LAY IN A HOSPITAL BED. THE FLOWER arrangement sent by the staff and residents of Shadow Oaks freshened the air. She sipped water through a straw and then closed her eyes. *Alone. No visitors. No family. What's to become of me?*

The pain medication eased her discomfort but made her thinking fuzzy. She dozed lightly and images from her past appeared in her mind. She was back in college.

May 1969

THE OPENING RECEPTION AT THE COLLEGE ART GALLERY started at seven o'clock in the evening. Nina's classmates and teachers drifted into the exhibit space in groups. Long hair, bell-bottom pants, and peace sign necklaces were the common look. Strangers from the local community mingled with the college students. She greeted each guest with a firm handshake and a smile.

"Welcome. Please enjoy the collection," she said.

The crowd grew and the noise level in the gallery rose. Visitors wandered around the room and paused before different pieces.

Nina beamed at the sight of her pictures framed and

hanging on the beige gallery walls. The last art show of the spring semester traditionally was reserved for a senior, but the planning committee had selected her—a college sophomore—to display her collection.

The graphite sketches captured the sights of Europe, from German castles and Paris cafés to Italian vineyards. The pen-and-ink florals reflected her time in Japan. The water-color landscapes were from her moves across the United States. The newest additions to her collection included the oil portraits she had done this year in Professor Rivero's class.

With his hand-carved cane and maroon beret set at an angle on his head, Professor Rivero arrived with a pale, older woman at his side. "Mrs. Wallace, let me introduce the featured artist for this exhibit, Kanina Koscielniak."

The woman extended her hand but never smiled.

"Nina," Professor Rivero said. "Mrs. Wallace is the art critic of the *Coastal Creatives* magazine."

Nina shook the woman's hand. *A limp fish hand*, Nina thought. "Pleased to meet you. If you have questions about any of the collection, I'd be happy to explain each piece."

"That won't be necessary." Mrs. Wallace walked toward the far corner of the gallery.

Nina leaned toward her instructor. "Did I say something wrong?"

Professor Rivero held his hand up and shuffled after Mrs. Wallace.

Another classmate arrived. "This is so groovy, Nina. Can't believe you did all these paintings."

"Thanks," Nina said. "I've been creating art most of my life, but I never thought I would be good enough to have an exhibition."

"You're so talented."

Nina blushed and looked away from her classmate. She glanced at the art critic and watched Professor Rivero wave his arm toward the middle of the gallery. *I bet she doesn't like my work.*

"Enjoy the collection." Nina quickly left her classmate and headed toward the two people who were the center of her attention. They examined a piece she was pleased with—a moody portrait of a young man done in sepia tones.

Without wanting to appear anxious, she approached them by circling the room. As she got closer, she heard Professor Rivero say, "Those who can't do, teach."

Nina froze in place, her mouth open in shock. *Is that what he thinks I should do?*

"Indeed," Mrs. Wallace said. "I must be going."

Professor Rivero escorted the critic to the door and left with her.

Nina stood still. The room spun around her in slow motion. The street scenes and florals blurred. The portraits laughed at her, while the hum of voices around her grew distant. Her dream of being a professional artist puddled on the floor at her feet. *Those who can't do, teach.* The words swirled through her head. *I'm not talented enough to be a fine artist. Just an art teacher. Why did I waste my time trying to be a real artist?*

Chapter 24

Thursday, December 7, 2023

WHEN PENNY CAME HOME FROM SCHOOL, SHE FOUND HER mother playing with Jody in her half sister's bedroom. "Did the mail come yet?" Penny asked her mother.

Mom glanced up from Jody's kitchen playset. "Yes. Just some catalogs and a magazine for Steve."

Penny exhaled loudly. "It's been days, and she hasn't written."

"Honey, try writing to a different person at Shadow Oaks."

"Want some cookies and milk?" Jody asked, holding a plastic cookie toward Penny.

Penny accepted the make-believe food. "Something must be wrong. Why would she stop writing?"

"She could have gone to visit family in another state. Even if she continued to write, mail would take longer to get to you. Or she ran out of stamps."

"I could send her stamps."

"We can't afford to send stamps to someone we barely know."

"But I know her. She listens to me and talks to me like an adult. Since you won't let me do anything with my other friends, she's the only friend I have left. And now she's gone."

"Want another cookie?" Jody tugged Penny's arm.

"No thanks." She handed the plastic cookie back to her sister.

Shoving her hands in her pants pockets, Penny went into her bedroom. *Something must be wrong. She would write otherwise. I could call Shadow Oaks and ask to talk to her. Or did she get tired of writing letters to me?*

Penny paced around her bedroom. "Why isn't she writing to me? Did I write something that upset her? I don't even remember what my last letter was about." She went to her desk and picked up the sketch of Kanina. "Why did you stop sending me letters?"

I'm going to be grounded forever if I don't get more letters and get released from community service. She fell backward on her bed and swiped the back of her hand across her eyes. *I thought Kanina was my friend. My dad can't be counted on. Goku's gone. Now more than ever, I need someone I can talk to. There's no one.*

Before dinner, Penny took Jody for a walk to search for the missing cat. She held a bowl of cat food and called the cat's name as they passed different houses.

At first, Jody skipped along the sidewalk and sang a song from daycare. Penny didn't know the words or recognize the tune. After turning the corner to walk around the block, Jody slowed down and her singing grew quiet.

"Why did Goku leave?" Jody asked.

"I don't know. Maybe he saw another cat and wanted to visit. Or he was tired of being inside all the time."

"Will he come home?"

Penny glanced at Jody. *Do I tell her what I think or make her feel good?* "He may have forgotten how to find our house. That's why we're looking for him."

"Daddy says cats like places and Goku will come home because he likes our place."

"That's probably true." *I hope it's true.*

They walked along the street with Jody's hand holding Penny's. They called the cat's name again, and Penny shook the bowl of cat food. Then they continued in silence, looking for any sign of the gray cat.

"Penny, how come you call Daddy Steve?"

"He's not my dad. I call him Steve because that's his name."

Jody gripped Penny's hand tighter. "Where is your daddy? Did he run away, too?"

She seldom talked about her father. *Mom doesn't want to talk about him, and any questions are usually brushed away with a vague response.*

"My dad left a long time ago. Mom divorced him."

"What's divorced?"

"Let's talk about something else, like what do you do at daycare?"

Jody rattled off a list of activities that she liked to do. While Jody talked, Penny wondered where her father was. *He called and said we were going to get together and then he went to Vegas. He showed up at school yesterday but then disappeared. Mom says he left her for another woman and had gambling problems. I can't count on him.* Tears started running down her cheeks.

"Don't cry, Penny," Jody said. "Goku will come back."

Penny sniffled and wiped her sleeve across her face. "You're right."

They called for the cat several more times before

going back home.

"Goku could return tomorrow," Penny said. *But I don't think my dad will ever come back.*

* * *

NINA'S SENSE OF HER TIME IN THE HOSPITAL WAS BLURRY. *How long have I been here?* The patient in the bed next to Nina moaned. The sound carried through the curtain that separated them.

"Do you want me to call the nurse?" Nina asked.

"No," the other woman said. "I'm just sitting up. My husband is bringing our kids for a visit in a few minutes."

It must feel wonderful to have visitors. Nina stared at the ceiling. *To have a family that cares about you.*

The door swung open, and footsteps drew Nina's attention. Through the partially open curtain, Nina glimpsed a middle-aged man and two children entering the room.

One youthful voice rose in excitement. "Mama!"

Nina tried not to listen to their conversation, but their laughter carried through the curtain. She imagined the family holding hands, with the children gathered around their mother, perhaps sitting on the bed with her.

My students were my children. Hundreds and hundreds of children. But where are they now? Here I am— all alone. No one cares.

* * *

IN THE SCHOOL HALLWAY, PENNY SPOTTED DYLAN AND ASHLEY waiting by her locker. *Wonder what they want. They're the cool kids everyone admires. They don't usually even talk to me.*

As she approached, they looked around to make sure no one was listening.

"We have something planned for Saturday night, and we thought you might like to join us," Dylan said.

Thrilled to be included in their plan, Penny hesitated when she recalled the mascot statue disaster. She hung her jacket in the locker and selected the notebook for her next class.

"I'm grounded," she said.

Dylan snorted. "That's not a problem. Parents make all sorts of rules that don't make sense. Even they don't obey them."

Penny considered Dylan's comment. "I don't know if I should." *But it would be fun to do something different. Being grounded is so boring.*

"Come on," Ashley said. "Live a little. You can sneak out when your parents are asleep. What time do they go to bed?"

"Around eleven o'clock." Penny glanced at them cautiously.

"Perfect," Dylan said. "My brother can pick you up at the corner of Grand and Coastal at midnight tomorrow, and we'll drive you there."

"Drive where?"

Dylan checked over his shoulder again. "We're going down to the rail yard and spraying some graffiti on the railcars."

"The rail yard is dark," Ashley said. "No one will see us there. And imagine your artwork traveling all around the country on that railcar. Where else would you get that exposure?"

Penny got goosebumps. *Imagine people all over the country seeing my art.*

The bell rang, and the hallway filled with students hurrying to class.

"Until tomorrow night," Ashley said.

Dylan put his hand up for a high five.

Penny slapped his hand. "Tomorrow night." *I shouldn't do this, but it would be amazing. I'm surprised they want to include me. I'll think about it and see how I feel tomorrow.*

* * *

THE SHADOW OAKS SENIOR LIVING HOME ENTRANCE SIGN BY the road directed vehicles to the visitor parking area. Megan drove under the oak tree branches arching over the paved entrance road. Strands of Spanish moss hung from the trees. She pulled into an open spot in the empty visitor lot. *Must be no one is visiting today. I would have thought Friday would be a busy day.* She clutched the *Coastal Creatives* magazine and walked from her car to the covered entrance, admiring the beauty of the grounds.

For the past week, since I learned Miss K and Penny are pen pals, I've been debating whether I should come here. But I think I should face my past. Besides, Miss K would be an excellent judge for the art contest.

When she walked through the front door, the odor of medicinal and cleaning products greeted her. *This place has an institutional smell to it.* Quickly, she located the admissions office.

A young woman welcomed her. "May I help you?"

Megan smiled and shook hands with the woman. "I'm Megan Hinson. My daughter has been exchanging letters with one of the residents here, a Miss Kanina Koscielniak."

"Oh, yes. Nina has enjoyed receiving all the mail. I'm Emily Carson, the activity director. Please come to my office." She led Megan down a corridor to a small room. "Have a seat. What can I do for you?"

"I'd like to meet Nina. I was one of her students long ago, and I have a magazine I think she would like to have." Megan placed the *Coastal Creatives* magazine on the desk.

"I can see that she gets it."

"While I appreciate that, I would like to give it to her myself."

"I'm sorry," Emily said. "I'm afraid that can't be arranged."

"Isn't she allowed to have visitors?" Megan's smile wavered, and she leaned forward.

Emily sighed. "We have to respect our residents' privacy." She shuffled several papers on her desk.

"Does she have a phone number I can call to talk to her?"

The young woman shook her head. "Even if she did, I'm not allowed to release that kind of information. I really am sorry."

"But she has been receiving my daughter's letters?" Megan picked up the *Coastal Creatives* magazine.

"Oh yes," Emily said and stood up. "In fact, there's a bulletin board in the lobby with one of your daughter's drawings posted. Nina put it up for everyone to see. I'll show you."

I'm being ushered out. Megan rose and followed the

activity director back to the lobby. A corkboard covered with drawings, business cards, and thank you notes filled the wall near the front door.

"Here it is." Emily pointed to a drawing of a humming-bird. "I wish I could help you, but there's not much I can do at the moment." She walked away.

Megan nodded and stared at the picture. *Penny did this? It's beautiful.* Her eyes wandered to the other items pinned to the board.

An elderly lady in a shawl shuffled over to Megan. "My grandson did this one." She rested her hand on a drawing of superheroes.

"Very colorful," Megan said. "My daughter did this one." As she pointed to the hummingbird, her finger trembled.

"My friend, Nina, received that from her pen pal. Is your daughter Nina's pen pal?"

"Yes, and I was hoping to see Nina."

"She's not here. It was so sudden."

Megan spun around to face the elderly lady. "What happened?"

"Nina fell in the garden, and the ambulance took her away. She's in the hospital."

"Which one?"

"I don't know. They tell us she may be gone for a while." The old woman brushed a tear from her eye. "Falls are so bad for our old bones. I hope she didn't break her hip. My husband had a bad fall before he died."

Megan sensed a long story coming and said, "I'm sorry to hear that. Afraid I need to get going."

After making a hasty escape, she hurried back to her car. Once she was home, she started calling all the local hospitals to inquire about a patient named Kanina Koscielniak. After three calls, she had the name of the hospital.

WHEN PENNY CAME HOME FROM SCHOOL, MEGAN WAS EXCITED to update her on what she had learned, but she didn't get far before Penny reacted.

"What?" Penny frowned. "You went to Shadow Oaks without me?"

"Miss K was my teacher, and I had a magazine article to give her. I also wanted to ask her for some help. You were in school. I thought—"

"You should have waited until tomorrow, when I could have gone, too." Penny's voice rose in volume. "She's my pen pal."

Megan hesitated. *She's right. One more day and she could have joined me.* "I'm sorry. But listen—"

"You never think about me." Penny stormed out of the room; her footsteps thundered up the stairs. The slam of her bedroom door sounded throughout the house.

I didn't get to tell her about Miss K's fall. Megan closed her eyes. *Why is it Penny and I always wind up like this?*

When Penny didn't come down for dinner, Megan decided to let things cool off between them.

LATER THAT NIGHT, MEGAN'S FINGERS FLEW ACROSS THE KEY-board, typing the story of Miss K. She hit send and her email went to those who had any connection to Miss K. She turned to all her social media contacts and asked for get-well cards for her. *Here's hoping her former students read this and follow through.*

One last email went to the local paper. *No telling if*

they'll run a story about her, but forty-eight years of teaching art in the same high school deserve recognition.

She signed each message with her title: "Acting Executive Director, Community Art Center." *The art community needs to appreciate Miss K and save the Art Center.*

She had just sent the last message when she received notification of an incoming message from the local newspaper. *That was fast!* She scanned the message and jumped up, screaming.

Jody came running into the office with her stuffed dog under her arm. "Mommy?"

Megan picked her up and swung her around the room in a celebratory dance.

"The paper wants to run an article about the Art Center and also do a piece on Miss K."

Chapter 25

Saturday, December 9, 2023

WHEN PENNY WOKE UP, SHE TEXTED LACEY. U THERE? When there was no response, Penny scrolled through her contact list. *I need to talk to someone about this midnight rail yard thing tonight.* She passed Ashley's name and kept scrolling. She stopped at Daddy. *He said not to call, but he's my dad. I should be able to ask him for advice.* She placed the call and listened for an answer.

"Yeah." His voice was harsh.

"Daddy?" *I feel like a little kid.*

"Don't call me that."

"But . . ."

"Why are you bothering me?"

Penny hesitated. "I need some advice."

"Go talk to your mother." He ended the call.

Penny threw her phone on the bed. "I thought having a father in my life would make me happy, but not like this."

She rubbed her hands over her face. *I don't need him. He doesn't have time for me. I don't have time for him. And I can't trust Mom—she went to Shadow Oaks without me. Dylan and Ashley are right that adult rules are a waste of time. I'll do what I want and show them all!*

Going to her chest of drawers, she pulled out her black leggings and black hoodie. *This should work for tonight.*

* * *

NINA LISTENED TO THE NURSES CHATTING OUTSIDE HER DOOR, talking about their holiday plans. *I have no plans. Perhaps that's what's wrong. I need to have a plan for what I want to do. Yes. What I want to do! Not just what other people want to do.*

Her eyes followed the wire to the nurse's call button. Taking the call box in her hand, she pressed the button. When the nurse arrived, Nina smiled and asked, "Could I get a piece of writing paper and a pen?"

"We don't have anything like that," the nurse said.

"Any paper will do, even if it's the back of something you're throwing out."

The nurse headed toward the door. "Let me see what I can find. I can't give you anything with patient information on it." A few minutes later, the nurse returned with a triumphant smile on her face and a sheet of paper in her hand. "I raided the printer paper."

"Thank you." Nina took the paper and pen the nurse offered. She laughed at the floppy flower taped to the top of the pen.

"So it doesn't disappear," the nurse said.

With her hospital bed adjusted and the tray in front of her, Nina wrote a letter.

Dear Penny,

 Sorry I haven't written recently. A friend died, then I fell and have been in the hospital. While I have been limited to lying in bed, I've thought about my future and my past.

 I taught high school art for forty-eight years and loved all of it. Since retiring, I've felt lost. I now know that I need to be teaching again. Not in high school, but to those people where I live. I tried to teach a class, but no one came. I'm not giving up. I'm going to try again.

 You shouldn't give up either. Don't give up on yourself, your mother, or Steve. All will be well. I feel it in my old bones.

Your friend,
Nina (Kanina Koscielniak)

She read the letter and nodded with satisfaction. Folding the paper in half, she frowned. *I don't have an envelope or Penny's address.* She set the letter aside. *I'll mail it when I get back to Shadow Oaks.*

* * *

"GOOD NIGHT, MOM. NIGHT, STEVE." PENNY WENT UP THE stairs. *I'll wear my black hoodie and leggings to bed. Then when Mom and Steve go to sleep, I'll come down and go out the kitchen door. Dylan said his brother has a white van.*

That should be easy to see in the streetlights. She ignored the nagging feeling that what she was about to do could get her into even more trouble.

She lay in bed and waited. The house grew silent, and the sound of footsteps in the hallway faded away. Her bedside clock showed 11:35 p.m. She willed the butterflies in her stomach to go away. The minutes dragged by. Soon the clock read 11:50 p.m. She slipped out of bed and grabbed her boots. With sock-covered feet, she crept down the steps. In the kitchen, she stopped to put her boots on.

She twisted the doorknob and opened the door from the kitchen to the backyard. The hinges groaned. She held her breath and listened for footsteps from upstairs. Hearing none, she slipped through the door.

Once outside, she exhaled. The moon shone high overhead. *Full moon.* She hurried around the house and down the street to the corner they had agreed on. The white van was there with the engine idling.

The van's side door slid open, and Dylan stuck his head out.

"Get in, Stretch."

"It's Poison Pen to you."

"That's so cute," Ashley said.

Penny climbed into the back row of the van. "It's not supposed to be cute." She sniffed at the smell of old gym clothes, french fries, cigarettes, and weed.

"That's my brother, Rob, who's driving," Dylan said. He pulled the van door closed.

"Yo! Next stop, the rail yard."

The van traveled through the downtown business section, to the warehouse district, and toward a part of town

Penny didn't know. She peered out the window at the broad rail yard with the dark mass of railcars looming ahead.

Rob steered the van into an alley and turned off the lights. "Everyone out."

Dylan jumped out of the van and carried a duffel bag with him. Metal cans clinked together.

Ashley giggled. "This is awesome. Come on, Poison Pen."

Penny emerged from the van and pulled her hoodie tight around her face. The moonlight cast a blue tint over everyone.

"This way," Rob said, leading the group toward the rail yard. "If we get spotted, split up, and meet back here by the van."

They slipped through an opening in the chain-link fence, then passed tractor-trailers and metal shipping containers. Soon they were stepping over the metal rails. The hulking shapes of railcars towered across the tracks. A cloud drifted past the moon and the night grew darker.

"Boxcar or tankers?" Rob asked.

Dylan snorted. "Boxcars."

Rob led them to the left and under a tanker car. Before them was a row of flat cars. "This way." He climbed over a coupling and offered Ashley a hand.

Penny clambered over the coupling on her own. *This is crazy. Why did I say I would do this?*

A boxcar side rose high before them, blocking the moon. Dylan pulled a flashlight out of his duffel bag. "This one will work. Here's a can for each of you." He handed cans of spray paint to Rob first, followed by Ashley, and Penny last.

Dylan aimed his flashlight at each can and called out

a color. "Rob has blue. Ash, yours is green. Stretch, you get red."

"It's Poison Pen!"

"Sure. Now pick your spot and get to it."

Rob climbed the ladder at the end of the boxcar and walked along the roof. He crouched down and leaned over the side. Ashley and Dylan ran together to the door of the boxcar.

Without the flashlight, Penny struggled to find a spot she could reach that wasn't already covered with graffiti. She put her hand against the side of the railcar and inched her way toward the ladder Rob had used. She stumbled and dropped her spray paint can. It clanged against the rail. In the dark, she groped for the can. Her fingers scraped against the rough gravel. Her pulse thumped louder in her ears. With a frantic sweep of her arm under the boxcar, she felt the cylindrical shape and grabbed the can. She popped the top off and aimed toward the side of the car. *Since I can't see what I'm doing, I'll keep it simple. Just a smiley face.*

She pressed the nozzle. The spray of red droplets with the familiar paint smell hissed against her chest and neck. A bit of paint fanned across her cheek. She fell backward, landing on her back. The spray can flew out of her hand and hit the ground with another hiss.

A dog barked, followed by another. Then a police siren wailed in the night.

Rob slid down the ladder and jumped the last few feet to the ground. "Run. It's the cops."

As Dylan and Ashley ran past her, Penny scrambled to her feet. She searched for the paint can but couldn't find it. She took off at a run, trying to keep up with Dylan and Ashley.

They dodged past the railcars and leaped over the rails. Bits of gravel went flying.

The flashing blue lights pulsed through the night. *Run. Got to get back to the van.* A chorus of dog barks and growls grew louder. Her boots pounded against the ground. She gasped for air with each stride. The fleeing figures of Dylan and Ashley disappeared. Penny kept running. A sharp pain shot through her side.

The alley lay ahead. The van's engine revved, and the side door was open. She dove into the welcome safety of the van. Dylan slammed the door shut and Rob gunned the engine. The tires squealed, and they raced away from the rail yard. Penny scrambled into the last row of seats, her heart racing.

With several miles behind them, Rob and Dylan started laughing. "That was awesome."

Ashley gave a nervous giggle. "Do you think they'll find us?"

"No way," Rob said.

Penny trembled. In the light from the streetlights they passed, she could see the swatch of red paint covering her hoodie and her hands. She rubbed her face but couldn't tell how much paint was there.

Rob dropped her off where the adventure had started.

"Don't tell anyone," Dylan said. "It's our secret."

Penny didn't say a word. *At least we didn't get caught. I'm not doing that again.*

When the van drove away, Penny headed home. As she hurried along the sidewalk, she yawned. *It must be almost two o'clock, maybe later.* The windows of the houses she passed were dark. Shadows from trees and shrubs loomed closer to the sidewalk.

This is creepy. Penny increased her pace.

At the house on the corner of her street, a dog barked. Penny knew the dog—a fierce German shepherd. *Quiet, Donovan. You'll wake up the whole neighborhood, and I don't need that.*

* * *

Megan rolled over in bed and snuggled against Steve. Her sleep had been troubled for days now, and tonight was no exception. *Stop thinking about paying bills. We'll be fine. I'll find a paying job soon.* She sighed. The alarm clock display read 2:12 a.m. *I'm not getting to sleep anytime soon.* Quietly, so as not to disturb Steve, she got out of bed and put on her robe.

Without turning on the light, she wandered down the stairs to the family room. The streetlights outside the house gave the room a soft glow. She sank onto the couch and picked up the remote. *I don't want to watch TV.* She put the remote down and rested her head against the couch cushion with her eyes closed. Within minutes, she slipped into a troubled sleep.

Her eyes flew open at the click of the kitchen door latch and the groan of the hinges. *Someone's breaking into the house. Call 911.* She reached beside her on the couch and groped for her phone in the dim light. Her hand closed around a smooth object. *Damn! It's the remote. The phone's charging by the bed.*

Soft footsteps approached from the kitchen. Megan got up from the couch and searched for something solid to use as a club. She grabbed the statue of an angel from the coffee table. *It isn't very heavy.* "Steve," she screamed. "Steve!"

A female scream answered hers. Steve's heavy footfalls sounded overhead. From the top of the stairs, Steve flicked on the lights and yelled, "What's going on down there?"

At the sight of Penny standing in the kitchen doorway and splashed with red, Megan dropped the angel and it shattered on the floor. "Penny, what are you doing out at this hour?" She hurried over to her daughter. "Is that blood? What happened?"

"It's spray paint." Penny looked down. "Some kids were going to do graffiti on the railcars."

"How could you? That's vandalism." Megan put her hand to her mouth. "You could get killed out there at night."

Steve came to Megan's side. "You scared your mother and me. Don't you understand what grounded means? We should tell the principal about this latest stunt."

"Please don't," Penny begged. "I'm sorry. I don't want to go to juvenile detention."

"You should have thought about that before you broke the law." Megan's voice quivered with anger. "You're such a disappointment."

"Go upstairs, Penny," Steve said. "We'll discuss this in the morning."

Crying, Penny ran past them and up the stairs.

With Steve's arm around her, Megan burst into tears. *How did I go wrong with her?*

Chapter 26

Sunday, December 10, 2023

In the morning, Penny's cell phone alerted her to an incoming text message from Lacey. Penny rolled over in bed and groaned. The pain in her back increased when she moved. *Oh yeah. The fall in the rail yard.*

Carefully, she sat up and read Lacey's text message. Hear u had a wild night.

She typed a question mark.

Painting.

Penny frowned. U know?

Yes. Everyone knows.

She typed another question mark.

Ashley. We need to talk.

Penny was typing a message when a loud knock thumped against her door.

"Penny, we want to see you downstairs," Mom called through the door.

With a sigh, Penny stepped over the paint-covered hoodie and leggings piled in a heap on the floor. *What a mess.* She threw on a pair of jeans and a baggy sweatshirt. After a fast bathroom stop to scrub the red splatters off her face and hands, she trudged down the stairs.

As she entered the kitchen, all eyes turned toward her. Mom and Steve sat at the kitchen table with Jody.

"I'm really sorry." Penny shifted her weight from foot to foot. "It won't happen again."

"That's what you said after vandalizing the school's statue," Mom said.

"Your mother grounded you and you disobeyed her," Steve said. "It's time for harsher punishment to get your attention. No computer time except for homework."

Penny looked from Steve to her mother.

"And give me your phone." Mom held her hand out.

"My phone?"

"Yes. Now." Mom stood up and continued to extend her hand.

Penny pulled the phone out of her pocket and threw it on the kitchen table. "Maybe you want to lock me in my room, too."

She ran back upstairs and slammed her bedroom door. She shut her eyes, fighting back tears. *How am I going to stay in touch with my friends?*

AS A NEW GROUP OF STUDENTS BOARDED THE SCHOOL BUS ON Monday morning, Penny craned her neck to find Lacey. When she spotted her friend, she smiled and took her backpack off the empty seat beside her. Lacey walked right by her.

What's going on? "Lacey, I'm right here."

Lacey sat in the row behind Penny and crossed her arms.

Penny twisted around to talk to her. "What's wrong?"

"I don't think you're someone I want to be seen with," Lacey said.

"Is this about Saturday night?"

"Of course!" Lacey looked out the bus window.

Grabbing her backpack, Penny changed rows and slid into the seat beside Lacey. "Let me tell you what happened."

"Oh, and make me an accessory to your crime? No, thank you."

Penny glanced around and leaned closer to Lacey. "Saturday night, I went out at midnight with Dylan and Ashley to the rail yard. When I got home, Mom and Steve caught me. They took my phone away."

"That's why you didn't answer my messages this morning." Lacey showed Penny her most recent messages.

"I don't even know when I'll get my phone back."

Lacey gasped. "That's a really mean punishment."

"I guess I had it coming." Penny played with the zipper of her backpack. "They were really mad."

"You need to stay away from Dylan and Ashley. They're going to get you in serious trouble."

Penny sighed. *Lacey is right. I keep getting in trouble because of things they want to do.*

The bus swayed to a stop at the high school. Penny and Lacey were separated when the kids crowded the aisle.

"See you later," Penny called to Lacey over her shoulder.

"Text me when . . . Sorry, I forgot," Lacey said.

Yeah. Without a phone, I won't be texting anyone.

AFTER RETURNING FROM SCHOOL, PENNY STARED AT THE BLANK page in her sketchbook. She twisted her pencil between her fingers. Her eyes wandered over the items on her desk and paused at a framed photo of Goku the cat.

"I miss you, Goku. Why did you run away? Why haven't

you come back?"

She picked up the picture and scrutinized the photo. Goku's green eyes stared off into the distance. The soft gray tabby stripes contrasted with the white chin and pink nose. "You always liked your neck scratched."

Penny placed her pencil on the open page and began sketching an image of Goku. The pencil marks curved across the paper with increasing speed. The cat's features materialized, and she added shading to deepen the shadows. When Penny was done, she sat back and assessed her work. *That's more realistic than I usually draw.*

"Penny, dinner's ready," Mom called from downstairs.

Leaving the drawing behind, she headed down to the kitchen with light steps. As she walked into the room, Steve entered from outside. "Look who I found," he said.

Repeated loud meows filled the kitchen.

"Goku!" Penny ran to the gray tabby and scooped him in her arms, holding him tight.

The cat purred and rubbed his head against Penny's face.

"Don't you ever do that again," Penny said. "You're skin and bones. Mom, we need some cat food right now. Goku must be starving."

With the kitty bowl full, Goku devoured the food. Penny hovered over the cat, beaming with happiness. *This feels like a rebirth.*

* * *

Tuesday morning, the nurse wheeled a cart into Nina's hospital room. "I don't know what you did, my dear, but you have become a celebrity on our floor. You've received more cards than anyone else here." She handed Nina a sizable stack of brightly colored envelopes in different sizes. "My guess is there must be close to fifty. Probably even more. Have fun reading all of these."

"They're all for me?" Nina asked. "I don't have any family and don't know many people."

"I haven't checked them all, but the mailroom is seldom wrong when they sort the mail." The nurse rolled the cart out of the room.

Nina picked up the top envelope on the stack, a bright pink envelope with a baby bird in the lower-left corner. It was addressed to her and the return label was from Tina Brookside in Allendale, Tennessee. *I don't know anyone with that name or from Tennessee.* She opened the envelope and pulled out a card.

A little birdie told me you were not feeling well.
Get well soon.

It was signed by Tina, class of 1998. *Oh, Tina! Tina with the purple-rimmed glasses and the big smile.*

She opened one card after another to discover best wishes for a quick recovery from many of her former students. *How did they find out I'm in the hospital?*

It took her all afternoon to open and read every card. She was exhausted at the end, but thrilled. *They haven't forgotten me.*

She was about to fall asleep when a nurse delivered a flower arrangement to her room. "This is a beautiful bouquet with lovely sunflowers. They're so happy."

"Who are they from?" Nina asked.

"There's a card here. It says, 'From the gang in room 111.'"

"Room 111 was my art classroom for forty-eight years."

"At Bridgewater High School?"

Nina nodded.

"My oldest brother was in your class. Tony Dillenbeck. Do you remember him?"

Nina thought back to her many classes of students. Then she remembered.

"Yes, I do."

Tony. His parents said he was slow. They wanted him in art class so he didn't have to study or work hard. I was such a new teacher, and his parents' attitude made me angry. But Tony was unique. He saw shapes and angles, shades of colors, shadows, and depth. He had a gift, and I helped him explore it. He did beautiful, detailed drawings.

Nina smiled at the memory of that parent-teacher conference. *His parents were astounded when I showed them his portfolio. "He did those?" His father couldn't believe it.* She shook her head. *I encouraged Tony to keep developing his talent—even got him a few commissions drawing people's pets. His clients loved his work. I wonder how he fared after school. His family moved, and I lost track of him.*

"How is he?" she asked.

"I'm afraid he passed away several years ago, but your art class was the best thing that ever happened to him. He left us many fantastic drawings."

"I'm sorry. He was an extraordinary person."

"And so are you. He always told us that Miss K loved him."

Nina's eyes misted. *I have been blessed.*

Chapter 27

Tuesday, December 12, 2023

NINA ROUSED AT THE KNOCK ON HER HOSPITAL ROOM DOOR. The door cracked open and a middle-aged woman with bobbed hair peeked in.

"May I come in?" the woman asked.

"Certainly."

The woman entered and sat in the chair beside Nina's bed. She placed a portfolio on her lap. "I'm Megan Hinson. Do you remember me?"

"Hinson?" *So many students. So many years.* Nina furrowed her brow.

"It was Megan Brown in 2000."

Her memory of young Megan returned. "Oh, yes. You didn't stay in my class very long."

"No, I'm afraid I wasn't smart enough to realize you were trying to help me."

"So, tell me, are you still doing art?" Nina watched the expression on Megan's face change.

"I found the sketchbook you had us keep. It had all your notes in it. I've used it to get started sketching again."

"Excellent!" Nina gave her a thumbs-up.

"And I'm volunteering at the Community Art Center."

"I hope that works out for you. I tried to interest them in showcasing student artwork, but they weren't cooperative."

"If I can, I'll try to change that." Megan opened her portfolio. "While I was doing some cleaning at the Art Center, I came across a magazine that had an article about you. I thought you might like to have it. I marked the page where the article starts. It's a well-written piece."

Nina took the *Coastal Creatives* magazine without opening it and put it on the tray beside her bed. "That was a long time ago. It was thoughtful of you to bring it."

Opening her portfolio again, Megan hesitated. "I also brought this." She handed Nina a piece of art paper.

When Nina turned the paper over, she clutched her chest. "The portrait you did of me. How did you get it? I sent it to a young girl."

"My daughter."

Nina blinked in disbelief. "Penny is your daughter?"

Megan's head bobbed up and down. "She had to write letters for community service hours. Until she showed me that drawing, I never made the connection between you and her pen pal."

"Amazing. I'm at a loss for words."

"She was worried when you stopped writing. I visited Shadow Oaks to find out what had happened. The people there were pleasant and explained about your fall. Penny's at school or she would be here, too."

Nina reached over to her tray. "I have a letter for her. It's somewhere under all these cards." She found the letter she had written and handed it to Megan. "You wouldn't know why I received all these cards from former students?"

The color rose in Megan's face. "When I found out you

were here, I went online and let a few alumni know. You have a lot of fans."

"It was quite a delightful surprise." *More like a shock.*

"Miss K, I have one request. When you're feeling better, I'm hoping you could be a judge for an upcoming art contest at the Community Art Center."

Nina rubbed her hand against the bed coverings. "I don't know yet when I'll be able to walk."

"We could bring the entries to you. It would mean a lot to the Art Center to have someone of your caliber as our judge."

Nina exhaled slowly. "The honor would be mine." *Truly.*

When Megan left, Nina pondered how much had changed in the space of one day. She eyed the old *Coastal Creatives* magazine resting on her tray. *It was thoughtful of Megan to bring it, but I wish she hadn't. I don't need to relive the anguish of that exhibition.* She reached for the magazine, found the article Megan had bookmarked, and slowly opened the pages. The smell of age rested between the covers.

Before her was a two-page spread entitled "College Phenomenon." *That's a strange title.* She began reading and stopped, returned to the beginning of the piece, and started over. *This isn't what I expected.* She got chills when she read herself described as a future art superstar.

"Kanina has a rare gift for art."

I thought the art critic didn't like my artwork. Even Professor Rivero said, "Those who can't do, teach." I never even looked at the article back then. I knew it would hurt too much.

She kept reading, and when she got to the part where

the professor was quoted, she froze. *I misunderstood what he said. He wasn't talking about me; he was talking about himself. He was teaching because he couldn't do art. All these years, I thought I wasn't good enough to succeed as an artist. So, I taught.*

She read the article again. *I love teaching. I love helping others learn to draw and paint. But I should have been creating my own art, too.* She put the magazine back on the tray and smiled. *There's still time.*

* * *

STANDING IN THE KITCHEN AFTER SCHOOL, PENNY TOOK THE paper Mom handed her. "What is it?"

"It's a letter from your pen pal," Mom said.

Confused, Penny glanced at the paper again. "But it's not in an envelope."

"She gave it to me in person."

Penny rocked back in surprise. "You saw her?"

Mom nodded. "I visited her at the hospital today."

With growing anger, Penny narrowed her eyes. "She's in the hospital and you went without me? She's my pen pal."

"You were in school, and I had to talk to her."

"You could have waited until I came home." Penny opened the paper. "And I suppose you read this, too."

"No. I didn't." Mom put her hands up in a defensive way.

Shaking, Penny glared at her. *Why would she go without me?* Then her thoughts turned to Kanina. "How is she?"

"She's recovering and tires easily."

With a curt nod, Penny took the letter upstairs and sprawled across her bed to read it. "She says don't give up on yourself, Mom, or Steve. And all will be well. I don't believe her. It doesn't feel like everything will be okay."

Penny took the paper to her desk and added it to the collection of other letters from Shadow Oaks. Looking at the stack, she sat down and counted them. "Thirty-eight. Thirty-nine. I only need one more and I'm done."

* * *

THE NEXT DAY, MEGAN PREPARED FOR THE TELEVISION INTERVIEW at the Art Center. Looking in the bathroom mirror, she put on her pearl necklace and brushed her hair into place.

"The interview today is a wide-reaching way to get the word out about our upcoming art contest and art classes," she said in a loud voice.

"You'll do a great job," Steve said from the bedroom. "We'll have to record the broadcast when it airs."

"It'll probably be online before I get home." Megan walked into the bedroom. "How do I look?"

Steve whistled. "Gorgeous. You have a professional presence with an artistic flair."

"You, sir, are a flatterer. And I love you." She gave him a quick kiss and headed toward the bedroom door. She paused and went back to stand before Steve. "I'm enjoying my role at the Art Center and was thinking that if I continue, we could downsize to a smaller house."

"You mean a cheaper house," Steve said. "Stop worrying about the finances."

"I'm not worried, but I think we can simplify our lives.

Find the things that bring us joy and focus on those."

"That sounds like a family decision," Steve said. "Let's talk with Penny about it. Moving to a smaller house might mean changing schools for her. High school is a tough time without adding a change in school."

Megan wrapped her arms around Steve. "You are more than a flatterer. You are a keeper."

"I try." Steve stroked her face. "While you're being a television star today, I'll be meeting with upper management to see if the cost-cutting measures have been enough to save my store."

"We'll have a lot to talk about over dinner tonight." She straightened Steve's tie.

When Megan stepped into the Community Art Center classroom, the television crew had already set up their cameras. Megan had arranged for volunteers to sit at the tables drawing and painting a vase of sunflowers. The crew wired Megan with a lapel microphone.

"We'll start with some basic questions," the reporter said. "Don't be nervous. If you have trouble, we'll repeat the question. The video will be edited in the studio."

Megan smiled and nodded. *I've done dozens of media interviews in the past. I won't have trouble.*

"Okay, we're recording. This is Jamie Lynn, and this is 'All About Our Town,' reporting from the Community Art Center. Today we're talking to the Center's acting executive director, Megan Hinson. Megan, you've been hard at work spreading the word about the Art Center to the community. What new programs can we expect to see in the coming months?"

Megan launched into her overview of the nonprofit's purpose and programs. She highlighted the details about entering the art contest and the range of classes being offered.

"How does the Art Center respond to the embezzlement of funds by the former executive director?" the reporter asked.

Megan stayed calm. *Glad I discussed the situation with Matt Greer and we agreed on an answer.* "This unfortunate situation has allowed the Art Center to put tight controls in place to prevent a repeat of that incident."

"Has the Community Art Center lost sponsors and funding partners?"

"Yes. Sadly, that's true. We are rebuilding our relationships and have many sponsorship opportunities for those who have a vision for the arts in our community."

"Mrs. Hinson, what makes you qualified to be the executive director?"

Without hesitating, Megan launched into a summary of her many award-winning projects. "But most important of all, I really appreciate those who have artistic talent or want to grow their artistic ability. The Community Art Center is a place where the arts are encouraged to flourish."

"Have there been many entries in the art contest?"

Megan shook her head. "Not yet, but we've only recently announced the window is open for entries." Her throat tightened with the fear that not enough artists would submit their artwork.

"And that concludes our report here at the Community Art Center. Come experience the arts here. Remember it's 'All About Our Town,' and I'm Jamie Lynn. Thank you for watching. Join us tomorrow for another visit in our town."

With the cameras and recording devices packed up, the reporter approached Megan. "Sorry to have to ask you those challenging questions, but we have to protect our viewing public."

"I understand. It's natural to be skeptical about a non-profit that had funds stolen by an employee. I can assure you, we won't let that happen again."

When the television crew left, Megan thanked the volunteers and admired their artwork.

"I hope you can save the Center," one volunteer said. "I would miss the Center if it wasn't here."

"Me, too," another volunteer added.

"I'm going to do my best to save it," Megan said. *I'm working the plan. Let's see how this exposure works out.*

A few minutes later, the phone rang at the Community Art Center, and Megan answered it. *It's unreal answering as the acting executive director.*

"Hi. I'm Mrs. Silsbury, the art teacher at Bridgewater High School, and I have a few questions about the art contest. Our school's Art Club has some students who are interested in entering."

"That's wonderful. We have a youth category for any artist eighteen and under." Megan quickly calculated. *Fifteen youth entries at ten dollars per entry would generate $150, which would cover the prizes for that group.* "Mrs. Silsbury, I would be glad to come speak to your Art Club to explain the contest and answer questions."

"Our next meeting is this afternoon at three o'clock. Is that too soon?"

"I can do that."

"I appreciate your willingness to speak to our students,

especially on such short notice. I'll meet you in the front office just before three."

When the call ended, Megan couldn't believe her luck. *This is a fantastic opportunity to get more youth entries.*

* * *

PENNY CARRIED THE REBIRTH ART CONTEST FLYER INTO THE Art Club meeting. Mrs. Silsbury had not arrived yet. More students were in the room than at the first meeting.

Chatting with the student beside her, Penny missed seeing the art teacher enter the classroom.

"Students," Mrs. Silsbury said, "I'm delighted to bring you a guest speaker today."

Penny turned around and her mouth dropped open. *Mom!*

"This is Mrs. Hinson, the acting executive director of the Community Art Center. She's going to talk to us about the Rebirth Art Contest. Please welcome her."

The students clapped, but Penny sat motionless, still in shock. *She never told me she was coming here. How could she do this to me?*

Her mother stood at the front of the room. "The Community Art Center is holding our first ever art contest, and we would like you to enter. You will be judged in the youth category. Entries can be in pencil, charcoal, ink, watercolor, pastels, or oils. The deadline is December twenty-first. There is a small fee to enter. All the details are on the form I'll be giving you."

"Several students have asked about the theme," Mrs. Silsbury said. "Can you explain what that is?"

"Of course. The theme for this contest is rebirth. Your art should reflect a new beginning of some sort. Can anyone think of an example of a rebirth?"

Three students raised their hands. Penny's mother pointed to a girl with braces.

"A caterpillar turning into a butterfly."

"Yes. That's right. Terrific example."

Penny kept her head low and avoided her mother's gaze. *She should have warned me she was coming today.*

Mrs. Silsbury distributed the entry form. "Does anyone have questions?"

When there were none, Penny's mother said, "Thank you. I'm looking forward to seeing your entries. Penny, I'll see you at home."

All heads turned in her direction, including Mrs. Silsbury's. Penny sank lower in her seat. *How could she embarrass me like that?*

Chapter 28

MEGAN HAD THE DINNER TABLE SET WHEN STEVE CAME home from work. "What an incredible day I had," she said.

"I have some good news, too." Steve hugged her. "But I'm starving. I didn't get lunch today."

"We can share our news over dinner," she said. In a raised voice, she called Penny and Jody. "Dinner's ready."

After Megan brought the casserole to the table, they filled their plates and bowed their heads to say grace.

"Thank you, Lord, for all your bountiful blessings," Steve said. He raised his head, and a broad smile lit his face.

"What's your news?" Megan asked.

"You know how I told you cost-cutting measures were being taken. Well, my store did so well with cutting costs and generating additional sales that I've been promoted. You're looking at the new regional manager of sales efficiency."

"Congratulations!" Megan reached over and squeezed his hand. *That's a true blessing. At least one of us has a pay-check.* "Isn't that great news, Penny?"

When Penny didn't say a word, Megan glanced at her. *She looks sullen. Unhappy.*

"The even better part is it comes with a ten percent pay increase, stock options, and a company car," Steve said. "I thought we could hold on to my old car for Penny, if she's interested, since she'll be driving soon."

Megan waited for Penny's reaction, but there wasn't one. She watched her daughter push the macaroni and cheese around her plate. *That's not like her at all. She loves mac and cheese.*

Steve continued talking about his new role, then he changed subjects. "Megan, you said you had an incredible day. How did the interview go?"

"It went well, and I was invited to speak at the high school Art Club about the upcoming contest. I was happy to see Penny there."

Penny pushed her plate away. "Why didn't you tell me you were coming?"

"Mrs. Silsbury called me, and it was a spur-of-the-moment thing. I didn't know this morning I would be going to your school."

"And embarrass me in front of my friends."

"What did I do that embarrassed you?" *Other than saying I would see her at home, I didn't single her out at all.*

"All the students looked at me."

"Penny, you're being kind of mean to your mother," Steve said. "The others probably looked at you because they were impressed your mother is running the art contest."

"I'm sorry if my being there embarrassed you, Penny. That wasn't my intention. The art teacher said there were questions, and I thought going to the Art Club in person might help. When I accepted, the meeting was within hours of the call." *Here we go again, butting heads.* "In fact, I don't recall you even mentioning that you were in the Art Club. I don't even know if you're going to enter the contest."

"I got the Art Club started," Penny said.

"You did?" *I had no idea she did that.* "I'm impressed."

"Sounds like the two of you need to communicate a little more," Steve said in a calm voice.

Megan and Penny stared at each other.

Jody held up her plate. "More macaroni, please."

Steve scooped some more cheesy pasta onto Jody's plate. "See how easy it is when it's clear what someone wants?"

Megan and Penny both looked at him and started laughing.

"Sorry, Mom," Penny said. "It just surprised me when you came. You did good explaining about the contest."

"Thanks, Penny. If you had your phone, I could have sent you a message. We need to consider returning your phone. Steve and I will talk about that."

Jody held her plate up again. "Can I have dessert now?"

Laughter burst out around the table.

* * *

"Miss Koscielniak, thank you for agreeing to this interview." The reporter flipped his notepad open.

Nina gave a half smile. "I'm not sure why you want to write about me."

"From what I've already researched about your background, you were a much-loved high school art teacher for many years."

"Forty-eight." She chuckled. "I would have kept teaching, but the school district has a mandatory retirement age."

"What was the most satisfying part of your time spent

teaching?" The reporter's pen hovered over his paper.

Nina considered her answer for a moment. "Helping each student find and explore his or her artistic talent. Everyone has some gift for art, whether it's to create it or appreciate it. As an art teacher, I was privileged to work with many young people. Sometimes they had difficulty communicating their feelings, but art was a way for them to express themselves."

When the reporter was finished scribbling his notes, he turned the page in his notebook. "You were named Teacher of the Year. What was the secret to your success?"

"I wish I knew. I was selected Teacher of the Year three times. It still amazes me that I was granted such an honor." Nina shifted in her hospital bed, easing her knee into a more comfortable position.

"If you could give art advice to students, parents, or other teachers, what would it be?"

Closing her eyes, Nina gathered her thoughts. "I used to start each class with the same message. 'Together we will do great art.' I wanted them to know they were never alone. By working together, we can create unique works of art."

After several more questions, the reporter thanked Nina and left. She leaned her head against the pillow. Talking about all those years of teaching brought back memories of students from the past. *I loved teaching.* She fell asleep with warm thoughts about her classroom days.

* * *

THE NEXT MORNING, WHEN THE ALARM SOUNDED, PENNY rolled over to find Goku's green eyes staring at her.

"I bet you're glad to be home. I sure missed you. I even drew a picture of you."

She got up and retrieved her sketch. In the morning light, the image appeared flat. *It's boring. How did I think it was so good yesterday?*

Carrying the sketchbook back to bed, she compared the drawing to the purring cat rubbing against her.

"Tomorrow, I'm going to draw you again and see how that looks."

"Hey, Poison Pen!" Dylan's voice carried down the high school corridor. "We've been looking for you."

Penny stiffened. "Who's we?"

"Ash and me. My brother's going on another rail yard run tonight. We thought you could join us again."

"I don't think so," Penny said, walking away from him.

Dylan ran in front of her and stopped. "You afraid?"

"Yes. I got caught coming home last time. Now I don't have a phone."

"You don't need a phone to be famous. You can put your message on a railcar and have it speeding around the country."

"That's damaging someone else's property."

Dylan sneered at her. "Since when did you get all legal on us?"

"It's just not right, and it's dangerous." Penny walked around him. Her heart thudded against her chest. When he didn't follow her, she relaxed. *I did it. I stood up to him and the world didn't end.*

At lunch, Ashley bumped Penny's elbow in the cafeteria line. "We need to talk," Ashley whispered. "I messaged you, but you ignored me."

"My phone was taken away after the other night's disaster," Penny said.

"Dylan tells me you're not coming with us tonight."

"Nope." Penny carried her tray to a table and sat down.

Ashley followed and settled across from her. "We want you to come. It'll be fun."

"No, it won't. I'm not going through that again. Running from the police in the dark. Trespassing." She searched for the right word. "Vandalizing railcars."

"Everybody does graffiti on those boxcars."

"Not everybody, and not me." Penny's fingers tightened around her fork.

"You have to." Ashley's face reddened.

"No, I don't. What are you going to do? Tell my parents? They already caught me. You should be more worried that I'll tell someone how you and Dylan were involved."

"You wouldn't."

Penny's jaw tightened. "Are you sure?"

Ashley got up and left her tray behind.

Penny loosened her grip on her fork. *Hopefully, that's the last of that.*

On Saturday, after dinner, Penny took a fresh piece of art paper and ran her fingertips over it, noting the texture of the page. She sharpened her pencil and examined the point. Then she positioned her desk chair to see Goku better.

The cat lay on her bed with his tail wrapped around his body. His green eyes glowed, rimmed with flecks of golden yellow and black. A narrow black pupil filled the center of each eye. Penny studied the eyes closely until Goku closed them.

With the image of his eyes still fresh in her mind, she sketched them. Then she added the outline of the nose. She continued drawing the shape of the cat. *Something's missing.*

Penny put her pencil down and studied Goku sprawled on her bed. Leaving her desk, she kneeled beside the bed and rubbed his head. The cat purred and extended his neck. He opened his eyes, and Penny sighed.

"I missed you so much. You always listen to me. While you were gone, I didn't have anyone to talk to. I wrote some letters to an old lady, but there wasn't anyone here to listen to me."

Goku butted his head against Penny's hand.

"You love the attention. Don't you?" She scratched his chin and his eyes closed again. "That's the emotion I want to capture. Contentment."

Penny returned to her desk and opened the bottom drawer. She searched through the long-neglected contents and found the unused watercolor paints, brushes, and paper she had received as a Christmas present two years ago. She put them on her desk.

"Let's try some color, Goku."

She swished her paintbrush in a cup of water and swept the brush across the pan of yellow paint several times. With her brush loaded with paint, she stroked the color across her pencil drawing.

Hours later, she set her brush down and turned off the desk lamp. "That's enough for tonight. Goku, you need to move over so I can go to bed."

THE DEADLINE FOR SUBMISSION OF ENTRIES TO THE REBIRTH Art Contest was in less than three days, and Penny still had not decided whether she was entering the contest.

Her watercolor painting of Goku had turned out better than she expected. *I can't believe I painted this. But is it good enough to enter a contest?*

She still had to frame the painting. *Mom offered to pay the entry fee, even though I haven't shown her the painting. Since she worries so much about money, that's a big deal. Maybe she's afraid there won't be many entries.*

Penny's stomach did somersaults at the idea of her artwork hanging on a gallery wall for people to see and comment on her amateurish efforts. *What if they hate it?*

She put the painting in a large envelope and carefully placed it in her backpack. *I'll get Mrs. Silsbury's opinion.*

On Tuesday morning when Penny entered the art classroom, she showed her painting to the teacher.

Mrs. Silsbury closely examined the piece, then grinned. "Penny, you had a breakthrough!"

Penny shrugged. "What do you mean? Because of the color?"

"This is the first piece I've seen you create that has genuine emotion."

"Like what?" She looked more carefully at her painting.

"Those eyes let us look into the cat's peaceful spirit."

Penny blushed. "I'm thinking of entering it in the art contest."

Nodding, Mrs. Silsbury said, "It needs to be matted and framed. You'll want a frame that complements the painting's colors and mood. There are some mats and frames in the supply room. I bought them at a second-hand shop. Pick out a few to try."

Penny selected three frames from Mrs. Silsbury's

collection. She auditioned the painting in each one. As soon as she saw it in the rustic frame with an antique-stain finish, she knew it matched the feeling she had for the painting. *That's the one!*

The framed painting of Goku gave her goosebumps. *I love it! Usually, I hate my art, but this I love.*

"It's wonderful, Penny," Mrs. Silsbury said. "Regardless of whether you win the contest, you've already won by tapping into a deeper level of expression."

Penny smiled and took a satisfied breath.

When Penny came home from school, she called for her mom, excited to share Mrs. Silsbury's comments.

"I'm in the kitchen," her mother answered.

Penny hurried in with the framed picture. "I have my entry for the art contest."

Her mother took the painting and gazed at it. Then she looked at Penny and back at the painting. "You did this?"

Penny nodded. "It's Goku. I'm calling it 'Contented Cat.'"

With a sniffle, her mother brushed the corner of her eye.

"Is something wrong?"

"No, Penny. This is gorgeous. I was expecting you to do one of those cartoon characters."

"Mom! They're called manga."

"I thought I was going to have to disqualify your entry because it isn't original, but this certainly is original."

"Mrs. Silsbury, my art teacher, said I had a breakthrough." *This is the longest conversation I've had with Mom in a long time.*

"You certainly did."

"I thought Goku coming home was a kind of rebirth. Is that close enough to the theme?"

"It's definitely an example of rebirth. On the entry form, there's a spot to explain how your art meets the theme. You can share the story of Goku's return." Mom still held the painting. "I can't get over how you've captured the intensity of his eyes. Great job, Penny."

"Thanks." She headed to her room to fill out the required form. *I'll have to write to Kanina about this.*

Chapter 29

Thursday, December 21, 2023

MEGAN SAT AT THE FRONT DESK, TALLYING THE NUMBER OF entries for the art contest. Today was the last day for entries and she expected a few last-minute artists to arrive with pieces that might still have paint drying. The freshly painted colorful walls of the front room were bare, ready to display the entries.

She looked up when the front door opened. "Welcome to the Community Art Center," she said with a broad smile. "Are you interested in entering our art contest?"

The couple who approached the desk were well dressed. The gentleman walked with the aid of a cane. The woman moved with grace and poise.

"Heavens, no," the man said. "We're collectors of art, not artists."

"I'm sorry, our gallery is empty. We haven't hung the entries for the art contest yet. But once we do, you're welcome to visit the exhibition."

"Thank you," the woman said, "but that's not why we're here."

Megan waited, noting the body language of the two individuals before her. *Confident. Assured. Cultured.* "I'm

Megan Hinson, acting executive director of the Center. What can I do to help you?"

"I'm Claude Bennett and this is my wife, Franny. We met in our high school art class years before you were born. Our teacher instilled a love of great art in both of us. I became an architect, and Franny an interior decorator. We both had profitable careers, and we owe it all to the art teacher who encouraged us to find art in our own way."

Megan felt a chill run up her arms. "Would your art teacher have been Miss K?"

They both chuckled.

"Yes," Franny said. "Anyone who attended that school knew Miss K. We saw the news coverage about her and even visited her in the hospital. We would like to do something to honor her years of teaching."

"Depending on how much you have in mind, we have some naming opportunities," Megan said.

"We would like to do a one-million-dollar annuity."

Megan's pulse jumped. "Did I hear you correctly?"

The couple grinned and nodded. "Our attorney will draw up the paperwork. We know nonprofits struggle to raise funds, and no one wants their donations to go to administrative expenses, but we understand keeping qualified professionals on staff, whether instructors or executive directors, takes money. Our annuity should address that concern."

Megan blinked and struggled to think of an appropriate response. "Thank you. Thank you so much. You have no idea how much this means to the Center."

"We're glad to hear that," Claude said.

"This is such an incredible gift. Would you like the Center to be named after you?" Megan asked.

"No, never!" the couple said in unison.

"We were thinking the classroom should be named after our wonderful art teacher," Franny said. "But we don't think the 'Miss K Room' is the right recognition."

"I think 'Nina's Classroom' would give it the warmth and friendliness she always shares," Megan suggested. "And students will still be able to pronounce the name."

"We'll have our attorney add that to the funding agreement."

"What can we do to recognize your generosity?" Megan asked.

"We prefer to remain anonymous. If the word gets out that we've given a gift of this size to one nonprofit, every worthy cause in town will be after us."

"I can understand that. Thank you again. You have no idea how much this means."

The woman leaned closer to Megan. "Lovely choice on the wall colors. I always thought the white walls were too cold for a place that should celebrate creativity."

"Thank you. My daughter, Penny, helped me select the colors." Megan's chest swelled with pride.

* * *

A NURSE WOKE NINA TO TAKE HER VITAL SIGNS. "THE DOCTOR will be in to see you tomorrow morning to review your options."

Nina licked her lips. "Options? What does that mean?"

"The doctor will explain that in more detail," the nurse said. "Make sure you keep drinking water."

Nina nodded and reached for the cup of water. *I*

thought I'd be going back to Shadow Oaks. I'll miss my walks in the garden. Walking may not be an option anymore. She watched the slow drip from the IV to the tube that disappeared under the tape across the back of her hand.

The next morning, the doctor arrived in his crisp white jacket.

"I'm Dr. Ben Gerhart. I've reviewed your X-rays, the MRI scan, and your medical records. You sustained a slight concussion from your fall. The good news is the X-rays show no broken bones; however, the MRI showed you had a torn meniscus in your left knee. We drained the fluid from your knee that was causing the swelling, but unfortunately, you have an infection. The IV you're receiving is an antibiotic. I'll be monitoring your condition, and you'll be released from the hospital once we get the infection under control. Your overall health appears to be good. I expect a routine recovery. You could be released as early as tomorrow. The question you need to consider is where you can go to meet your rehabilitation requirements after release."

"Can't I go back to Shadow Oaks?" Nina asked.

"They are not equipped for rehabilitation."

"Can I stay here?"

"I'm afraid not. This hospital does not provide rehabilitation services. Do you have a family member who can help you explore availability at different rehab facilities?"

Nina shook her head. "I'm all alone. I don't have any family."

The doctor jotted down a note on his chart. "Social services may provide some assistance. I'll pass your name along to them. But you'll be released soon and need to go somewhere."

When the doctor left, Nina swallowed hard. *Lord, I haven't prayed in a long time, but I need your help. I've been able to teach and travel on my own, but this I can't do alone.* She recited a prayer she remembered from her childhood. *Thy will be done.*

CHAPTER 30

Saturday, December 23, 2023

WITH THE LAPTOP VOLUME ON HIGH, PENNY LISTENED TO her favorite song on the Cosmic Dreams playlist. She shuffle-danced to the beat until the prolonged ringing of the doorbell intruded on her music.

Guess I better see who's at the door.

She continued bobbing and rocking to the song while she bounced down the steps to the first floor. She glanced through the side window and groaned.

Steve's parents. They weren't supposed to be here until tomorrow. Why isn't Mom here?

The doorbell rang again. Penny faked a smile and opened the front door.

"Merry Christmas," Grandmother Hinson said in a cheery voice. "My! How grown-up you look." She held her arms open for a hug.

Penny gave her a halfhearted embrace. "Come in. Mom's not here right now, Steve's at the store, and Jody's at daycare."

The elegantly dressed woman swept past Penny, followed by her husband with a bundle of Christmas presents in his arms.

"Hi there, young lady," he said. "Santa got lost and left some gifts at our house." He winked.

Penny laughed politely. *He must think I'm Jody's age.* She led him to the decorated blue spruce tree in the family room.

"Mom and Steve weren't expecting you until tomorrow."

Grandmother Hinson helped place the colorfully wrapped presents under the tree. "We chartered a flight, rather than deal with the crowds at the airport."

"It's the best way to travel these days," Steve's father said. He settled into the recliner.

Penny nodded. *Now what do I say?* "Steve said you were staying at a hotel."

"We've already checked into the Grand Royale. Comfortable suite on the top floor." He leaned back in the recliner and raised the footrest.

Grandmother Hinson cleared her throat. "You know, Penelope, you should call him something more endearing."

"Endearing?" Penny raised an eyebrow. *I hate when she calls me Penelope. She's the only one who uses my full name.*

"Dad. Daddy. Father. Pop. Something like that."

"Leave it alone, Gloria," Steve's father said. "It's none of our business."

Penny stared at him. *That's right.*

Grandmother Hinson wandered around the family room and examined the framed photographs on the wall. "Jody is adorable. She resembles Stevie when he was that age."

That's why Jody is your favorite. Penny twisted her fingers together. "Would you like to see the mural I painted on Jody's bedroom wall?"

"I heard all about it. You must be quite talented," Grandmother Hinson said.

The front door swung open, and small footsteps raced across the floor.

"Grandma! Grandpa!" Jody ran into the family room, and Grandmother Hinson scooped her into a warm embrace.

Mom followed and gave both their guests a kiss on the cheek. "Mother and Father Hinson, what a surprise to see you today. Steve called and told me you flew in early. He'd love to be here, but with Christmas so close, he can't get away from the store right now."

"We can visit him and get some last-minute shopping done," Grandmother Hinson said.

"We can do that," Mom replied.

"Guess I'll drive you ladies to the store." Steve's father got up from the recliner and rubbed his hands together. "Who wants to go?"

Not me. Penny glanced at her mother.

"Jody isn't usually that cooperative when I go shopping. Penny, can you stay here with her?"

"Sure can." *What a relief!*

Penny gestured for Jody to follow her. "Let's go in the kitchen and eat some Christmas cookies."

* * *

WITH ONLY A DAY AND A HALF UNTIL CHRISTMAS, THE FRANTIC shoppers hurried past Megan and her mother-in-law to complete their last-minute shopping. Steve had taken his father for a walking tour of the store, while Megan led the way to the children's clothing department.

Mother Hinson held up an emerald-green dress with layers of tulle. "This would be darling on Jody."

"It is pretty, but it looks like a pageant dress. Not one she would wear to daycare."

"She could wear it on Christmas. It would be lovely in a family photograph."

Megan spotted the price tag and shook her head. "This costs too much."

"Nonsense, Megan. My granddaughter deserves the best."

After reading the price tag on another dress, Megan pulled a cotton floral-print dress from the rack. "This is charming. Jody would like this."

"Then let's get both for her."

"I didn't mean she needs two dresses."

"Of course she does." Mother Hinson took the print dress from Megan and held it with the tulle dress. "Now how about Penelope?"

"Penny?" *Nobody calls her Penelope.*

"She needs to dress up for the family photograph."

I don't see that happening. "Penny doesn't dress up much."

"We bought her a kimono for Christmas. I hope she'll wear it while we're here."

"That was kind of you."

"We found it when we were in Tokyo earlier this year. It's made of pure silk, hand stitched. But she needs a festive dress for Christmas."

How do I tell her Penny won't wear anything we buy? "Penny's sixteen. It's a difficult age."

Mother Hinson headed into the Junior Department. She perused the merchandise and flagged down a young sales representative.

Megan lagged behind her. *The Juniors section always feels like a carnival to me. Wild colors and styles. Music blaring. Not a single tailored item in sight.*

"I'm looking for an anime-inspired cosplay dress for my granddaughter," Mother Hinson said to the salesperson.

"Here's a navy-blue sailor dress. It has a pleated skirt, a white blouse with short puffy sleeves, and a red ribbon tie."

"That's perfect!" Mother Hinson took the hanger and examined the front and back of the dress.

Megan eyed the outfit skeptically. "It's short, and Penny's tall."

"She can wear leggings," Mother Hinson said.

How does she know so much about the way young people dress? "That could work. If she's willing to wear it."

Mother Hinson tilted her head and gave Megan a questioning stare. "You're being rather hard on her."

With her temper rising, Megan took a deep breath. "We've had some trouble with Penny recently. I'd rather not discuss it here."

"I can understand that. Stevie told me about the problems she's had. However, I want to buy her this dress. If she won't wear it, my feelings won't be hurt. I would have preferred to have her here with us, but she's babysitting Jody. That's convenient for you and Stevie."

I hadn't thought about that. I do take for granted that Penny can babysit whenever I need her.

Steve and his father walked into the Junior Department. They were deep in a conversation about LED lights.

"Stevie, here's what I found." Mother Hinson held up the three dresses.

"Your money is no good in my store," Steve said with a broad smile.

Mother Hinson shook a finger at her son. "Humor a grandmother."

Megan followed them to the checkout counter. *I've been taking Penny for granted. It's time for me to thank her more.*

CHAPTER 31

Monday, December 25, 2023

NINA'S MOVE FROM THE HOSPITAL TO THE REHABILITATION center had gone smoothly yesterday. From her bed, she stared at the ceiling in the new room and let her eyes wander along the edge of each ceiling tile. With the bed next to her empty, she had no one to talk to.

The staff and surroundings are pleasant here, but this is the worst Christmas I've ever experienced. I'm used to being alone, and that part never bothered me before. But being confined to a bed makes me feel worthless.

She closed her eyes and recalled many of her past Christmas trips. *I enjoyed finding new places to visit while school was closed for winter break.* She spent the rest of the day recalling her favorite December vacations.

* * *

THE CHRISTMAS TREE LIGHTS BLINKED RANDOMLY, CHANGING colors from white to blue. Soft music played in the background, while the Hinson household gathered in the family room to open presents. Grandmother and Grandfather Hinson sat on the couch, Steve in the recliner, Mom in an armchair, and Jody and Penny on the floor. Clad in her pajamas, Jody giggled and ripped the gift wrap off her present.

"Merry Christmas, Jody." Grandmother Hinson handed a large box in red wrapping paper to the four-year-old.

Penny shifted position to get a better view of Jody opening her gift. *She always gets the best stuff.*

With a flurry of bits of paper, Jody tore the package open. She squealed in delight. "A baby doll."

"That's really lifelike," Penny said.

"I had it customized, based on Jody's baby photos."

"I'm glad you didn't use the photos the day she was born." Steve laughed. "Her face was all red and squinched like a prune."

"Shame on you, Stevie. Don't talk about my granddaughter like that." The old woman's eyes sparkled with humor.

"I love her, Grandma." Jody hugged the doll and ran to show Mom.

Grandfather Hinson rose from the couch and retrieved a long rectangular package covered with shiny green paper and an elaborate white bow. "Penny, this one is for you. We think you'll like it."

"Thanks." She took the box and felt the weight of something substantial. Carefully, she removed the bow and set it aside. Then she slipped a finger under the tape at the end of the package.

"I'll help you," Jody said and ripped the corner of the gift wrap. She tore a wide strip of paper off the top of the box.

"Jody," Mom said. "Penny can open her own present."

"It's okay. She can help." *She's more excited than me to see what's in here.* Penny lifted the lid off the box to expose a layer of tissue paper.

Jody clapped her hands. "Let me see."

Slowly, Penny peeled back the layers of tissue paper. Her eyes widened, and she sucked in her breath. She ran her fingers over the red silk, pausing at the gold embroidery outlining a white bird. *A Japanese crane. This must be a kimono!* In shock, she glanced from one step-grandparent to the other.

"This is for me?" She lifted the kimono out of the box.

"Of course, darling," Grandmother Hinson said. "We heard you're interested in Japanese art and culture. This kimono was handmade in Japan."

"It's gorgeous." Penny blinked, fighting back tears. *Why am I crying?* Her fingers caressed the fabric.

"We're glad you like it." Steve's parents beamed.

"Thank you so much." Penny's voice quivered. *I didn't think they cared about me.*

"Can I open another one?" Jody asked.

Everyone laughed, and Grandmother Hinson handed both Jody and Penny another present. "These are for the family photo later today."

"Can I wear the kimono in the photo?" Penny asked.

"Why don't you see what's in this box first," Mom said.

Jody opened her box with exuberance. "Look, Mommy." She twirled around the room holding the tulle dress.

Penny gasped at the dress in her box. "I love it."

"You do?" Mom's eyebrows rose.

"Sure. It's like Usagi Tsukino's outfit." Penny grinned at Mom's startled expression.

"Who?" Mom looked from Penny to Grandmother Hinson.

"Sailor Moon." Penny smiled at her step-grandparents. "Thanks. I can use it for cosplay, too." *This is the best Christmas ever.*

* * *

LATER THAT DAY, MEGAN SHEPHERDED THE FAMILY over to the fireplace for the annual Christmas photograph. *Penny's missing.*

"Penny!" she called up the staircase, then returned to the family room. "Steve, please stand over here, next to your parents."

She guided Jody to a spot beside Steve. "Stay here, sweetie."

Megan returned to her camera, mounted on a tripod, to check the viewfinder. "Penny, hurry down. Everyone's ready."

The quick tread of Penny's footsteps on the stairs grew closer. A moment later, she burst into the room with a broad smile on her face.

"What do you think?" She held her arms out and spun around. Then she hurried over to the fireplace and slipped behind Jody.

"You look amazing," Mother Hinson said.

Megan examined the schoolgirl dress Penny wore. *The best part is the smile on her face.* "You look happy."

Megan checked the viewfinder again and set the timer for the photo. She hustled over to stand between her two daughters. "Smile everyone."

The camera flashed twice, and Megan blinked.

"With all these smiling faces, this should be a most

festive photo," Steve said.

Megan checked the final image and gave everyone a thumbs-up.

"It looks wonderful." *This is a photo I will cherish forever. And to think I was dreading the arrival of Steve's parents. They have made such a difference in Penny's attitude and helped me see that I haven't been treating her right.*

THE NEXT DAY, AFTER THE HINSONS HEADED TO THE AIRPORT, Megan put on her running shoes and went for a jog. With each stride, she reviewed her shortcomings in raising Penny and vowed to do better.

As she headed back to the house, she realized she owed Steve an apology, too. *He's been treating Penny better than I have.* When she entered the house, Penny bounded down the stairs to meet her.

"Hey, Mom. Since I'm grounded, can Lacey come here?"

Megan grinned. *Now would be a good time to end her grounding.* "Sure, but would you two like to go to the movies?"

"Really?" Penny's eyes widened.

"Yes." Megan took her daughter's hands in hers. "You've done a great job with your letter writing. You agreed there would not be another rail yard incident. So, I think it's time to drop the grounding."

A broad smile brightened Penny's face. "Fantastic!"

"I want you to know I'm sorry for the way I've been treating you. You look so much like your father. I'm afraid I've been holding that against you. I'm sorry." Megan's voice trembled. "You didn't deserve that." She searched Penny's face for a reaction.

"I thought you loved Jody more than me."

"Oh, Penny. No." Megan tightened her hold on Penny's hands. "I love you both. I've done a terrible job of coping with the changes we've gone through. Can you forgive me?" A tear trickled down Megan's cheek.

Penny's lips quivered, and she nodded.

"We've been through a lot. I promise to make things better from now on." Tears continued to slide down Megan's face, and she brushed them away.

Penny flung her arms around Megan and sobbed.

"I love you, baby," Megan whispered, clinging to her daughter. *We haven't been this close in years.*

After a few minutes, she pulled away from Penny and said, "I'm going to give your phone back. Why don't you call Lacey and see if she wants to go to the movies. I'll drive you both there."

The wide grin on Penny's face warmed Megan's heart. She enjoyed the newfound connection with her daughter.

Penny raised the returned phone to her ear. "Hi, Lacey. I'm not grounded anymore. Want to see that movie that just came out?" She flashed a smile at Megan before dashing upstairs.

Listening to her daughter's excited chatter with her friend, Megan marveled at the positive change in her relationship with Penny. *Who knew it could be so easy?*

CHAPTER 32

Wednesday, December 27, 2023

Nina swallowed the pain pill. She lay back and waited for it to take effect. The throbbing of her knee eased, and her breathing slowed. *That's better. Who knew rehab would hurt this much?*

There was a knock at the door to her room. "May I come in?"

She raised her head. *Who could that be?* "Come in."

"Miss K, how are you feeling?"

"Ah, Megan. You found me again. First at the hospital and now at the rehab facility."

"I'm persistent," Megan said. "We've received a good number of entries for the art contest."

"I'm afraid I can't go there to judge," Nina said.

Megan pulled a tablet from her handbag. "That's what I figured. I have photos for you to look at. When you narrow them down, I'll bring you the originals to review in person."

Nina pressed the control to raise the head of her bed. "You have photos on that thing?"

"Let me show you." Megan selected the professional entries. She scrolled through the images, holding the screen for Nina to see.

Nina studied each photo and shared her impressions with Megan. "This one I would like to see the original." A few more photos later, she pointed again. "This one, too. It speaks rebirth so well."

They completed the professional and adult amateur entries, then turned to the youth category. Nina's knee ached. *The pain meds must have worn off.* She had Megan scroll through the youth entries quickly. "I'd like to see the cat, the coastal scene, and the motorcycle."

"Thank you, Miss K. I appreciate you agreeing to help the Art Center."

"You received some beautiful pieces of art," Nina said. "There are many talented artists in our community."

"I'll be back tomorrow with the first group of entries you requested."

"God willing, I'll still be here." She yawned. "Sorry, the pain pill makes me sleepy."

"I'll see you tomorrow morning." Megan left quietly.

It is nice having a visitor. So many talented artists . . . Nina drifted off to sleep.

* * *

Friday, January 12, 2024

The evening of the Community Art Center's opening reception arrived with clear skies. At the Center, Megan made a final round of inspections. The caterer had trays of appetizers prepared. *Getting the caterer to reduce her prices for sponsorship recognition was an extra benefit.*

"I can't believe how grand the place looks," Matt Greer

said. The awe in his voice was clear.

Before the front door opened for the artists' reception, Megan took one last glance around the gallery. The bright-colored walls enriched the space, and the framed artwork looked stunning. Youth entries were hung together. Professional entries had a prominent location, immediately visible to those entering the Center. The amateur entries—many so good they could be professional—filled the rest of the gallery. Each entry had a small sign with the artist's name, the title of the piece, media, and purchase price.

The judge's awards were ready to be distributed. Megan knew the winners and could barely contain her excitement. *Nina did an outstanding job as the judge.*

Megan swung the front door open, and people strolled in. The crowd grew, and the sound of cheerful voices filled the air. She kept looking toward the door in anticipation.

* * *

As the sun set, Nina leaned on her cane and stepped carefully onto the Shadow Oaks shuttle bus. She had been back from the rehab facility only a few days and was already going on an outing. *An outing I'm excited about.*

Andy helped her navigate the step into the vehicle. "It's a pleasure to have you back with us, Miss Nina."

"I'm glad to be back."

Rosemary waved to her. "Come sit by me. I want to hear all about being a judge for this art contest."

Nina settled into the seat across from Rosemary and Emmett. "It was quite an honor to be asked."

"You were holding out on us what a celebrity you are.

Imagine having a newspaper article written about all those high school students you taught."

Streetlights popped on and the shuttle turned toward downtown.

"This is such a treat to be going at night," Rosemary said. "And such fun to be dressing up for an art gallery reception."

Nina nodded. She remembered how excited she had been at her own exhibit reception. *I still could kick myself for jumping to the wrong conclusion about Professor Rivero's comment.*

* * *

"TIME TO GO, GIRLS," STEVE CALLED. "YOUR MOM EXPECTED US to be there by now."

Penny hurried down the stairs, with Jody behind her.

"Going to Mommy's art show," Jody sang.

At the bottom of the stairs, Steve stood with a wrist corsage for each of them. "You two are looking spectacular." He handed Penny the larger corsage with red roses and helped Jody with the pink carnation corsage.

Penny grinned. She wore a brand-new white top that she and Mom had purchased together. The neckline was covered by a row of lace, and her mother's pearl necklace nestled against the lace. The burgundy skirt swirled around her, showing her knees in the front and dipping down to mid-calf in the back. She wore her favorite black boots and a bright red beret. *I feel like a butterfly.*

In a mock formal fashion, Steve held out both arms. "It is my pleasure to escort two lovely ladies to the art gallery."

Giggling, Jody took one hand, and Penny put her arm through Steve's other arm. *Is this what a father does?*

Together they promenaded to the car, laughing and putting on airs.

"May I open the door for you, madam?" Steve bowed deeply.

Penny curtsied. "You most certainly may."

"And you, little princess, must sit in your booster seat."

Jody pouted but climbed into her assigned seat.

They carried on a lively banter for the short drive through the dark to the Community Art Center. The conversation kept Penny distracted, and she appreciated that. *Otherwise, I'd be a nervous wreck.*

"We have arrived," Steve announced.

Penny stared at the tiny twinkling lights around the entrance to the Art Center. *It looks magical!*

A crowd of people was already circling through the gallery. Penny tried to catch a glimpse of her painting, but without success. All the artwork she saw looked breathtaking, and her gut tightened. *My little cat picture isn't as good as these. I think I'm going to be sick. This is scary.*

Steve picked Jody up. "Let's go find Penny's masterpiece. I believe the youth entries are to the left. Then we'll find your mother."

Penny followed him, afraid to look at the art pieces around her.

"There it is," Jody said with glee. "There's Goku. Look, Penny."

Lifting her head, Penny saw the royal hunter-green wall before her. *I helped Mom pick the colors. This wall looks great.* In the middle of the wall was her rustic frame with Goku's green eyes staring out into the gallery. A chill ran down her spine, and she walked past Steve to get a better view.

"It looks great," she whispered. *I can't believe I created that.*

"It most certainly does," Steve said. The pride in his voice made Penny turn to look at him.

"Do you like it?"

"It's incredible, Penny. I'm proud to be your stepfather."

A second chill ran up her spine. *Wow!* She hugged him.

Jody giggled. "Hug sandwich!"

"Let's find your mom. She's probably wherever the food is." His laughter was loud and genuine.

Penny regarded him in a new light. *He's acting like my dad.*

* * *

THE SHUTTLE PULLED UP IN FRONT OF THE COMMUNITY ART Center. Emily and Andy assisted everyone off the bus.

"We'll be leaving at eight thirty sharp," Emily said.

When Nina hobbled through the front door, a swell of people greeted her. *My former students!* She straightened up and leaned on her cane less. She greeted each person with a warm smile.

* * *

MEGAN SAW STEVE ARRIVE WITH PENNY AND JODY, BUT SHE was talking with one of the board members and could not leave. Then she lost sight of them. *Hope they find Penny's entry.* She glanced at the front door again.

The Shadow Oaks shuttle pulled in front of the Center and the residents streamed out of the vehicle. Megan went to greet them. Nina, looking radiant in a purple scarf and a ribbon wound through her signature single braid, was the last. Megan hugged her. "I'm glad you could come."

"I wouldn't miss it." Nina moved carefully around the gallery, leaning on her cane.

Megan raised her voice. "May I have your attention, please?"

The crowd quieted and turned toward her.

"On behalf of the board of directors of the Community Art Center, I'm delighted to welcome you to the first annual Rebirth Art Contest. I'm Megan Hinson, the executive director." She smiled in celebration of dropping "acting" from her title.

"We have an announcement to share with you before we award prizes for the entries. Thanks to an exceptionally generous anonymous donation, we are proud to reveal the new name of our classroom. In recognition of her almost fifty years of service to art education in our local high school, we are delighted to recognize Kanina Koscielniak by dedicating our classroom as Nina's Classroom."

Matt Greer removed the cloth covering the plaque affixed to the wall beside the classroom. The crowd applauded and cheered.

"Many of you know her as Miss K. I'm also pleased to announce that Nina, Miss K, was our judge for this inaugural year of our art contest." Megan pointed to the blushing art teacher. "We'll announce the winners in a few minutes. In the meantime, please circulate and be sure to enter your selection for the People's Choice Award."

The guests applauded, and Megan beamed with happiness. *The evening is shaping up to be a success.*

* * *

PENNY HEARD HER MOTHER'S VOICE OVER THE SWIRL OF conversations around her. The crowd silenced.

"Thank you for coming to the inaugural art contest of the Community Art Center," Mom said over an amplified sound system. "We had a tremendous response from the artists in our community."

Penny stood on the tips of her toes, trying to get a glimpse of her mother, but the bobbing and weaving of heads between them made it impossible.

"We were hoping for a robust response and were not disappointed. As you wander around the gallery, you will see the range of talent we have living in our town. Many of the pieces of art are for sale. Perhaps you will consider adding one of them to your home decor. A portion of the proceeds will be retained by the Art Center to help us put on future events such as this."

Applauding, the crowd shifted positions. Penny glimpsed her mother holding a microphone. Jody, high in Steve's arms, waved to Mom.

"Our judge for this show is none other than Miss Kanina Koscielniak."

The crowd cheered and clapped for minutes.

Is she here? Penny jumped up, hoping to spot her.

"She did a wonderful job of evaluating the range of mediums. We will take a photo of each winner with their entry after all the awards are announced. Now, let's start with the youth division. Honorable mention goes to Becky Stone for her pastel entitled 'Summer in Maine.'"

Penny's heart beat faster. *She's announcing who won. What if I win? What if I don't?*

After the applause died down, her mother continued, "Second place and a cash prize of fifty dollars goes to Evan Orser for his pen and ink entitled 'Motorcycle.'"

More applause, and Penny felt like she might faint.

"First place and a cash prize of one hundred dollars goes to Penny Davis for her watercolor entitled 'Contented Cat.'"

Time slowed down, and Penny grinned at the crowd's cheers. *I won! I really won!*

Steve gave her a big hug. "Congratulations, sweet pea!"

"Thanks, Dad." She pulled back. *Did I just call him Dad? I did.* She smiled at him.

"That means a lot, Penny." Steve ducked his head.

Jody clapped and sang, "Happy, happy, happy."

The rest of the announcements were a blur to Penny. Her mother's final words were "Thank you for coming. Enjoy the art. Winners, please go to your entry, and we'll be around to present the ribbons and take a photo."

Penny felt Steve's hand on her back, guiding her to the youth section. She moved in a numb daze.

Her mother appeared with a big blue ribbon and an envelope. She handed both to Penny and hugged her. "I'm proud of you."

"Is she here? Is Kanina here?" Penny asked.

"Yes. She's surrounded by people right now, but we'll get you over to meet her in person as soon as the last of the prizes are distributed. First, we need to take a picture of you beside your painting with your ribbon."

A man with glasses motioned Penny to move closer to her painting.

"Go ahead, Matt," Mom said.

Penny smiled and held the ribbon close to the framed painting. *Thank you, Goku, for being such a handsome subject.*

* * *

Nina watched the cluster of people circulating around the Art Center, the winners having their photographs taken with their winning entries and the glasses of champagne being clinked together. *Seeing so many of my former students is incredible. So many memories.* A tear trickled from the corner of Nina's eye. She brushed it away quickly.

A young woman with her hair in a ponytail approached Nina. "Miss K, I'm Brooke Silsbury. I'm not sure if you remember me."

Nina tried to recall her face in a classroom setting. "Brooke Silsbury . . . I'm afraid I don't remember."

"My name was Brooke Willis back then."

"Oh yes, Willis. You sat behind Jim Vernon and wore big hoop earrings."

The young woman blushed. "Yes, that was me. I wanted to thank you for being an outstanding role model. I became a high school art teacher because you inspired me."

"That's quite a compliment," Nina said.

"All three of the youth winners are my students."

Nina held her hand out to her former student. "You are

doing an excellent job with young talent."

Mrs. Silsbury took Nina's hand. "As you did with me."

"May I give you one piece of advice?" Nina pulled her closer.

"Certainly."

"If anyone ever says to you, 'Those who cannot do, teach,' don't listen to them, for they are wrong."

* * *

JODY LEANED HER HEAD AGAINST STEVE'S SHOULDER. SHE yawned and her eyelids drooped.

"I think I need to get this little princess home to bed," Steve said. "Penny, do you want to stay longer or come home with me?"

"I'd like to meet the lady who judged the contest," Penny said. "My pen pal."

"Sure. You can ride home with your mother."

With all the photos taken and the crowd thinning, her mother came over to Penny. "Want to meet Miss K?"

"Yes."

As they walked toward the center of the gallery, Penny caught sight of Kanina. She sat at the table in the center of the room. A bright purple scarf circled her neck, and her hair was braided in a single long strand over her left shoulder. *She looks familiar.*

"Miss K, this is Penny, my daughter," Mom said.

The old lady smiled. "We've met before."

"You have?" Mom looked confused.

"At the art museum," Penny said. *She was the lady on the bench.*

"Yes," Kanina said. "And in letters."

They all laughed.

Kanina held up her hand. "I want you to understand that when I judged the art pieces, I did not know who the artists were. Your first-place win is because it was the best in the youth category."

"Thanks. That makes me proud," Penny said.

* * *

"I'd like to talk to both of you, but I need a quieter place," Nina said.

"Let's go to Nina's Classroom," Megan said.

When they were seated, Nina looked from Megan to Penny. "We are all creative spirits. Megan, you left my class because I challenged you to go deeper with your artistic skills. Penny, you started writing letters to me because you used your creative talent in the wrong way. And I buried my creativity because I misunderstood what my teacher meant. The creative spirit must be nurtured. Promise me you both will free your potential to make the world a better place."

"I regret I didn't stay in your class," Megan said. "That was a mistake."

"I made a mistake, too. Two of them," Penny said. "I'm sorry, Mom."

As mother and daughter embraced, Nina smiled. *What an evening this has been!*

Megan and Penny turned to Nina and in unison said, "I promise."

All three of them laughed until tears ran down their cheeks.

314

"Now, let's go enjoy this gallery of lovely art," Nina said, rising slowly to her feet.

* * *

PENNY WATCHED SEVERAL ELDERLY VISITORS HEAD TO THE Shadow Oaks shuttle parked outside the front door.

"I'm afraid I have to go," Nina said.

"Can I come visit you at Shadow Oaks?" Penny asked eagerly.

"That would be lovely."

Penny followed her pen pal to the door and held it open for her.

"Thank you again for your encouragement and all the letters. I need one more to finish my community service."

"I can send Miss Poison Pen a note of congratulations on her win." She winked and limped slightly to the shuttle.

"She's an amazing woman," Mom said, coming up behind Penny.

"Yes. She is one of a kind." Penny turned to her mother. "And so are you." *I'm pretty lucky!*

CHAPTER 33

Saturday, January 13, 2024

WHILE AT BREAKFAST THE DAY AFTER THE OPENING reception for the Rebirth Art Contest, the Shadow Oaks residents chatted happily about the evening event.

"Mike, you should have come," Rosemary said. "There was a young boy who did a picture of a motorcycle that you would have loved."

"There was a motorcycle? I thought it was an art show." Mike looked dubious.

"It was an art show, but the lad did a detailed drawing of a motorcycle."

"It was a vintage Indian Chief motorcycle," Emmett said. "Wouldn't think a boy that young would even be familiar with such a fine machine."

"And Nina was the star of the show," Rosemary said.

Nina blushed. "The stars were the artists. There is a lot of talent in town."

"It must have been hard to pick winners, but that cat with the green eyes was adorable." Rosemary picked up her teacup. "Made me miss my little Flossie."

"Nina, did you have a picture in the show?" Mike asked.

"No, I was the judge. I couldn't enter."

"I bet if you entered a painting, you would have won," Rosemary said.

Nina lowered her head. "I haven't painted that much original work. I mostly taught students and painted the same things repeatedly to demonstrate for the classes."

The words from the old *Coastal Creatives* magazine swam through her thoughts. *I should try an original piece.*

That afternoon, Nina carried her art supplies into the gathering room and selected a table near the window. She set up her paints, two jars of water, the set of brushes, and the block of art paper. Gazing out the window, she studied the row of stately oak trees with Spanish moss hanging from the lower limbs. *This is the view Liz liked so much.*

She dipped her paintbrush in the water and spread water over the paper. She added blue for the sky and swirls of green for the trees. With her brush, she moved the paints across the paper, intensifying colors in some spots and lifting them in other places. Mixing several colors, she added more hues to the painting.

The light shifted as the sun moved and she deepened the shadows. Finally, she sat back and regarded the finished piece. *Not bad. Especially since I haven't painted since my fall.*

"That's gorgeous," Emily said from behind Nina.

"Oh, I didn't realize you were there."

"I've been watching for a few minutes. I'm amazed that you can turn a blank piece of paper into a masterpiece."

Nina laughed. "It's hardly a masterpiece."

"I love it."

Nina looked at the expression on Emily's face. *She really means it.* "Would you like it?"

"You're going to give it to me?"

"What else am I going to do with it?" Nina laughed.

"You could sell it."

Nina removed the painting from her pad. "It's yours."

"Thank you. I'm going to get it framed and hang it in my office."

Nina massaged her right hand. *Not sure how many paintings I have left in this tired old hand, but perhaps a few more. A few could go to the Community Art Center for sale. Half the money would go to the Center, and I can use the rest to buy more supplies.*

January 2024

Before breakfast each day, Nina decided on a new art theme. She took her art supplies to the gathering room and worked on a painting by the window. Other Shadow Oaks residents would stop to watch her progress. At first, she cringed, embarrassed that others would criticize it, but with time, she relaxed. Her painting style grew looser, and the paintings glowed with freedom of expression.

"I wish I could do that," one resident said.

Nina didn't know the woman's name. "You can. I teach an art class here every Monday morning at ten o'clock. Come and learn."

Gradually, the weekly art class increased in size. Laughter and fun filled the gathering room. Nina taught basic drawing lessons, and residents asked her to hold more frequent classes.

"Once a week is not enough," Rosemary said.

Nina smiled. "You can practice without me." *I need time to do art for myself. Yes. I can do art.*

Saturday, February 3, 2024

Nina wore her fanciest dress and draped a scarf over her shoulders. She walked to the lobby without her cane. Her steps were careful but more confident. She glanced out the front door and grinned when she saw Megan's car drive up to the entrance.

Rosemary came up beside her. "Where are you going, Nina?"

"My pen pal and her mother are taking me out to lunch."

"How sweet. Is that her?"

Penny came running up to the front door. She wore her bright red beret at an angle.

"Yes, that's the girl who started as Poison Pen."

After opening the door, Nina greeted Penny and strolled to the waiting car. "How is Art Club going?"

"Great," Penny said. "My art teacher, Mrs. Silsbury, convinced the principal to let us do a mural in the cafeteria."

"I'm glad to hear that. Murals make quite a statement."

At the car, Penny opened the door and waited while Nina got settled.

"You are looking lovely today, Miss K," Megan said.

"Please call me Nina. I'm not Miss K anymore."

Megan drove them to a small farm-to-table restaurant in the next town. Along the way, they passed meadows with wildflowers in bloom.

"Notice how the contrast between the bright wildflowers and the green grass sets off the colors of the flowers," Nina said, pointing to the scenery.

"That sounds like a Miss K observation," Megan said.

Nina chuckled. "I guess once a teacher, always a teacher."

At the restaurant, they enjoyed a pleasant lunch while looking over a small river.

"This looks like a postcard." Penny snapped a photo with her phone.

"You should try painting it." Nina watched Penny's reaction.

"That's what you said at the art museum."

"Yes, and did you?"

"I did, but it didn't turn out like Vincent van Gogh's."

"He practiced for years. He even painted over canvases he had already used."

Penny cocked her head. "You also said I should go to Paris."

"And you should."

"You hear that, Mom. She says I should go to Paris."

"We all should," Megan said with a laugh. "But until then, I have a request."

Nina rubbed her hand over her mouth. "And that request is?"

"We're creating a series of classes at the Art Center. My friend, Abbie, has agreed to teach Intro to Photography. I've lined up an art journalist to teach a class. Would you consider teaching a beginning drawing class?"

Nina looked down. *I can do, and I teach, too.*

Megan kept talking. "My husband can pick you up

from Shadow Oaks and bring you to the Art Center, and take you back, of course."

"My dear, you are making an old lady feel very appreciated. I would be delighted to teach a class. It is the purpose of my life."

* * *

Friday, March 22, 2024

PENNY DIPPED THE TIP OF HER BRUSH IN THE PAINT TRAY and applied a thin line of gunmetal gray to the wall. She stepped back and assessed the image of the Eiffel Tower. The faintest smile crossed her lips. *I think that finishes it. It looks a lot like the scene Kanina sent me.*

She crossed the empty high school cafeteria to view the mural from a greater distance. The Paris street scene with the Eiffel Tower in the distance decorated the wall opposite the cafeteria entrance. Her smile broadened. *It's done.*

Mrs. Silsbury came up beside Penny. "It looks terrific. Magnifique!"

"Thanks." Penny beamed with pride. "But it was a team effort."

"You've brought a bit of Paris to our school."

Penny nodded. "I'm going to go there one day."

"I'm sure you will. With your talent, travel the world and capture its beauty for all to see."

Principal Nelson joined them. "Wow, Mrs. Silsbury! The students are going to like this new look when they come back from spring break."

"It's all Penny's doing," the art teacher said.

Penny's face grew warm at the compliment, and she looked down at her shoes.

"What's next?" Principal Nelson asked.

The art teacher looked at Penny. "Go ahead and tell him."

"We're going to paint a polar bear in the gym."

The principal broke into a long, deep laugh. "That's a suitable spot for the school mascot. Penny, you've come a long way."

In more ways than you'll ever know. And with people in my life who care about me.

* * *

Monday, April 1, 2024

IN THE AFTERNOON'S QUIET, NINA SAT BY THE WINDOW, looking out at the garden, and watched the birds fly from the stately oak trees to the feeder in the butterfly garden. *Liz spent hours sitting here.*

The activity director hurried over with a manila envelope. She pulled a chair beside Nina. "Miss Nina, I have the best news. Management has decided to repaint the interior of Shadow Oaks. The old wallpaper will be removed, and we get to choose the new color scheme for the common areas."

"That will be an improvement," Nina said. *Since the first day I came here, I've hated the colors.*

"I want you to help me pick the color scheme." Emily opened the envelope and removed a ring of color swatches.

For the next hour, Nina and Emily discussed an overall color strategy for Shadow Oaks and went room by room, selecting colors.

"Thank you, Miss Nina. This has been very helpful." Emily hesitated. "I have one more request."

Nina cocked her head. "What is it?"

"I know it's a big request. I'd like to replace the artwork on the walls with portraits of our residents and staff. If we provide the art supplies, could you draw or paint a portrait for each person?"

Nina looked down at her hands. "That is quite a compliment." She flexed her fingers. "I would be glad to, but arthritis has slowed my hands."

"You can work at your own pace. Will you do it?"

With a smile, Nina nodded. "Perhaps I could start with a wedding picture?"

Emily's eyebrows raised. "Of who?"

Nina pointed to the engagement ring on Emily's finger, and Emily blushed.

"You are truly an angel, Miss Nina."

"I haven't earned my wings yet, but I'm working at it."

* * *

Saturday, April 6, 2024

IN A FADED PAIR OF JEANS AND A SHIRT THAT COULD DOUBLE AS an artist's smock, Megan hurried down the stairs. "Come on, Jody. Let's go paint."

Jody followed her, jumping from step to step and chanting in her singsong voice, "Here we go to painting."

Megan grinned at her daughter's delight in their Saturday morning activity. *I'm glad the board of directors agreed to try "Painting with Parents and Peeps" as a community outreach event. I know classes for parents and children together will be a success. I still can't believe Miss K agreed to teach for us.*

Arriving early at the Art Center, Megan unlocked the front door and opened it as Steve pulled up to the curb with Nina. "Welcome. We have a full class this morning, and everything is all ready for you."

"Thank you for inviting me." Nina moved slowly. "I hope I won't disappoint the students."

"Never. Come right this way."

Jody skipped out of the classroom and stopped in front of Miss K. "Are you drawing, too?"

Megan took Jody's hand in hers. "Nina, this is my youngest daughter, Jody. She's one of your excited students."

"Wonderful. And yes, Jody, I will draw, too."

Together they entered the classroom and Megan helped Nina settle into the teacher's desk in the front of the room. Within minutes, other parents and children arrived. Megan leaned over to Jody and whispered, "This is going to be fun." *These are moments money can't buy.*

"Welcome, everyone. I'm Miss K, and together we will do great art."

THE END

Author's Notes

Letters from Shadow Oaks is a fictional account of three women, but the ideas behind the novel were inspired by real people and situations.

Over a decade ago, when it was common to sit with the local newspaper and scan the obituaries to see if anyone you knew had passed away, my attention was captured by a grainy black-and-white photo. It was an image of a woman in a long coat and hat riding a bicycle away from the photographer, while holding an umbrella. The photo in the obituary section was unusual, since the typical entry included only a head shot of an individual, often from an earlier time. I paused to read the obituary of this person I did not know.

Known as "Miss T" to her students, Rosemary Trefethen (1930-2014) was an art instructor for forty-eight years in Hillsborough County, Florida. She rode her bicycle to school daily and frequently traveled the world. She was reported often to say to her many admiring students, "My art is teaching." Her obituary made no mention of family, and there was no funeral.

I saved the newspaper clipping and filed it away, thinking that she was an unusual personality who might be intriguing to write about. Years passed, and I forgot about the photo. Then, in 2020, the COVID pandemic occurred, and lockdowns were instituted. Many nursing homes eliminated visits for the elderly residents. It was a lonely time for many people.

One creative nursing home started posting photos on social media requesting pen pals for their residents. Each person was photographed holding a sign that listed their personal interests or hobbies. I began corresponding with a few individuals. It was the first time I became a pen pal.

Gradually, the idea of combining these two elements—a retired teacher and writing letters to an elderly person—morphed into *Letters from Shadow Oaks*. Nina and Penny's community service project were created as a result.

My love of art is also an important aspect of the story. I have dabbled in watercolors, graphite, and colored pencils. My daughter and I attended several movies and exhibits about Vincent van Gogh, fueling a love of his art.

When a social media site offered a fall writing contest that included a sunflower as a prompt, I was immediately drawn to it. The very first piece of *Letters from Shadow Oaks* was a short scene that featured an old lady, a teenaged girl, and a van Gogh sunflower painting. That piece was incorporated into the museum scene in Chapter 16.

I love all the characters in *Letters from Shadow Oaks*. Each one has a bit of someone I know or myself molded into their life story. Even Goku the cat is based on my barn cat Rose, a gray tabby with green eyes.

Thank you for reading. Reviews are always appreciated.

Acknowledgments

There are many people to acknowledge and I'm sure I've missed someone. Know that I appreciate all your help and support.

- My family has been a constant source of love and encouragement.

- My beta readers, Cheryl, Mary Lu, and Mary Ann, provided their honest feedback and suggestions.

- My online writing community has been a wonderful source of knowledge and advice about the writing and publishing process.

- Cayce Berryman and Crystal Burton of Kingsman Editing shaped the words and pages into a polished novel.

- Lidia Puccetti created the book cover with special care.

If there are any errors in this book, they are my responsibility.

About the Author

K. L. SMALL is the author of novels for young readers and those who are young at heart. She was born in Queens, New York. She started college as a Creative Writing major and spent most of her professional career doing business writing.

She is a four-time winner of Royal Palm Literary Awards for her fiction, including *A Dress to Remember* and *The Magic Carousel* (originally entitled *Rust Boy and the Brass Ring*). Several of her short stories have been published in anthologies.

Her childhood dream was to own a horse and be an author. She is living her dream in Brooksville, Florida, with her husband, Rick, on a ranch called Carousel Acres. They own two horses (Rory and Skylark) and four barn cats (Blanche, Dorothy, Rose, and Stan).

You can follow her on the Web at https://kathleenlsmall.com, and sign-up for her newsletter to get updates on her writing activities. Other novels are coming soon.

Books by K. L. Small

A Dress To Remember: A Fairy Tale

The Brass Ring Series

The Magic Carousel
The Christmas Carousel
The Haunted Carousel

*The Dark Horse and Other Short Stories
with a Touch of Magic* (coming in 2025)

A Carousel for Shade Tree (coming in 2026)

Reviews of her books are always appreciated. Reader feed-back helps shape future writing projects. Suggested sites for reviews are Amazon and Goodreads.

To receive updates on upcoming activities and stories, please subscribe to K. L. Small's monthly newsletter at:

www.kathleenlsmall.com